WHERE SHADOWS DANCE

THE SEBASTIAN ST. CYR SERIES

What Angels Fear

When Gods Die

Why Mermaids Sing

Where Serpents Sleep

What Remains of Heaven

WHERE SHADOWS DANCE

A Sebastian St. Cyr Mystery

C. S. HARRIS

AN OBSIDIAN MYSTERY

OBSIDIAN
Published by New American Library,
a division of Penguin Group (USA) Inc.,
375 Hudson Street, New York, New York 10014, USA
Penguin Group (Canada), 90 Eglinton Avenue East, Suite 700, Toronto,
Ontario M4P 2Y3, Canada (a division of Pearson Penguin Canada Inc.)
Penguin Books Ltd., 80 Strand, London WC2R 0RL, England
Penguin Ireland, 25 St. Stephen's Green, Dublin 2,
Ireland (a division of Penguin Books Ltd.)
Penguin Group (Australia), 250 Camberwell Road, Camberwell,
Victoria 3124, Australia (a division of Pearson Australia Group Pty. Ltd.)
Penguin Books India Pvt. Ltd., 11 Community Centre,
Panchsheel Park, New Delhi - 110 017, India
Penguin Group (NZ), 67 Apollo Drive, Rosedale, North Shore 0632,
New Zealand (a division of Pearson New Zealand Ltd.)
Penguin Books (South Africa) (Pty.) Ltd., 24 Sturdee Avenue,
Rosebank, Johannesburg 2196, South Africa

Penguin Books Ltd., Registered Offices:
80 Strand, London WC2R 0RL, England

First published by Obsidian, an imprint of New American Library,
a division of Penguin Group (USA) Inc.

First Printing, March 2011
1   3   5   7   9   10   8   6   4   2

Copyright © The Two Talers, LLC, 2011
All rights reserved

OBSIDIAN and logo are trademarks of Penguin Group (USA) Inc.

LIBRARY OF CONGRESS CATALOGING-IN-PUBLICATION DATA:
Harris, C. S.
Where shadows dance: a Sebastian St. Cyr mystery/C. S. Harris.
p.   cm.—(An Obsidian mystery)
ISBN 978-0-451-23223-6
1. Great Britain—History—George III, 1760–1820—Fiction. 2. London (England)—Fiction.
3. Murder—Investigation—Fiction. I. Title.
PS3566.R5877W4755   2011
813'.54—dc22   2010040930

Set in Weiss
Designed by Elke Sigal

Printed in the United States of America

To my mother,

Bernadine Wegmann Proctor,

1917—2010

The old tree groans to the blast;
The falling branch resounds.
The wind drives the clung thorn
Along the sighing grass;
He shakes amid the night.
Dark, dusky, howling is night,
Cloudy, windy, full of ghosts;
The dead are abroad; my friends
Receive me from the night.

—from "The Six Bards,"
James MacPherson, 1736–1796

WHERE SHADOWS DANCE

Chapter 1

A cool wind gusted up, rustling the branches of the trees overhead and bringing with it the unmistakable clatter of wooden wheels approaching over cobblestones. Standing just outside the open gate to the alley, Paul Gibson doused his lantern, his eyes straining as he peered into the fog-swirled darkness. Thick clouds bunched overhead, obscuring the moon and stars and promising more rain. He could see nothing but high, rough stone walls and a refuse-choked muddy lane curving away into the mist.

A dog barked somewhere in the night. In spite of himself, Gibson shivered. It was a dirty business, this. But until the government revised its laws on human dissection, anatomists like Gibson could either resign themselves to ignorance or meet the resurrection men in the darkest hours before dawn.

Paul Gibson was not fond of ignorance.

He was a slim, dark-haired man of medium height, Irish born and in his thirty-second year. Trained as a surgeon, he'd honed his skills on the battlefields of Europe. But a French cannonball that shattered the lower part of one leg had left him with recurring pain and a weakness for the sweet relief to be found in poppies. Now he shared his knowledge of anatomy by teaching at hospitals like St. Thomas's and St. Bartholomew's, as well as working out of his small surgery here at the base of Tower Hill.

The dog barked again, followed this time by a man's low curse. A two-wheeled cart loomed out of the mist, the rawboned mule between the poles snorting and jibing at the bit when the driver drew up with a guttural, "Whoa there, ye bloomin' idiot. Where ye think yer goin'? We got one more delivery t' make before ye can head home t' yer barn."

A tall, skeletally thin man in striped trousers and a natty coat jumped from the cart and tipped his top hat in a flourishing bow. As he straightened, a waft of gin underlaid with the sweet scent of decay carried on the wind. "We got him fer ye, Doctor," said Jumpin' Jack Cochran with a broad wink. "Mind ye, he's not as fresh as I like me merchandise t' be, but ye did say ye wanted this particular gentleman."

Gibson peered over the cart's side at the bulky, man-sized burlap sack that lay within. Another name for the resurrection men was the sack-'em-up boys. "You're certain you've got the right one?"

"It's him, all right." Cochran motioned at the sturdy lad who accompanied him. "Grab the other end there, Ben."

Grunting softly, the two men slung the burlap-wrapped merchandise off the back of the cart. It landed heavily in the rank grass beside the gate.

"Careful," said Gibson.

Cochran grinned, displaying long tobacco-stained teeth. "I can guarantee he didn't feel a thing, Doctor."

Hefting the heavy sack between them, the two men carried the merchandise into the stone outbuilding at the base of Gibson's overgrown garden and heaved it up onto the granite slab table that stood in the center of the room. Working quickly, they peeled away the mud-encrusted sack to reveal the limp body of a young man, his dark hair fashionably cut, his hands soft and well manicured, as befitted a gentleman. His pale, naked flesh was liberally streaked with dirt, for the body snatchers had stripped off his shroud and grave clothes and stuffed them back into his coffin before refilling the tomb. There was no law against carting a dead body through the streets of London. But stealing a cadaver *and* its grave clothes could earn a man seven years in Botany Bay.

"Sorry about the mud," said Cochran. "We've had a mite o' rain today."

"I understand. Thank you, gentlemen," said Gibson. "Here's your twenty guineas."

It was the going price for an adult male; adult females generally went for fifteen, with children being sold by the foot. Cochran shook his head and hawked up a mouthful of phlegm he shot out the door. "Nah. Make it eighteen. I got me professional pride, and he's not as fresh as I like 'em t' be, even if he was kept on ice afore he was planted. But ye would have this one."

Gibson stared at the pallid, handsome face of the body lying on his dissection table. "It's not often a healthy young man succumbs to a weak heart. This gentleman's body has much to teach us about diseases of the circulation system."

"Weery interestin', I'm sure," said Cochran, scooping up his muddy sack. "Thank ye kindly fer the business, and a weery good night t' ye, sir."

After the men had left, Gibson relit his lantern and hung it from the chain suspended above the table. The lantern swayed gently back and forth, the golden light playing over the pale flesh of the body below. In life, his name had been Alexander Ross. A well-formed gentleman in his mid-twenties, he'd had long, leanly muscled arms and legs and a broad chest tapering to a slim waist and hips. He looked as if he should have been the epitome of health. Yet five days ago, his heart had stopped as he slept peacefully in his own bed.

The delicate dissection of the defective heart would need to wait until daylight. But Gibson set to work with a bowl of warm water and a cloth, sponging off the mud of the graveyard and casting a preliminary practiced eye over the corpse.

It was when he was washing the soil from the back of the man's neck that he found it: a short purple slit at the base of the skull. Frowning, Gibson reached for a probe and watched in horror as it slid in four inches, easily following the path previously cut through living flesh by a stiletto.

Taking a step back, he set aside the probe with a soft clatter, his teeth sinking into his lower lip as he brought his gaze back to the young man's alabaster face. "Mother of God," he whispered. "You didn't die of a defective heart. You were murdered."

Chapter 2

*T*he first rays of the rising sun caught the heavy mist off the river and turned it into shimmering wisps of gold and pink that hugged the wet rooftops and church spires of the city. Standing beside his bedroom window, Sebastian St. Cyr, Viscount Devlin, cradled a glass of brandy in one hand. Behind him lay the tangled, abandoned ruin of his bed. He had not slept.

He was a tall man, leanly built. Not yet thirty years of age, he had dark hair and strange yellow eyes with an unnatural ability to see clearly at great distances or at night, when reality was reduced for most men to vague shadows of gray. Now, as the world outside the window brightened, he brought the brandy to his lips only to hesitate and set it aside untasted.

There were times when memories of the past tormented his sleep and drove him from his bed, times when his dreams echoed with the crash of cannonballs and the screams of mangled men, when the cloying scent of death haunted him and would not go away. But not this night. This night, he was troubled more by the present than by the past. By a life-altering truth revealed too late and a future he did not want but was honor bound to seek.

He reached again for his brandy, only to pause as the sound of frantic knocking reverberated though the house. Jerking up the sash, he leaned out, the cool air of morning biting his bare flesh as he shouted down at the figure on the steps below, "What the bloody hell do you want?"

The man's head fell back, revealing familiar features. "That you, Devlin?"

"*Gibson?*" Sebastian was suddenly, painfully sober. "I'll be right down."

Pausing only to throw on a pair of breeches and a silk dressing gown, he hurried downstairs. He found his majordomo, Morey, dressed in a paisley gown of astonishingly lurid reds and blues, and clutching a flickering candle that tipped dangerously as he worked at drawing back the bolts on the front door.

"Go back to bed, Morey," said Sebastian. "I'll deal with this."

"Yes, my lord." A former gunnery sergeant, the majordomo gave a dignified bow and withdrew.

Sebastian yanked open the front door. His friend practically fell into the marble-floored entrance hall. "What the devil's happened, Gibson? What is it?"

Gibson leaned against the wall. He was breathing heavily, his normally jaunty face haggard and streaked with sweat. From the look of things, he hadn't been able to find a hackney and had simply hurried the distance from the Tower to Mayfair on foot—not an easy journey for a man with a wooden leg.

He swallowed hard and said, "I have a wee bit of a problem."

Sebastian stared down at the pale body stretched out on his friend's granite slab and tried to avoid breathing too deeply.

The sun was up by now. The wind had blown away the

clouds and the last of the mist to leave the sky scrubbed blue and empty. Already, the day promised to be warm. From the corpse before him rose a sickly sweet odor of decay.

"You know," said Sebastian, rubbing his nose, "if you'd left the man in his grave where he belonged, you wouldn't have a problem."

Gibson stood on the far side of the table, his arms folded at his chest. "It's a little late now."

Sebastian grunted. To some, they might seem unlikely friends, this Earl's heir and the Irish surgeon with a passion for unraveling the secrets of the human body. But there had been a time when both had worn the King's colors, when they'd fought together from the West Indies and Italy to the mountains of Portugal. Theirs was a friendship forged in all the horrors of blood and mud and looming death. Now they shared a dedication to truth and a passionate anger at the wanton, selfish destruction of one human being by another.

Gibson scrubbed a hand across his lower face. "It's not like I can walk into Bow Street and say, 'By the way, mates, I thought you might be interested to hear that I bought a body filched from St. George's churchyard last night. Yes, I know it's illegal, but here's the thing: It appears this gentleman—whose friends all think died in his sleep—was actually murdered.'"

Sebastian huffed a soft, humorless laugh. "Not if you value your life."

The authorities tended to turn a blind eye to the activities of body snatchers, unless they were caught red-handed. But the inhabitants of London were considerably less sanguine about the unauthorized dissection of their nearest and dearest. When word spread of a body snatching, hordes of hysterical relatives had a nasty habit of descending on the city's churchyards to dig up the remains of their loved ones. Since they frequently discovered only empty coffins and torn grave clothes, the resultant mobs then turned their fury on the city's hospitals and the homes of known anatomists, smashing and burning, and savaging any medical men unlucky enough to fall into their clutches.

Gibson was well-known as an anatomist.

Sebastian said, "Perhaps Jumpin' Jack dug up the wrong body."

Gibson shook his head. "I plan to check the Bills of Mortality later today to make certain, but my money's on Jumpin' Jack. If he says this is Alexander Ross, then this is Alexander Ross."

Sebastian walked around the table, his gaze on the pale corpse.

Gibson said, "Do you recognize him?"

"No. But then, to my knowledge I've never met anyone named Alexander Ross."

"I'm told he had lodgings in St. James's Street, above the Je Reviens coffeehouse."

Sebastian nodded. St. James's was a popular locale for young gentlemen. "Who told you he died of a defective heart?"

"A colleague of mine at St. Thomas's—Dr. Astley Cooper. He was called in to examine the body. Swore there were no signs of any violence or illness; the man was simply lying dead in his bed when his valet came to rouse him that morning. Cooper was convinced he must have had a weak heart. That's why I was so eager to dissect the body—to observe whatever malformation or damage might be present."

Sebastian hunkered down to study the telltale slit at the base of the man's skull. "Your Dr. Cooper obviously didn't think to look at the back of his patient's neck. But surely a wound like this would bleed. Wouldn't the pillow and sheets have been covered in blood?"

"If Mr. Ross were killed in his bed. Obviously, he wasn't. Someone must have gone through a great deal of trouble to make this death look natural."

"And if not for you, he would have succeeded." Sebastian straightened and went to stand in the open doorway overlooking the unkempt garden that stretched from the stone outbuilding to the surgery beyond.

Gibson came to stand beside him. After a moment, the Irishman said, "Looks like a professional's work, doesn't it?"

"It could well be."

"I can't pretend I didn't see this."

Sebastian blew out a long breath. "It's not going to be easy, investigating a murder no one knows occurred."

"But you'll do it?"

Sebastian glanced back at the pallid corpse on Gibson's dissection table.

The man looked to be much the same age as Sebastian, perhaps a few years younger. He should have had decades of rewarding life ahead of him. Instead he was reduced to this, a murdered cadaver on a surgeon's slab. And Sebastian knew a deep and abiding fury directed toward whoever had brought Ross to this end.

"I'll do it."

Chapter 3

*T*he milkmaids were still making their rounds, heavy pails swinging from yokes slung across their shoulders, when Sebastian climbed the shallow front steps of his elegant, bow-fronted establishment on Brook Street.

"A note arrived a few moments ago from the Earl of Hendon," said Morey, meeting Sebastian at the door with a silver tray bearing a missive sealed with the St. Cyr crest.

Sebastian made no move to pick it up. Until a week ago, he had called Hendon father. Sebastian supposed that he might eventually adjust to the brutal realization that he was not in truth the person the world still believed him to be, that far from being the legitimate son of the Earl of Hendon he was in fact the by-blow of the Earl's beautiful, errant Countess and some unnamed lover. Perhaps in time he would learn to understand and forgive the lies Hendon had told him over the years. But Sebastian knew he could never forgive Hendon for allowing him to believe that the love of his life was his own sister. For that lie had turned their love into something sordid and wicked and driven the woman Sebastian had hoped to make his wife into a loveless marriage with another man.

"Send Calhoun to me," said Sebastian, leaving the note on the tray as he headed for the stairs.

The shadow of some emotion quickly suppressed flickered across the majordomo's face. "Yes, my lord."

Sebastian took the steps two at a time, stripping off his coat of dark blue superfine as he went. He was in his dressing room, pulling a clean shirt over his head, when Jules Calhoun, his valet, appeared in the doorway.

"I'd like you to find out what you can about a gentleman named Mr. Alexander Ross," said Sebastian. "I understand he had lodgings in St. James's Street."

A small, slim man with even features, Calhoun was a genius of a valet, uncomplainingly cheerful and skilled in all manner of refined arts. And since he had begun life in one of London's most notorious flash houses, some of his more unusual talents were of considerable use to a gentleman who had made solving murders his life's passion.

Calhoun picked up Sebastian's discarded coat and sniffed. The faint but unmistakable odor of decay lingered. "I take it Mr. Ross has been murdered?"

"By a stiletto thrust to the base of his skull."

"Unusual," said Calhoun.

"Very. Unfortunately, the world believes he died peacefully in his sleep, so this one's going to be rather delicate."

Calhoun handed Sebastian a fresh cravat and bowed. "I shall be the model of discretion."

Lifting his chin, Sebastian looped the cravat around his neck and grunted.

Calhoun cleared his throat. "About the other matter you asked me to look into . . ."

Sebastian felt an unpleasant sensation pull across his chest. He ignored it. "Yes?"

"I have it on excellent authority that Miss Hero Jarvis will be patronizing the opening of the New Steam Circus north of Bloomsbury this morning."

"The what?"

"The New Steam Circus, my lord. It's an exhibition of Mr. Trevithick's latest steam locomotive. I believe the gate opens at eleven o'clock."

"I should be back before then. Have Tom bring my curricle around at a quarter till." Sebastian adjusted his cuffs. "Tell, me: How, precisely, did you discover this?"

"Miss Jarvis's maid, my lord," said Calhoun, holding up a fresh coat of navy Bath cloth.

Sebastian eased the coat up over his shoulders. "Did you woo her, or bribe her?"

"Pure filthy lucre, my lord."

Sebastian frowned. "That's not good."

"I thought the same, my lord. I mean, there's not many who've my way with the ladies, if I do say so myself. But that woman'll talk to anyone who's willing to pay her price."

Charles, Lord Jarvis, stood beside the window of the chambers set aside for his exclusive use in Carlton House, his gaze on the palace forecourt below.

Since old King George had slipped irrevocably into madness some eighteen months before, the center of authority in London had shifted away from the ancient brick courtyards of St. James's Palace to this, the extravagantly refurbished London residence of the Prince of Wales. And Jarvis—cousin to the King, brilliant, ruthless, and utterly dedicated to the preservation of the House of Hanover—had emerged even more prominently as the acknowledged power behind Prinny's weak Regency.

In his late fifties now, Jarvis was a big man, both tall and fleshy. Despite his heavy jowls and aquiline nose, he was still handsome, with a wide mouth that could smile in unexpected brilliance. It was a gift he used often, both to cajole and to deceive.

"I tell you, it's madness," grumbled the Earl of Hendon, one of two men who had come here, to Jarvis's chambers, to discuss the current state of affairs on the Continent.

Jarvis glanced over at Hendon but kept his own counsel. He'd long ago learned the power that comes from listening while other men talk.

"It's far from madness," said the second gentleman, Sir Hyde Foley, Undersecretary of State for Foreign Affairs. "Our troops under Wellington are making rapid progress in Spain. At the rate they're going, we could be in Madrid by the middle of next month. And do you know why? Because Napoléon in his arrogance has now attacked Russia and is, as we speak, advancing on Moscow. How is it madness to send British troops to aid the Czar's defenses?"

"It's madness for the same reason that Napoléon's invasion of Russia is madness," said Hendon, his face dark with emotion. Chancellor of the Exchequer under two different prime ministers, he was a sturdily built, barrel-chested man in his late sixties, with a shock of white hair and the brilliant blue eyes that were the hallmark of his family, the St. Cyrs. "We simply don't have the manpower to fight the French in Spain and in Russia, defend India, and still protect Canada should the Americans decide to attack us there."

Foley made a deprecating sound. A wiry man in his mid-thirties, with dark hair and a narrow, sharp-boned face, the Undersecretary was proving to be a capable—and formidable—force in the Foreign Office. "The Americans have been threatening to attack us anytime these last four years. It hasn't happened. Why should it happen now, when we've revoked the Orders in Council they found so odious?"

"Because the bloody upstarts want Canada, that's why! They have some crazy idea that God has given them the right to expand across the whole of the Continent, from the North Pole to the Pacific Ocean and the Gulf of Mexico."

Foley threw back his head and laughed. "Those rustics?"

Hendon's cheeks grew darker still. "Mark my words if they don't do it—or try to."

"Gentlemen," said Jarvis softly. "These arguments are premature. Discussions with the Czar's representatives are still at the preliminary stage."

It was a lie, of course. The negotiations with the Russians had been nearly complete for more than a week. Only Hendon's continuous, vociferous objections had prevented their finalization.

"Just so," said Hendon. He glanced at the ormolu clock on the mantel. "Now you must excuse me. I have a meeting with Liverpool in a quarter of an hour."

"Of course," said Jarvis, at his most gracious. He paused, then added with feigned concern, "I was grieved to hear that an unfortunate estrangement appears to have arisen between you and your son, Viscount Devlin."

Hendon's jaw hardened. "No."

"Indeed?" Jarvis reached for his snuffbox. "Then I must have been misinformed. You relieve me, my lord."

Hendon bowed politely to first Jarvis, then Foley. "Good day, gentlemen."

After Hendon had gone, Foley came to stand beside Jarvis, his gaze, like Jarvis's, on the scene below. As they watched, the Earl of Hendon emerged from the palace and walked rapidly across the paved forecourt.

"He doesn't know?" said Foley.

"He suspects."

"You think he may be a problem?"

"He may." Jarvis raised a delicate pinch of snuff to his nostril and sniffed. "But don't worry. I can deal with him."

Chapter 4

$\mathcal{T}$he coffeehouse known as Je Reviens occupied the ground floor of a gracefully proportioned sandstone-faced building of four stories on the western side of St. James's Street. Through the coffeehouse's elegant oriel window, Sebastian could see a paneled room crowded with cloth-covered tables and chairs filled even at this early hour with men drinking coffee or chocolate. It was an animated scene, the muted roar of the men's voices and laughter spilling into the street as they passionately discussed everything from the latest horse race to Napoléon's invasion of Russia and the new threats of war from the United States.

He stood for a time on the footpath, breathing in the scent of freshly roasted coffee and watching quietly. Beside the door to the coffeehouse stood a second door. Pushing it open, he found himself in a well-scrubbed hall containing a steep, straight staircase that swept up to the rooms above. The stairs were of marble, uncarpeted. As Sebastian climbed to the first floor, his footsteps echoed hollowly.

Since he had no knowledge of which rooms had once belonged to Alexander Ross, he knocked at both doors on the first floor. From behind the panels to his right came a surly male voice slurred with sleep. *"Go away.* You'll get your money next week, I said!"

The second door was opened by a middle-aged housemaid with an enormous bosom and a crown of curly, fiery red hair inadequately restrained by a freshly starched mobcap. "Mr. Ross?" she said in a rasping Scottish brogue, in answer to Sebastian's question. "Ach, no; it's old Mrs. Blume what lives here, sir. Ye'll be wanting the forward rooms upstairs." She jerked her head toward the staircase and leaned closer to add, "Only, ye won't find him at home, I'm afraid. Died in his sleep just last Saturday, he did."

She stared at Sebastian expectantly, obviously more than willing to talk about the incident. Sebastian was quite happy to oblige.

"Yes, I had heard," he said. "We were friends. The thing is, you see, that I lent Ross a book a few weeks ago and was hoping to get it back."

"Ah, well, Mr. Ross's man is up there still. Sir Gareth is paying his wages until the end of the month."

"Sir Gareth?"

"His brother, Sir Gareth Ross." She drew her head back, her gray eyes narrowing with suspicion. "I thought ye said ye was his friend?"

"Oh, of course, Sir Gareth!" Sebastian affected a self-deprecating laugh. "I keep forgetting Gareth has inherited the title now. And how is he?"

She gave a sad *tsk.* "Not well, poor man. They say he's never recovered from his injury, you know. He was able to travel down from Oxfordshire for Mr. Ross's funeral, but he was that uncomfortable the whole while. Left for the Priory again just this morning, he did. He's had to leave Mr. Poole to pack up everything for him."

Sebastian nodded understandingly. "So Poole is still Mr. Ross's valet, is he?"

"Oh, yes. Or I suppose we should say he *was*. He's terribly broken up about poor Mr. Ross's death." She made an impish face and dropped her voice as if sharing a secret. "But then, seeing as how he'll now need to be finding a new position, he would be, wouldn't he?"

"True," said Sebastian. "Still, I expect Poole found Ross easy enough to work for." He was fishing, of course; for all he knew, Alexander Ross could have been the very devil of an employer.

An unexpected glow came over the maidservant's full, ruddy face. "Oh, Mr. Ross was a lovely gentleman. Ever so charming, he was. Always giving the children at the greengrocer's up the street rides on his shoulders and bringing them little treats. Why, he even carried a scuttle of coal up the stairs for me once, when I mentioned me back was hurting. I was ever so grateful."

If the Scotswoman had been young and winsome, one might suspect the late Mr. Ross of having had designs on her virtue. But under the circumstances Sebastian decided the dead man could be acquitted of any such ulterior motives.

Sebastian heaved a melancholy sigh. "They do say the good die young. I'd no notion he had a delicate heart."

"Nor had anyone. A more handsome, robust gentleman you never did see."

"Did he go out the night he died, I wonder, or have a quiet evening at home?"

She frowned with the effort of memory. "I can't rightly say. I think I did hear footsteps up and down the stairs a few times that night. But then, Mr. Ross was a great one for having visitors."

"And there's always the other residents of the second and third floors, I suppose," said Sebastian.

She shook her head. "Oh, no. Old Mr. Osborne on the third floor is quite the recluse—and as deaf as Mrs. Blume here, to boot—while Mr. Griffen next to him spends his summers in the country."

"And the other set of rooms on the second floor?"

"They've been empty these past two weeks."

"I see." Sebastian held his hat in his hands and gave her an elegant bow. "Thank you, Miss—"

"Jenny," she supplied.

"Thank you, Jenny. You've been most helpful."

He mounted the stairs to the second floor as light-footedly as he could, curious to see if it might be possible to minimize the racket. He was reaching the top step when the nearest door jerked open and a nattily dressed gentleman clutching an unwieldy bundle of clothes maneuvered through the opening and out into the hall.

A softly plump man, he had rounded shoulders, a thin mustache, and a spreading bald spot made all the more conspicuous by his attempts to cover it with what was left of his long, straight dark hair. At the sight of Sebastian, he let out a shriek and staggered back, the bundle sliding to the floor with a soft plop.

"Merciful heavens," said the man, groping for his handkerchief and pressing the snowy folds to his loose lips. "You startled me. How long have you been standing there?"

Sebastian mounted the final step. It was obviously possible, with care, to climb the stairs very quietly indeed. He said, "I've only just arrived, actually. I take it you're Poole?"

The valet gave a crisp bow. He looked to be somewhere in his forties or fifties, with heavy jowls and a second chin and dark brown eyes that reminded Sebastian of a sad puppy dog. "Noah Poole, yes. How may I be of service?"

Sebastian's gaze dropped to the bundle at their feet. "Off to the clothes fair in Rosemary Lane, are you?"

The valet's pale cheeks suffused with color, as if he'd been accused of doing something improper. He pulled back his round shoulders and said with a lisp that might or might not have been affected, "Sir Gareth has instructed me to dispose of Mr. Ross's clothing here in London."

"Makes sense," said Sebastian, pushing past the man to enter the drawing room beyond uninvited.

It was a typical gentleman's abode, all fine dark wood and burgundy and navy silk. Beyond the elegant chamber used as a combination drawing room and dining room, Sebastian could see a second chamber, a bedroom. From the looks of things, Ross might have just stepped out for a visit to his club. Noah Poole was obviously in no hurry to complete his assigned task.

"Actually," said Sebastian, "I'm here to retrieve a book I lent Ross a couple of weeks ago. Scott's *Lady of the Lake*. Have you seen it?"

Poole blinked at him a few times. "And who might you be, if I may be so bold to ask?"

Sebastian withdrew one of his cards and held it out between two fingers. "Devlin."

Poole's well-trained jaw hung slack. There were few in this part of London—either above- or belowstairs—who had not heard of Viscount Devlin.

The valet took the extended card with trembling fingers and gave another bow, this one considerably deeper and more obsequious than the first. "Oh, of course! Lord Devlin! I do beg your pardon." He cleared his throat nervously. "I don't recall seeing such a book, but I can assure you I will be more than happy to send it on to you should I come across it."

"That would be helpful, thank you."

Sebastian wandered the room, his gaze taking in the fine Adams cabinetry, the lyre-backed chairs covered in striped silk, the engraved invitations tucked into the frame of the gilded mirror over the hearth. Pausing, he found himself studying an invitation to that evening's reception for the Russian Ambassador at St. James's Palace.

Behind him, Poole cleared his throat. "I understand you have something of a reputation for solving murders."

Sebastian glanced over at him. "Yes."

"But . . . Mr. Ross died in his sleep. I discovered him myself."

"Must have been quite a shock for you."

Poole fumbled again for his handkerchief. "Indeed it was. You've no notion. I fear I've yet to recover my equilibrium."

Sebastian continued his slow perusal of the room. He would need to come back later tonight for a more thorough—and private—search. "Had Ross done anything unusual the day of his death? Anything that might have taxed his heart?"

"Not to my knowledge, no. He was out most of the previous evening, so he arose a trifle later than normal. But Sir Hyde was never too particular about that sort of thing."

Sebastian swung around to stare back at the round little man. "Sir Hyde? You mean, Sir Hyde *Foley*?" Sir Hyde Foley was the Undersecretary of State for Foreign Affairs. Which meant that the murdered Mr. Ross must—

"But of course," said Poole. "Mr. Ross worked for Sir Hyde at the Foreign Office."

Chapter 5

*S*ebastian's gaze went again to the invitation to that evening's reception at St. James's Palace. The quiet murder of the unknown Mr. Ross had demanded investigation. But the stealthy assassination of a young gentleman from the Foreign Office opened up a host of disturbing possibilities.

"At what time did Mr. Ross return from the Foreign Office that evening?" asked Sebastian.

Poole frowned with the strain of remembrance. "A little later than the usual time, I believe. Although it's difficult to remember for certain, now."

"Did he go out again that night?"

"I couldn't say, my lord. You see, it wasn't long after his return that Mr. Ross informed me he wouldn't be needing me for the remainder of the evening." Poole hesitated. "Actually, I had the impression he was expecting someone later that night."

"A man or a woman?"

"I was not informed."

"Is your chamber here, on the second floor?"

Poole shook his head. "No, my lord; I am in the attic." He nodded to a bellpull near the hearth. "Mr. Ross could summon me whenever I was desired, but he did like his privacy."

"How long have you been with Mr. Ross?"

"Ever since his return from Russia."

"Ross was in Russia?"

"Yes, my lord."

Once again, Sebastian's gaze returned to the invitation tucked into the gilded frame. As heir to the Earl of Hendon, he had received a similar invitation. He'd had no intention of attending—before. But now . . .

He realized Noah Poole was still speaking. "And I've more than twenty years of experience as a gentleman's gentleman," he was saying, "so if you would by chance know of anyone who is in need of a valet, I've excellent recommendations." The valet stood with his hands together as if in prayer, his lower lip caught between his teeth, his eyes wide and hopeful.

"If I hear of anything, I'll be certain to pass your name along."

Noah Poole gave a grateful nod and bowed.

Sebastian was turning to leave when Poole cleared his throat again and said, "You might try speaking to Madame Champagne."

Sebastian paused to glance back at him. "Who?"

"Angelina Champagne—the proprietor of the coffee shop on the ground floor. She owns the entire house, actually. She sits by that oriel window most of the day—and half the night, as well." Poole swallowed, both his chins pulling back into his neck so that they nearly disappeared. "In my experience, there is little that escapes her attention."

"Thank you. That might be helpful," said Sebastian, and went in search of Madame Champagne.

But when he entered the fragrant, noisy coffee room on the ground floor, it was to be told that *madame* had stepped out and was not expected back until late in the afternoon.

Sebastian slipped his watch from its pocket and frowned. It was nearly eleven o'clock.

Driving himself in his curricle, Sebastian arrived in Bloomsbury to find the big square just to the north of the New Road filled with an enormous circular wooden enclosure that looked for all the world like some primitive fortress in the wilds of America. Vertical boards twelve to fifteen feet high discouraged the efforts of a motley crowd of curious onlookers from sneaking a peek at the steam locomotive without actually paying to enter the gate.

"If I'm more than ten minutes, walk 'em," Sebastian told the young groom, or tiger, who clung to his perch at the rear of the curricle. From the far side of the palisade came a belch of steam and the shriek of a whistle. The chestnuts snorted and tossed their heads nervously.

"Easy, lads," crooned Tom, scrambling onto the seat. A half-grown urchin of thirteen years, he was gap-toothed and scrappy and utterly devoted to Sebastian. "Maybe I'd best walk 'em now."

"As you wish," said Sebastian, hopping down. "Actually, you might use the time to see if you can discover where Foreign Undersecretary Sir Hyde Foley takes his nuncheon."

"Aye, gov'nor."

Dutifully handing over his shilling entrance fee, Sebastian pushed his way into the vast enclosure to find an open space circled by a single line of tracks laid just inside the wall. On the far side of the ring stood a small black steam engine mounted on wheels, with a modified open carriage bolted behind it. The engine's boiler smoked and steamed, filling the air with the hot pinch of burning coal.

Some forty to sixty brave souls ranging from well-dressed ladies and gentlemen to gawking artisans and apprentices milled about the enclosure. But the carriage remained empty. It was one thing, obviously, to pay one's shilling for a look at the throbbing, hissing machine, but something else again to actually risk life and limb by going for a ride.

Sebastian let his gaze drift around the assembled crowd, looking for Miss Hero Jarvis. It was nearly half past eleven; perhaps she had already come and gone.

"I'd no notion you took an interest in the advances of modern science," said a well-bred female voice behind him.

He turned to find Miss Jarvis regarding him with an expression he found impossible to decipher. She was a tall young woman, nearly as tall as her powerful father, Lord Jarvis. No one would ever describe her as "pretty," although she was handsome in her own way, despite having also inherited her father's aquiline nose and haughty expression. She wore a carriage gown of soft moss with a matching parasol she held tipped against the glare of the sun, and a jaunty, velvet-trimmed hat from which escaped wisps of soft brown hair. A frightened-looking abigail hovered behind her, for a single gentlewoman never went anywhere without her maid.

"We don't know much about each other, do we?" said Sebastian. He did, in fact, have a passing interest in modern science—but not, as it happened, a fondness for steam engines.

"True." She let her gaze rove the crowd of curious onlookers. "Mr. Trevithick hasn't attracted much of a crowd, I'm afraid. And even those who've paid to take a look seem to lack the courage to actually go for a ride."

"Perhaps they're waiting for someone else to be the first?"

She brought her gray eyes to his face and smiled. "I'm game if you are."

He stared at her. "*Me?*"

"Surely you're not afraid too?"

Sebastian studied the engine's fiercely glowing fire. "You do know why Watt insists on the use of low-pressure steam, don't you?"

"Yes. Because high-pressure steam engines can be danger-ous. But they can be made so much smaller. *This*"—she gestured with one elegantly gloved hand toward Trevithick's steaming engine—"*this* is the future."

Sebastian rubbed the side of his nose with his bent knuckles. "I hear one of his engines exploded, killing four men."

Her lips tightened. "That was an earlier design. I tell you, one day engines such as this will propel passenger-carrying ve-hicles on our roads."

"I like horses," said Sebastian.

"So do I. But I also recognize their limitations. Imagine what working steam locomotives could accomplish—*if* people could only learn to accept them."

With a wry smile, Sebastian stepped to the side of the empty carriage and held out his hand. "Very well, Miss Jarvis; shall we set an example?"

She put her hand in his.

"Oh, Miss Jarvis!" cried the abigail, her fists clenched tight against her bosom. "You're never going to make me ride in that thing?"

Miss Jarvis glanced back at her. "You may await me here. It's no different, surely, from going with his lordship for a drive around the park."

The abigail heaved a visible sigh of relief. "Oh, *thank you*, Miss Jarvis."

As Sebastian scrambled up behind Miss Jarvis, a tall, dark-haired man with a craggy face dominated by a large nose nod-ded to the engineer. A shrill whistle cut through the air, eliciting a shriek from those nearby. The engineer opened a valve. There was a rush of steam, and the engine's wheels began to turn. With a sharp jerk, the carriage lurched forward.

"How fast can it go?" shouted Sebastian over the *whoosh* of steam leaving the cylinders and the roar of the crowd.

"Twelve miles an hour," she shouted back, her hand tightening on the handle of her parasol. "But you didn't come here to talk to me about steam engines, did you, Lord Devlin?"

Sebastian met her gaze squarely. "You know why I'm here."

Two months before, they had faced death together, trapped in the subterranean vaults beneath the abandoned gardens of a long-vanished Renaissance palace. In a moment of desperate weakness, they had sought comfort in each other's arms. Only, they had cheated death. And now it had become apparent that those moments of unexpected intimacy had resulted in an unintended consequence.

Thus far, Lord Jarvis's indomitable daughter had determinedly resisted all Sebastian's efforts to convince her to accept the protection of his name. But he was not one to give up so easily. He said, "Have you reconsidered my proposal?"

She held his gaze without flinching, although he noticed her throat tightening as she swallowed. "In point of fact, I have."

"And?"

"I have decided you are right; it is in the best interests of all concerned that I accept your generous offer. Therefore, I would be honored to be your wife, my lord." She paused, then added, "Preferably as soon as possible."

Chapter 6

*H*er response caught Sebastian so completely by surprise that for a moment he could only stare at her in stunned silence.

A wry sparkle lit up her eyes. "Didn't expect that, did you?"

"To be honest? No. But believe me when I say that I will never give you cause to regret this decision."

She responded with what sounded suspiciously like a derisive snort. "Personally, I've no doubt we shall both have multiple occasions on which to ponder the wisdom of this moment."

He huffed a soft laugh. Then his smile faded. "What made you change your mind?"

When she'd refused his offer, before, she told him she'd decided to leave England. Travel the world. Give birth to their child in some exotic locale and then return after several years, claiming the infant as an adopted foundling. It was a suggestion that had revolted Sebastian on many different levels—not least because it touched on the secret but raw wound of his own cloudy parentage.

"It would not have been"—she hesitated, as if searching for

the right word—"good for my mother had I left England. She needs me here."

Sebastian had heard that in her youth, Lady Jarvis was a pretty, vivacious thing, dainty and gay and different from her daughter in most ways imaginable. Then an endless series of miscarriages and stillbirths had ruined her health and debilitated her mind, leaving her easily frightened and more than a little addlebrained. Of the relationship between mother and daughter he realized he had no knowledge at all.

"Will she be unhappy to see you wed?" he asked.

"My mother? Hardly. The first time she sees you, she will doubtless fall on your neck and shower you with her undying gratitude. She never could understand my refusal to marry."

"Most women do wish to see their daughters established in life."

She started to say something, then obviously changed her mind and looked away.

He studied her carefully schooled profile and acknowledged a moment of deep disquiet. They may have faced death together; they may have joined their bodies to create a new life. Yet they were still, in essence, wary strangers—while he and her father were sworn enemies. He said, "I thought I would ask the Archbishop to officiate. Would sometime next week suit you?"

"Arrange the time and place, and I will be there."

"I suppose it only appropriate that I also formally approach Lord Jarvis."

Something flickered in her eyes, although whether it was amusement or a quite different emotion he could not have said. "That should be an interesting encounter, seeing as how in the past eighteen months you have at various times broken into his house, held him at gunpoint, and thrown a knife at him."

"Don't forget that I also kidnapped his daughter," Sebastian reminded her. It's how they had first met, when Sebastian had been a fugitive unjustly accused of murder and Jarvis had been doing his best to avert a scandal by having Sebastian summarily killed.

She said, "That too."

The steam engine's shrill whistle sounded again, drawing new shrieks from the crowd. She said, "I believe he has meetings with the Prince early this afternoon. But he should be in his chambers at Carlton House later."

Belching steam and soot, the engine picked up speed, chugging round and round the tightly circling tracks, the carriage swaying rhythmically from side to side. Sebastian kept his gaze on the woman before him. "I don't intend to give him the option of forbidding the match."

"I should think not. I am five-and-twenty, after all."

"He could disinherit you."

"He won't. You are hardly unsuitable. Just . . ."

"His enemy."

"My father has many enemies."

The carriage swung around the track, and she adjusted her parasol against the shifting angle of the sun. "I should like to make it clear at the onset that I have every intention of continuing with the various projects in which I am currently involved."

He found himself smiling. Miss Jarvis's "projects"—which ranged from an analysis of the economic stresses driving women into prostitution to an ambitious study of possible ways of improving the survival rates of infants left on the parish—alternately puzzled, infuriated, and bemused her father. Sebastian said, "I would not have expected otherwise, Miss Jarvis. After all, I intend to continue with my own involvement in murder investigations."

She regarded him with interest. "Are you involved in an investigation now?"

"No one's been murdered, have they?"

"Not to my knowledge."

A great cracking noise cut across the circle. The craggy-faced, dark-haired man started forward with a shout. The wheels of the engine froze with a sliding screech.

Sebastian craned around. "What the hell?"

"I believe the track has broken," said Miss Jarvis calmly as the carriage lurched sideways. The bench pitched wildly to the right, and she flung out a hand to maintain her precarious perch. "I heard Mr. Trevithick expressing some concern that the engine might be too heavy for the rails."

A great gasp went up from the crowd of spectators as the steam engine and its carriage came to a shuddering, lopsided halt.

Sebastian said, "Are you all right?"

She used the back of her wrist to push her hat out of her eyes. "Quite all right, thank you. But I fear for the success of Mr. Trevithick's New Steam Circus."

"Keep a smile on your face," said Sebastian, sliding off the seat. Boots firmly on the ground, he reached up to help her alight.

She came down beside him in an unruffled swirl of petticoats and artfully balanced parasol. "Oh, that was such fun," she exclaimed loudly for the benefit of the excited, jabbering crowd.

He leaned forward to whisper, "One of the staves of your parasol has snapped."

"Oh." She quickly closed it. "Thank you."

"My dear Miss Jarvis!" exclaimed the craggy-faced man, descending on them. "Please accept my heartfelt—"

"No, no, Mr. Trevithick, let me thank *you*," she said, cutting him off. "What a wonderful experience! And do let me know when the tracks are repaired so that I may have another ride around your amazing circus."

"You can't be serious," whispered Sebastian as they pushed

their way through the crowds rushing forward to gawk at the steaming, hissing engine.

"But I am." She drew up just inside the palisade's gate, her gaze scanning the crowd for her abigail. "Where is that woman of mine?"

Sebastian spied the harried, pale-faced maid threading her way toward them. He said, "I'll let you know the details once I've spoken to the Archbishop."

Miss Jarvis nodded, her gaze on the abigail.

He found himself studying the woman beside him. She had a streak of soot across her cheek; a lock of soft brown hair had escaped from beneath her hat. The combination made her look both less formidable and considerably more likeable.

"You won't regret this," he said suddenly.

She brought up a hand to shove the stray lock of hair back up under her hat with a brisk motion. "It was always my intention to never marry. To be forced to do so, now, seems somehow a defeat."

He reached out to wipe the smudge of soot from her cheek with the pad of his thumb. "Yet you also told me that your one regret was that you would never have children."

An uncharacteristic rush of color tinged her cheeks, and she tightened her grip on her parasol. "Yes, well . . . We have already remedied that, have we not?"

"Oh, Miss," exclaimed the abigail, rushing up to them. "What a frightful thing! You could have been killed!"

Miss Jarvis turned toward her maid. "Nonsense, Marie. I am quite all right." She nodded to Sebastian with what struck him as a regal inclination of her head. "My Lord Devlin."

He tipped his hat. "Miss Jarvis."

He stood at the gate, his gaze following her across the square. He was still watching her when Tom drew up the curricle beside him.

"What did you discover?" Sebastian asked, leaping up to take the reins.

Tom scrambled back to his perch. "Yer Sir 'Yde Foley takes 'is nuncheon at a public house on the corner o' Downing Street. The Cat and Bagpipe."

Ancient and low ceilinged, its atmosphere permeated with the wood smoke and spilled ale of centuries, the Cat and Bagpipe had once echoed with the shouts and bawdy songs of medieval pilgrims to the nearby shrine of Edward the Confessor in Westminster Abbey. Its current patrons were considerably more sedate, being drawn largely from the government offices occupying the warren of old houses fronting Downing Street and St. James's Park.

Pushing his way through the early afternoon crowd of clerks and MPs, Sebastian found Sir Hyde Foley eating a plate of sliced boiled beef at an age-darkened oak table near the pub's vast stone hearth. A slim man with pale skin and dark hair, he watched Sebastian's progress across the hazy room with narrowed eyes.

"Let me tell you right off," he said as Sebastian drew up beside his table, "that if you are here as your father's emissary—"

"I am not." Without waiting for an invitation, Sebastian drew out the opposite chair and sat. "I'm told Mr. Alexander Ross worked for you."

Foley cut a slice of beef. "He did. Why do you ask?"

Sebastian studied the other man's thin, sharp-boned face. "You don't find the sudden death of a healthy young man at the Foreign Office cause for concern?"

Foley chewed slowly and swallowed. "Mr. Ross died of a defective heart."

Sebastian caught the eye of the plump, middle-aged barmaid

and held up two fingers. "Mr. Alexander Ross died from a stiletto thrust to the base of his skull."

Foley hesitated with his fork raised halfway to his mouth. "How do you know this?"

"That, I am not at liberty to say."

"Indeed. So I am simply to take your word for it?"

Sebastian waited while the barmaid set two foaming tankards on the battered tabletop between them. Then he said, "When exactly did you last see Mr. Ross?"

Foley frowned as if with thought. "He died . . . when? Last Sunday?"

"Either early Sunday morning or sometime Saturday night."

Foley shrugged. "Then I suppose I must have seem him that Saturday, at the Foreign Office. Why?"

Sebastian took a long, slow swallow of his ale. "What precisely were Mr. Ross's duties with the Foreign Office?"

"He dealt with foreign nationals."

Sebastian raised one eyebrow. "Meaning?"

"Meaning that anything beyond that is none of your damned business."

Sebastian smiled and took another sip of ale. "What was your opinion of him?"

"Ross?" Foley shrugged. "He was a good man. A very good man. We were sorry to lose him. Too many young men in his situation would have treated his position in the Foreign Office with negligent indifference. Not Ross."

"'In his situation?' What does that mean, precisely?"

"Only that his brother, Sir Gareth Ross, is both childless and half-paralyzed from a carriage accident. As the heir presumptive, Alexander Ross would doubtless have inherited—had he lived."

"Sir Gareth's fortune is considerable?"

"Considerable? I wouldn't go so far as to say that. But comfortable, definitely comfortable. The family is an old one, while the estate—Charlbury Priory—is both ancient and widely admired."

"Ross was how old? Twenty-five? Thirty?"

"Six-and-twenty, I believe. He'd been with the Foreign Office since coming down from Cambridge."

"Always in London?"

Foley carved another slice of beef. "With the exception of a two-year stint at our embassy in St. Petersburg, yes."

"He was in Russia?"

"That's right."

"By which I can assume that some of the 'foreign nationals' he dealt with here in London were Russian?"

Foley raised his own tankard to his lips, his gaze meeting Sebastian's over the rim. "You may assume anything you like."

Sebastian leaned back in his seat, his arms crossed at his chest, and smiled. "I'm told Ross was expecting a visitor Saturday night. You wouldn't by any chance know who that was?"

Foley shook his head. "Sorry. No."

"Do you know if he had any financial difficulties? A mistress? Gambling debts, perhaps?"

"Hardly. We're pretty careful about that sort of thing."

"Know of anyone who might have wanted him dead?"

Foley set down his fork with a clatter. "You can't be serious about all this?"

Sebastian ignored the question. "No enemies?"

Foley held his gaze. "None that I am aware of, no."

"Any recent quarrels?"

Foley was silent for a moment.

"What?" prompted Sebastian.

The Undersecretary drained the last of his pint and gave a soft laugh.

Sebastian said, "So he did have an argument. With whom?"

Sir Hyde Foley reached for his hat, his chair grating across the old stone-flagged floor as he pushed to his feet. "Good day, my lord."

Quickly paying off his tab, Sebastian reached the flagway in time to see Foley turn to stride up Pall Mall, away from his offices in Downing Street.

Tom was waiting nearby.

"Get down and follow him," said Sebastian, leaping into the curricle to take the reins. "I want to know where he goes."

Chapter 7

Paul Gibson spent most of the morning dissecting Alexander Ross's chest cavity. He found no evidence of any heart disease or other natural disability. He was so engrossed in his task that he barely managed to grab time before his scheduled lecture at St. Thomas's to study the Bills of Mortality for London and Westminster.

Published weekly for more than two hundred years now by the parish clerks, the Bills of Mortality recorded the dead in each parish, along with their ages and causes of death. Originally designed to provide a warning against the onset of plagues, the Bills of Mortality were not infallible. But they were fairly reliable. The returns were compiled by old women known as "viewers" or "searchers of the dead," employed by each parish. Their job was to enter houses where a death had been reported. Since they were paid two pence per body, they tended to be thorough to the point of being aggressive.

Of course, the searchers' expertise in determining causes of death was limited. Gibson had no doubt that whatever searcher

recorded Alexander Ross's death had simply accepted the diagnosis provided by the renowned Dr. Cooper. But if Jumpin' Jack
had made a mistake—if the body lying on Gibson's slab belonged
not to Mr. Alexander Ross but to some other young gentleman
who was known to have encountered a violent death—then his
identity would be found in the Bills of Mortality.

Choosing a chair near a dusty window, Gibson quickly ran
through the compiled list of deaths by natural causes for the
previous week . . . *aged, 24; ague, 2; bloody flux, 1; childbed, 3; fever,
235; French pox, 1; measles, 5.* . . . Sighing, he skipped down to the
"unnatural deaths": *bites, mad dog, 1; burnt, 2; choked, none; drowned, 3;
shot, none; smothered, 1; stabbed, none.*

He checked the previous week, just to be certain. *Shot, one.
Stabbed, none.*

Leaning back in his chair, he scrubbed both hands down
over his face. Then he pushed to his feet, returned the Bills of
Mortality to the bored-looking clerk, and went in search of Dr.
Astley Cooper.

He met the surgeon turning in through the gates of St. Thomas's
Hospital.

An imposing man with dark eyebrows and thick gray hair
flowing from a rapidly receding hairline, Dr. Astley Cooper
was long accustomed to hearing himself described as London's
preeminent surgeon. In addition to lecturing on anatomy at St.
Thomas's, he was a member of the Royal College of Surgeons
and a professor of surgery at Guy's Hospital. But it was his flourishing private practice that earned him more than twenty-one
thousand pounds a year—a level of success he made no attempt
to keep secret.

"May I walk with you a moment, Dr. Cooper?" Gibson asked,
falling into step beside the famous man.

"As you wish," said Cooper, cutting across the quadrangle toward the chapel. He cast Gibson a quick, assessing glance. "I hear you are to lecture this afternoon on cerebral circulation. I trust you've consulted my own writings on the subject?"

Gibson schooled his features into an expression of solemn respect. "To be sure, Dr. Cooper. You are the expert, are you not?"

Cooper nodded, said, "Good," and kept walking.

Gibson said, "I wanted to ask you a few questions about Alexander Ross."

Cooper frowned. "Who?"

"The young gentleman who was found dead in his rooms in St. James's Street last Sunday. The one you said died of a defective heart."

"Ah, yes; I remember now. What about him?"

"I was wondering if you were told he had a history of pleurisy? Or perhaps carditis?"

Cooper shrugged. "How would I know? The man was no patient of mine."

"No one gave you a medical history?"

"I was told simply that he appeared healthy to all who knew him."

"And you saw no signs of disorder in the room? Nothing out of place?"

"What a preposterous question. The man died peacefully in his sleep. He wasn't thrashing about in his death throes, if that's what you're suggesting."

"There were no signs of blood on the sheets?

"Why on earth would there be? The man died of *morbus cordis*." The surgeon's eyes narrowed. "Are you questioning my diagnosis?"

"Not at all. Simply curious." Gibson drew up. "Thank you; you've been most helpful."

He started to turn away, then swung back around when a thought occurred to him. "Just one more question, Dr. Cooper—"

The surgeon tightened his prominent, bulbous jaw. "Yes? What now?"

"I was wondering who called you to Mr. Ross's bedside that morning."

"Who called me? Sir Hyde Foley. Why do you ask?"

Chapter 8

$\mathcal{S}$ir Henry Lovejoy, once the chief magistrate at Queen Square, now the newest of Bow Street's three stipendiary magistrates, drew a handkerchief from his pocket and pressed its snowy folds against his damp upper lip. The day had grown uncomfortably warm, the insects in the surrounding dank grass setting up a loud, maddening hum that seemed somehow to accentuate the foul stench of death and decay rising from the body before him.

Wrapped in a dirty canvas, the unidentified corpse lay half-hidden in a weed-choked ditch on the edge of Bethnal Green. A wretched, insalubrious area on the northeastern fringes of London, the district was a favorite dumping ground for dead cats and dogs, unwanted babies, and victims of murder.

"He ain't a pretty sight, I'm afraid," said Constable O'Neal, a stout, middle-aged man with florid jowls and a prominent nose. Slopping noisily through several inches of slimy water, he leaned over with a grunt to draw back a corner of the canvas and reveal a bloated, discolored nightmare of a face.

"Good God." Lovejoy bunched the handkerchief against his nostrils. "Cover it up again. Quickly, before the children see it."

The constable threw a skeptical glance at the knot of ragged, half-grown urchins who'd gathered nearby to gawk at them, and dropped the canvas. "Yes, sir."

Normally, the discovery of another body in one of the poorest districts of London was of no concern to Bow Street. But there were circumstances surrounding this man's death that Lovejoy found troubling. He said, "So what exactly have you discovered, Constable?"

"Not much, I'm afraid. You did notice his clothes, sir? They're uncommon fine. The local magistrate reckons the body musta been brought from someplace else and dumped here. Ain't no gentlemen missing from around these parts, sir."

Lovejoy sighed. "No identification on him?"

"None, sir."

Lovejoy turned to stare thoughtfully across the green, toward the dark, grim walls of the madhouse and, beyond that, Jews Walk. This was an area of marshy fields and tumbledown cottages, of Catholics and Jews and impoverished French weavers.

The constable cleared his throat. "And then there's the lad I was telling you about—Jamie Durban, sir."

Lovejoy brought his gaze back to the constable's jowly face. "Where is he?"

"Here, sir." The constable motioned to one of the ragged boys. "Well, come on, then, lad. Say your piece."

Jamie Durban—a scrawny, carrot-topped lad of ten or twelve—wiped the back of one hand across his nose and reluctantly stepped forward.

Lovejoy looked the boy up and down. He was barefoot, the flesh of his arms and legs liberally streaked with dirt, his ragged shirt and breeches two sizes too big for his slight frame. "So what have you to say for yourself, Jamie Durban?"

The lad threw a frightened glance at the constable.

"Go on. Tell him," urged the constable.

Jamie swallowed hard enough to bob his Adam's apple up and down in his skinny throat. "It were Saturday night o' last week, sir—or rather, I suppose you could say early Sunday mornin'."

Lovejoy fixed the boy with a hard stare. "Go on."

"I were 'eadin' 'ome along the east side o' the green, when I seen a swell carriage drawn up just 'ere—beside the ditch."

"What makes you think it was a gentleman's carriage and not a hackney?" asked Lovejoy. "It was rather dark last Saturday, was it not?"

"Not so much, sir. The moon was still pretty new, but it was clear and the stars was shinin' somethin' fierce. It was a gentry cove's carriage, all right. A curricle, drawn by a pair o' high-steppin' dark 'orses and driven by a cove wearin' one o' them fancy coats with all them shoulder capes."

Lovejoy studied the boy's pale, delicate features. "And?"

"I could see the gentry cove was wrestlin' with somethin' big and bulky 'e 'ad on the floor o' 'is curricle. So I nipped behind the wall o' the corner house there to watch, and I seen 'im dump it 'ere, in the ditch. It'd rained some that day, and I 'eard the splash when it 'it the water."

Lovejoy's gaze drifted back to the silent, canvas-covered body at their feet. "What did the gentleman do next?"

"Why, 'e got back in 'is curricle and drove off. Toward the west, sir."

"And what did you do, Jamie?"

Jamie dug the bare toes of one foot into the dirt, his gaze averted.

"Speak up, there, lad," barked the constable. "Answer the magistrate's question."

Jamie's jaw went slack with remembered horror. "I . . . um, I waited 'til I was sure the cove was long gone. Then I come and took a peek at what 'e'd 'eaved into the ditch."

"Are you telling me," said Lovejoy, "that you have known this body was here since last Saturday night? And you only just got around to telling the constables about it today?"

The boy took a step back, his eyes widening. "I kept thinkin' somebody was bound to find 'im. Especially once 'e started smellin'. But then 'e jist laid 'ere and laid 'ere, and finally it got so's I couldn't stand it no more. So I told Father Dean at St. Matthew's, and 'e said I should own up to what I seen."

Lovejoy frowned. "You're certain this was Saturday night?"

"Yes, sir."

"And when you first saw it, was the body fresh? Or was it already showing signs of decay?"

"Oh, 'e were fresh, all right. Why, 'e were still warm!"

Lovejoy frowned. "What time did you say this was?"

"Jist after three, sir. I remember I 'eard the night watchman calling the hour as I was crossin' the green."

Lovejoy and the constable exchanged glances. "And what were you doing out at three in the morning, lad? Hmm? Speak up there."

Jamie Durban took another step back, his previously pale face suddenly flushing scarlet.

"Go on, then. Answer the magistrate's question," urged the constable.

His nostrils flaring in panic, the boy whirled to take off across the green, arms and legs pumping, hair flashing golden red in the hot sun.

"Bloody hell." The constable lumbered up out of the ditch. "You want I should go after him, sir?"

Lovejoy watched the boy run. "No. Let him go. I assume you know where he lives?"

"Yes, sir. In Three Dog Lane. Lives with his widowed ma and three sisters, he does."

His handkerchief pressed once more to his nostrils, Lovejoy hunkered down beside the ditch. The weeds had been trampled by countless rough boots, the fetid water churned and muddied. Whatever evidence might have been recoverable days ago had been lost to the rain and the passage of time and careless men. He glanced up at the constable. "You've searched the area?"

"We have. Nothing, sir." The constable paused. "You want we should send the body to the dead house in Wapping, sir?"

Lovejoy frowned. London had several dead houses, or mortuaries, for unidentified or unclaimed bodies. But they were miserable, filthy places, most with little space for a proper postmortem.

He shook his head. "Fetch a shell from the dead house, but have a couple of lads carry the body to the surgery of Paul Gibson, on Tower Hill. Perhaps he'll be able to give us something to go on." He pushed to his feet. "And check the pawnbrokers' shops and fences in the area. See if young Mr. Durban has sold any men's jewelry or other items in the last week."

"You think he stole something from the body, sir?"

"How else did he know the corpse was still warm?"

"Aye, good point that, sir. Although I suppose—" The constable broke off, his gaze shifting to something over Sir Henry's shoulder.

"What is it?" Lovejoy turned to find a tall, bone-thin clerk hurrying toward them across the green. He drew up before them, his breath coming in noisy gasps.

"Sir Henry," said the man, his pale forehead gleaming with sweat. "A message for you from the Foreign Office. The Undersecretary, Sir Hyde Foley, wishes to see you. At once!"

Chapter 9

*S*ebastian's next stop was the Mayfair town house of the woman he still thought of as his Aunt Henrietta, although she was not, in truth, his aunt, or any other relation closer than a distant cousin.

Born Lady Henrietta St. Cyr, the elder sister of the Earl of Hendon, she had been married for fifty years to the Duke of Claiborne. A widow now for more than three years, the Dowager Duchess still occupied the vast family pile on Park Lane. By rights, the house belonged to her eldest son. But the new Duke of Claiborne was no match for his formidable mother. So while the current Duke raised his growing family in a much smaller house on Half Moon Street, the Duchess continued on as before, one of the acknowledged grandes dames of society—and a veritable walking *Debrett's Peerage*, who knew everything there was to know about the members of the Upper Ten Thousand.

Sebastian expected to find her still abed, or perhaps sipping chocolate in her dressing room, for the Duchess was famous for never leaving her room before one. But to his surprise, she was not only up and dressed, but in her breakfast parlor partaking of toast and tea and perusing a copy of the *Morning Post.*

"Good heavens," she said, sitting forward with a jerk that set her tea to slopping dangerously. "Sebastian."

"You're up early, Aunt," he said, stooping to plant a kiss on her cheek. "It's barely past noon."

"Blame Claiborne's eldest, Georgina. Takes after me, poor girl. But as I always say, just because a woman is not beautiful is no excuse for not being fashionable. Unfortunately, that silly nitwit Claiborne married can't dress herself properly, let alone a chit just out of the schoolroom. So there's nothing for it but for me to take the child to the cloth warehouses myself."

"Ah."

She reached for her quizzing glass and regarded him through it. "Why are you here, you fatiguing child?"

He laughed. "Two things, actually. First of all, I'd like to hear what you know about Sir Gareth Ross."

"Sir Gareth?" She looked intrigued. "Whatever has he done?"

"Nothing that I know of." Sebastian drew out the chair beside her and sat. "Tell me about him."

"Well . . . there's not much to tell, actually. He must be in his early forties by now, I suppose. Your typical country gentleman. Married some chit from Norfolk—a Miss Alice Hart, if I remember correctly—but she died in childbirth barely a year later, and her child with her. He never remarried."

"I take it he's something of an invalid?"

"That's right. Broke his back in a carriage accident a few years ago. He isn't exactly bedridden, but he doesn't get around much and, well"—she dropped her voice to a stage whisper and leaned forward—"let's just say, I've heard he won't be siring any sons."

"So his heir presumptive was his younger brother, Mr. Alexander Ross. And now?"

"A cousin of some sort. There were something like four or five daughters in the family, but only the two sons."

Sebastian turned sideways so he could stretch out his legs and cross his boots at the ankles. "What do you know about Alexander Ross?"

"Charming young man. Terrible tragedy, his dying like that." She opened her eyes wider. "Good heavens, is *that* why you're interested in the Rosses? Dear me."

It was beginning to occur to Sebastian that he had only to express an interest in someone who'd recently died for anyone hearing him to assume that individual had been murdered. He said, "That's all you can tell me about the younger Ross? That he was a 'charming young man'?"

Henrietta frowned. "Well, he'd recently become engaged to an heiress. Miss Sabrina Cox."

"Cox?"

"Mmm. Not one of the Coxes of Staffordshire, mind you. Her father was Peter Cox—the one who was Lord Mayor, and then Member of Parliament for London until his death."

"So he was a Cit?"

"A very rich Cit. The girl's mother was gently born, however. A sister of Lady Dorsey. But her father ran with the Hellfire crowd and plunged so deep that he was forced to sell his youngest daughter to the highest bidder."

"How high a bid are we talking about here?"

"Towed the old reprobate out of the River Tick—or so they say. In his day, Peter Cox was said to rival Golden Ball. Divided his wealth between his son and daughter."

Sebastian frowned. "Her brother is Jasper Cox?"

"Yes. You know him?"

"I've met him," said Sebastian noncommittally.

Henrietta huffed a sharp laugh. "And couldn't stand the man, obviously. Few can. But he's dreadfully well off. Manages his sister's portion until she weds, as well. Together they're major shareholders in the Rosehaven Trading Company, amongst other ventures. It was quite a brilliant match for Ross, even if the wealth does come from trade."

"Thank you, Aunt," said Sebastian, pushing to his feet. "You've been most helpful."

She frowned up at him. "You said you were here for two reasons; Ross is the first. What is the second?"

He leaned forward to kiss her cheek. "I'm getting married next week." He turned toward the door.

"You're what?" Her teacup hit its saucer with a clatter. "Sebastian, you come right back here and sit down. You can't just fling something like that at me and then walk away! Sebastian, it's not— Oh, Sebastian; you're not marrying Kat Boleyn?"

He paused with one hand on the doorframe to look back at his aunt, his jaw set hard. "She's already married, remember?"

He tried hard not to resent the ill-disguised relief he saw flood across his aunt's face. "Then who—" She broke off, her eyes widening. "Good heavens. It's Miss Jarvis, isn't it?"

It was his turn to stare. "How the devil did you know that?"

She raised her teacup to her lips and gave him an arch look over the brim. "Well, you have been seen together rather a lot lately."

They'd been seen together because they'd been discussing murder, but he wasn't about to tell his aunt that. He said, "I'd like you to be there for the ceremony, if you're willing."

"Don't be ridiculous. I shall be delighted." She hesitated. "You've told Hendon?"

"No."

"Sebastian . . . however difficult it may be for you to believe, you must realize that Hendon's love for you is real. You have always been his son in every way that counts. That has not changed, and it never will."

Sebastian swallowed the inevitable retort and turned away. "I'll let you know when the time and place have been finalized."

His next stop was Lambeth Palace on the south bank of the river Thames, home to John Moore, the aged Archbishop of Canterbury.

"So," said the Archbishop, pouring a shaky stream of tea into two delicate china cups. His movements were slow and deliberate, for he was an old man, pale and gray haired, his thin body racked by the final stages of consumption. "If you've already procured a special license from Doctors' Commons, you don't need me."

Sebastian stood before the marble mantelpiece in the Archbishop's chambers, his hands clasped behind his back. "Nevertheless, I would be honored to have Your Grace perform the ceremony. This is, if you feel you're up to it."

"It would be a pleasure." Moore paused to carefully set the heavy teapot aside. "Odd that the Duchess of Claiborne made no mention of any approaching nuptials when I encountered her in Bond Street yesterday." The Archbishop and the Duchess were old friends.

"She didn't know then. She does now."

"Ah. I see." Archbishop Moore held out one of the cups. "Well, here's to your health and happiness." He raised his own cup in a wry toast. "I wish it were something more suitable, but doctor's orders, you know. At any rate, cheers."

"Thank you, Your Grace." Sebastian took a polite sip of the tea.

The Archbishop's eyes crinkled into a smile. "If I might be so bold as to ask the name of the lady?"

"Miss Hero Jarvis."

The Archbishop choked on his tea and fell to coughing violently.

Sebastian started forward. "Are you all right, sir? Shall I call—"

"No, no." Moore put out a hand, stopping him. "One would expect that by my age I'd know better than to try to drink and breathe at the same time." He fortified himself with more tea. "Miss Hero Jarvis, you say? A fine young woman, to be sure." He cleared his throat. "And when would you like the ceremony to take place?"

"Sometime this week, if possible."

Moore nodded. "Thursday, shall we say? At eleven in the chapel here, at the palace. You may arrange the details with my secretary." He stared down at the murky liquid in his cup, a strange smile curling the edges of his lips. "Well, well, well," he said as if to himself. "How very interesting."

Chapter 10

*L*eaving the Archbishop's palace in Lambeth, Sebastian made his way back to the Je Reviens coffee shop on St. James's Street.

This time he found Madame Champagne seated at a small round table placed so that it caught the sun streaming in through the oriel window overlooking the fashionable thoroughfare. She was an attractive woman somewhere in her late forties or fifties, petite and slender, with pale blond hair just beginning to fade gracefully to white. Her features were fine boned and elegant, their delicacy thrown into sharp relief when she turned her head and he saw she wore a black silk patch over her right eye.

She watched him cross the room toward her, a wry smile curving her full, generous mouth. "Viscount Devlin, I assume?" She gave the title its French inflection, *vicomte*, her accent still pronounced despite the years of exile from her native land. "I was told you were inquiring after me."

"May I?" he asked, drawing out the chair opposite her.

She spread her hands wide. "Please. I know why you are here."

Sebastian sat. "You do?"

"Monsieur Poole and I had an interesting conversation." She gave a barely perceptible nod to the burly, gray-bearded man behind the counter, who set to work preparing two coffees. "Alexander Ross was murdered; is this not so?"

"I never said that."

"It was unnecessary." She tilted her head to one side, her remaining eye narrowing as she assessed him. He noticed she tended to keep the right side of her face turned away. She said, "I trust you have a good reason for this assumption?"

"I have."

She nodded. "Me, I suspected as much."

"Why is that?"

She shrugged. "When a healthy young man who is involved with dangerous people dies suddenly . . . Well, let us just say that if there's one thing I have learned in this life, it is not to take anything at face value."

Sebastian waited while the gray-bearded man placed the coffee on the table before them, then withdrew. "How long have you been in London?"

"Nearly ten years. I went first to Italy, then Majorca." She leaned back in her chair, her fingers playing with her cup, an enigmatic smile touching her lips. "I was acquainted with your mother, you know. You are quite like her in many ways . . . although not in all."

Sebastian held himself very still. Some eighteen years before, on a hot, joyless summer day after the death of Sebastian's two older brothers, the Countess of Hendon had staged her own death and disappeared to the Continent with her latest lover. He had mourned his mother for half his life before discovering that she was, in fact, alive.

It had been but the first of several unpleasant truths he had learned.

He'd tried in the months since that discovery to trace her fate. His agents had followed her to Venice and then to France, where they hit a wall built by war and an inexplicable, fearful silence.

Now he asked, his voice calm and casual and everything he was not, "You knew her in Venice?"

"Yes. She lived in a crumbling old palace on the Grand Canal with . . ." Her voice trailed off.

"Her lover?" he supplied.

A sad, sympathetic smile touched her lips. "Yes. She used to give wonderful musical evenings—it's how I came to know her. Her lover was a talented composer as well as a poet, you see. They were quite happy. But then, he died."

Sebastian nodded. According to the last report he'd received, Lady Hendon had eventually taken up with one of Napoléon's generals, but he had no way of knowing if that was still true.

Angelina Champagne reached out to touch her fingertips briefly, unexpectedly, to the back of his hand. "You need have no fear that I will speak of these things to others. The past is dead, and we who are left alive must go on, yes?"

She paused to take a slow sip of her coffee. There was a fragile, ethereal beauty to her features, a tautness that hinted at sadness and tragedy borne with a quiet stoicism and something else—something mysterious and well hidden. She said, "You know Ross was with the Foreign Office?"

"Are you saying you think his work at the Foreign Office had something to do with his death?"

"You doubt it? All of Europe has been at war for—what? More than two decades. Over the years, alliances have shifted and recombined, again and again. But it's my belief that one day, historians will look back on this summer and see it as a pivotal moment in time."

"You mean, because of Napoléon's invasion of Russia?"

"Even without the successes of Wellington in Spain, it was most unwise. But as the situation currently stands?" She pursed her lips with contempt. "It goes beyond folly to madness. Tens of thousands will die. Perhaps hundreds of thousands. We have lost too many already—so many dead, so much of what once made France great, destroyed. And now this."

He wondered how many relatives she still had in France, perhaps even serving in the legions that were marching on Moscow as they spoke. He said, "Napoléon claims the Czar left him no alternative."

She let out her breath in an elegant sound of disgust. "There are always alternatives. The Swedes and Russians have ended their war with the Treaty of St. Petersburg, while the Treaty of Bucharest has ended the Russo-Turkish War. With their northern and southern flanks thus protected, the Russians will be able to throw all of their forces against the French."

"Except they're not facing just the French," Sebastian reminded her. "Napoléon has succeeded in cementing a new alliance to bring the Prussians and Austrians with him against Russia."

"Only because Prussia's King Frederick William knew his choice was between a military alliance with Napoléon and the loss of his crown."

"And Austria?"

"Austria has little to lose and much to gain from a war between France and Russia. Metternich knows this."

She was an unusual woman, shrewd and well versed in current events and not the least hesitant to state her opinions. Sebastian studied the stark line of the tie for her eye patch, the sun-kissed skin of her cheek. In an age when most gentlewomen took excruciating pains to protect their delicate complexions from the sun, Madame Champagne obviously deliberately sought it out, and he found himself wondering why.

He said, "You take an interest in diplomatic affairs."

"War tends to make us all students of diplomacy, does it not? There is a story that Napoléon once told the widow of the Marquis de Condorcet that he detested women who meddled in politics. Do you know her reply?"

Sebastian shook his head.

"She said, 'You are right, of course, General. But in a country where one cuts off women's heads, it is natural that they should wish to know the reason why.'"

Madame Condorcet had been a widow because the Revolution sent her husband, the famous *philosophe* the Marquis de Condorcet, to the guillotine. Sebastian's gaze dropped to Madame Champagne's left hand. She still wore a simple gold band on her finger, but the dusky lilac silk of her gown told its own story, for lilac was the color of sadness and mourning.

As if aware of the train of his thoughts, she said, "My husband was Baron Jean-Baptiste Champagne. He was killed in the September Massacres, in 1792."

Sebastian had heard of Jean-Baptiste Champagne. Like the Comte de Virieu and Lally-Tollendal, Champagne had been an early supporter of the Revolutionary movement—before it turned violent and cruel and began devouring its own.

He said, "That's when you fled France?"

"As soon as I was able, yes."

Her voice quavered ever so faintly, and she turned her head, showing him only her flawless profile as she studied the flow of elegant carriages in the street, the endless parade of gentlemen on the strut. He found himself wondering about the life she'd once lived— and lost—in Paris, about the horrors she must have witnessed before she finally escaped it all and fled to Venice, and about all the lonely years she'd lived since then, bereft, with her memories.

They sat in silence for a moment, watching as a plump-cheeked dandy with exaggerated shirt points and a painfully nipped-in waist approached the adjoining door that led to the apartments above and disappeared inside. A moment later, the shuffle of his footsteps on the stairs could be faintly heard above the murmurs in the coffee shop.

Sebastian said, "These 'dangerous men' you say Ross associated with . . . Do you know who they were?"

"No."

"Then how do you know they were dangerous?"

Again, that faintly amused curving of the lips. "In my experience, men who turn up the collars of their coats and pull their hats low enough to hide their faces are generally to be avoided."

"Did such men visit Ross often?"

"Often enough."

"And the night he died?"

"You mean, last Saturday?"

"Yes."

"What makes you think I would remember such a thing now, a week later?"

"Because on Sunday morning, when you heard Ross had died, you were suspicious. I think you gave some thought as to what you might have observed the night before."

She raised her cup to her lips and took a sip. "You are very astute, are you not?"

Sebastian said, "Who visited Alexander Ross that night?"

She set her cup down with careful attention. "Well . . . Let's see. First there was a young woman. Or at least, I assume she was young, although it is difficult to be certain since she wore a cloak and had the hood pulled up."

"A well-dressed young woman?"

"Her cloak was plain, but well cut. I couldn't see more than that, since she also wore a veil. She was no woman of the streets, if that's what you're asking."

"Did Ross entertain women of the street?"

"Not in his rooms. I've no notion how he conducted himself elsewhere."

"How long did this woman stay?"

"Twenty minutes? Perhaps half an hour. No more. She left very quickly."

"She came by carriage?"

Madame Champagne shook her head. "Hackney, of course."

Sebastian nodded. St. James's Street was the gentlemen's preserve. For a gentlewoman simply to walk down St. James's Street was considered a social solecism. But for a woman of quality to be seen entering a gentleman's lodgings, alone, would mean swift and certain ruin. No wonder the woman—whoever she was—had taken care to hide her face. "And then?"

"An hour or two after the woman's departure, a gentleman in evening clothes went up."

"And he arrived—how?"

"Walking. But there's no use asking me anything more about him because I really couldn't tell you. He wore a hat pulled low and an opera cape with the collar turned up, and he took care to keep his head down."

Sebastian smiled. "One of Ross's 'dangerous men'?"

"Exactly."

"He stayed how long?"

"Longer than the woman. An hour. Perhaps longer. I'd say it was close to nine or ten when he left."

"There's nothing you can tell me about him?"

"Not really. He was neither remarkably tall nor short, corpulent nor excessively thin. His clothes were very much those of a gentleman—silk stockings and knee breeches. Oh—and he carried a walking stick."

Sebastian himself possessed an elegant ebony walking stick. The silver handle was artfully contrived to conceal a stiletto. He said, "Mr. Ross himself never stepped out that evening?"

"If he did, I didn't see him."

"Is there another way out?"

"There is a door to the court, but it doesn't lead anywhere." Madame Champagne sipped her coffee for a moment, then said, "Ross had one more visitor that night."

"Oh?"

She nodded. "Shortly before I retired for the evening, another gentleman went up. But he came back down almost immediately."

"You mean, as if he had found Mr. Ross not at home?"

"Yes. Or as if Mr. Ross were already dead."

Chapter 11

Sebastian studied the Frenchwoman's fine-boned face, the single, half-hooded eye. "And how was this second gentleman dressed?"

"Much the same as the first. Evening cape and knee breeches."

"Could they have been the same man?"

She frowned, as if considering this. Then she shook her head. "I do not believe so. They moved differently. Or at least, it must have seemed so to me at the time, for it never occurred to me that they might be the same man."

Sebastian said, "Had you seen these men visit Mr. Ross before?"

"Them, or men like them."

"But you've no idea who they might be?"

She started to say something, then hesitated.

"What?" he prompted.

She leaned forward. "Men may hide their faces but forget that their accents can tell their own story . . . to those who know how to listen."

"What kind of accents are we talking about?"

"Mainly Russian. But also Swedish and Turkish. And the occasional Frenchman, of course." She kept her gaze on his face. "You're wondering how I could know, yes?"

He gave a wry smile. "I doubt I would be able to identify a Swedish or a Russian accent. Or distinguish a Turk from, say, a Greek."

"My father was an official at Versailles when I was a child. I grew up surrounded by accents from all over Europe—and beyond. It was a game my brother and I played, imitating them."

Sebastian watched her nostrils flare on a quickly indrawn breath and he knew without being told that her brother, like her husband, was dead. He said, "You knew none of these men?"

"I recognized one of the Russians—a colonel attached to the embassy, by the name of Colonel Dimitri Chernishav. I understand he and Ross were friends from Ross's time in Russia."

The name meant nothing to Sebastian. "Anyone else?"

She made a face. "Well, there's Antoine de La Rocque."

"Who is he?"

"Once, he was a priest. He fled France in the first wave, more than twenty years ago now. He has something of a reputation as a collector of rare, old books. He has opened part of his collection to the public—to the paying public, of course, although he claims that is only to keep out the riffraff."

"Where is this?"

"Great Russell Street, near the museum. Although he can frequently be found prowling the bookstalls in Westminster Hall."

"Could de La Rocque have been one of the men you saw that night?"

"He visited Alexander Ross regularly. But was he one of the men I saw that night?" Again, that enigmatic smile. "Who knows?"

Sebastian was beginning to suspect she knew considerably

more than she was willing to reveal. But all he said was, "The second man—the one you say went upstairs and came back down again so quickly—at what time was this?"

"Somewhere around half past midnight. It was shortly before I retired for the night. I keep rooms in another house I own near here," she explained, "on Ryder Street. So it is always possible someone could have arrived to see Monsieur Ross after I left here. Or Monsieur Ross himself may have stepped out. I would not know."

Sebastian pushed to his feet. "You've been most helpful, Madame; thank you."

She gazed up at him thoughtfully. "Yet you wonder why, when I know your reason for asking these questions, I have given you the name of one of my countrymen—a fellow émigré. Hmm?"

He had, in fact, been wondering exactly that.

The skin beside her remaining eye crinkled with her smile. "For some time now, those of us in the émigré community have suspected that there is a traitor in our midst. One who claims to despise Napoléon and all the while secretly passing information back to Paris."

Sebastian had heard such rumors. He said, "You think de La Rocque could be the traitor?"

She pressed her lips together and shrugged. "He claims he fled France to avoid being put to death as a nonjuring priest." Tens of thousands of priests had fled Revolutionary France rather than take the antipapal oath of religion; those who stayed faced either death or deportation to a penal colony. "Yet he will also laugh and tell you he lost his faith in God at the age of ten. Both cannot be true."

"That doesn't make him a traitor," Sebastian said.

"No. But it makes him a liar. Remember that when you speak to him."

. . .

Hero Jarvis sat at the heavy oak table in the library of the Jarvis town house on Berkeley Square. She held a pen in one hand; piles of maps and books lay scattered about her. She had intended to devote the afternoon to a survey she was preparing on the few surviving traces of London's lost monastic houses. But the ink had long ago dried on the nib as she stared unseeingly at the garden beyond the room's tall windows.

She'd told Lord Devlin the truth when she said it had been her intention never to marry. She might work hard to change England's draconian marriage laws and the unconscionable powers granted husbands over their wives, but she was realistic enough to know that real change was still generations away. And so she had poured the energy that other women her age devoted to their families into studies and articles and draft legislation. She'd told Devlin she intended to continue her efforts, and she did. But she was no fool, and she suspected her life was about to change in ways she couldn't begin to imagine and didn't want.

There was also the matter of who would take over from Hero the management of her father's big house on Berkeley Square. Hero's grandmother, the Dowager Lady Jarvis, had long ago retired to her rooms on the second floor and rarely ventured forth to do more than complain or criticize; Hero's own mother, Annabelle, Lady Jarvis, was so feeble both physically and emotionally that the mere thought of trying to select a menu or deal with tradesmen was enough to send her tottering toward her couch, vinaigrette in hand.

Hero would need to find a companion for her mother, someone capable of both overseeing the household and sheltering her ladyship from the worst of her husband's venom. Jarvis did not suffer fools lightly, and Lady Jarvis's mental stability was always at best precarious. Hero was running a list of possible candidates through her head when the butler appeared bearing a sealed missive on a silver tray.

"A message from Lord Devlin, Miss Jarvis," he said with a bow, his face impassive.

"Thank you, Grisham." She set aside her pen but waited until the butler had withdrawn before breaking the seal and spreading open the single, folded sheet. The message was brief and to the point.

> *Brook Street, 24 July*
>
> *I have made arrangements with Canterbury for the ceremony to be held at eleven o'clock Thursday morning, in the Lambeth Palace chapel. Pls advise if this is convenient.*

The signature was a simple, scrawled *Devlin*.

She sat for a time, conscious of an uncharacteristic disquiet yawning deep within her. It was one thing, she'd discovered, to analyze the various unpleasant options available to one and choose what appeared to be the most reasonable course of action. But it was something else entirely to find oneself actually catapulting toward that fate.

Especially when that fate was marriage to a man like Devlin.

Resolutely refusing to allow herself to dwell on all such a marriage would involve, she dipped her pen in the ink and scrawled a simple, three-word answer.

It is convenient.

She sealed the note and entrusted its delivery to one of the footmen. Then she went in search of her mother.

Chapter 12

The ancient, well-worn paving of Westminster Hall bustled with self-important clusters of barristers and judges in wigs and gowns, who pushed their way through the motley crowds gathered around the stalls of the sempstresses and milliners, law stationers and old booksellers, who lined the entrance of the vast, soaring hall.

A few discreet questions brought Sebastian to a stall halfway down the eastern row, where a thin, middle-aged man dressed in gently worn buckskin breeches, a ruffled shirt, and an old-fashioned green velvet coat stared with thoughtful concentration at a slim volume bound in battered brown leather and marbled paper. He had a sallow complexion and wispy, straw-colored hair he wore cropped short, which had the unfortunate effect of accentuating his unnaturally long neck and small head.

"Monsieur de La Rocque?" asked Sebastian, walking up to him.

The Frenchman turned to give Sebastian an intense, unexpectedly hostile look. He had pale blue eyes and a narrow face, his nose high arched and long. "That's right," he said. "And you are . . . Devlin, no?"

"I am."

De La Rocque held up the volume and said in French, "An early copy of Newton's *Method of Fluxions*, from the library collected at the Château de Cirey by Voltaire and his mistress, the Marquise du Châtelet. Here it sits, at the stall of some ignorant secondhand book dealer on the banks of the Thames. Bizarre, no?"

"Will you buy it?" asked Sebastian, answering in the same language.

De La Rocque tucked the book back into its row of tattered old volumes and switched to English. "If it is still here tomorrow, perhaps."

They turned to walk together beneath the soaring medieval windows. Sebastian said, "I understand you trained as a priest."

De La Rocque gave a faint, polite smile. "Under the ancien régime there were but two careers open to a nobleman's son: the sword and the church. My three older brothers chose the Army. I was the bookish one, which meant I was consigned to the Jesuits at the tender age of seven. If things had worked out differently, I would have been a bishop by the age of thirty. Now—" He spread his arms wide, taking in the stalls displaying ribbons and gloves, the maids buying white scarves, the law students with their pale complexions and shiny coats, then dropped his hands back to his sides. "Behold my noble see."

"And would you have enjoyed being a bishop?"

Rather than answering, he simply smiled and let his gaze drift away. "As flattering as your visit is, Monsieur le Vicomte, I'm afraid I can't help but wonder why you have sought me out."

"I'm told you were acquainted with Alexander Ross."

"I was. But I fail to see—" The man's eyes suddenly widened, his lips puckering as he chewed distractedly at the inside of his cheek. "*Mon Dieu.* Ross was murdered? Is that it?"

"You obviously find the possibility somewhat disturbing," said Sebastian. "Why?"

"It is a natural reaction, is it not? To be troubled when one learns of the murder of a friend."

"Was Alexander Ross a friend?"

"Of a sort."

"And what sort was that?"

"Ross had a burgeoning interest in rare and old books."

Sebastian studied the other man's small, narrow face. There'd been a few books on Ross's shelves, but none of them had struck Sebastian as particularly old or rare. "He did?"

"Mmm. From time to time I came into possession of a choice volume that interested him."

"Any kind of books in particular?"

"Many of my books come out of France. With the dissolution of the monasteries there, countless volumes of astonishing antiquity have been thrown on the market."

"In France."

De La Rocque laughed. "Yes, well . . . there are ways, you know."

"When was the last time you saw him?"

De La Rocque shrugged. "Last week sometime, I suppose. Wednesday or Thursday, perhaps?"

"Not Saturday night?"

De La Rocque frowned as if with thought, then shook his head. "No. It was earlier. Wednesday. Yes, definitely Wednesday."

"Interesting. You see, I spoke to someone who rather thought they saw you leaving Ross's rooms last Saturday night."

It was a lie, of course. But it was curious to watch the Frenchman's reaction. Rather than appearing alarmed or angered at the possibility he might have been observed, he merely shrugged and said, "Saturday? No. Whoever told you that was mistaken."

"But you did sometimes visit Ross at his rooms?"

"From time to time."

"Any idea who some of his other sources of old books might have been?"

The Frenchman shook his head. "Sorry. No."

"How familiar were you with some of Ross's other activities?"

The Frenchman looked confused. "Other activities?"

"I think you know what I'm talking about."

De La Rocque paused at the top of the steps, his gaze on the crowded, noisy square below. "There is a diplomatic revolution under way in Europe at the moment," he said slowly. "The man who is your friend this morning may be your enemy this evening, and vice versa. That was Alexander Ross's world. If I were you, Monsieur le Vicomte, I would tread carefully. Very carefully, indeed. You are wading into treacherous waters."

"Is that a threat?"

"A threat?" The Frenchman twisted to face him, the light from the hot summer sun falling across his features. "*Mais non.* Consider it merely a friendly warning." He nodded across the square, to where the walls of the Houses of Parliament rose, tall and soot stained. "More than mere lives are at stake here. The fates of kingdoms hang in the balance. Russia. Sweden. Austria. Prussia . . . Believe me, nothing is as it seems."

It all sounded rather grandiose and flamboyant—like de La Rocque himself. Sebastian said, "Who would benefit from the death of Alexander Ross?"

"I suppose that would depend on what Ross knew."

"About what?"

De La Rocque's eyes narrowed with his smile. "Ah. But if I knew that, then I too would be at risk. And believe me, Monsieur le Viscomte, I am a man who believes in minimizing risks."

"Yet you're not, obviously, averse to taking risks, when necessary."

"When the odds are good."

"The odds? Or the price?"

Rather than being offended, the Frenchman laughed. "Both, actually." He hesitated a moment, then said, "There is one man you might find it productive to speak with. A Swede."

"A Swede?"

"Tall man, blond. Name of Lindquist. Mr. Carl Lindquist."

Sebastian frowned. "Who is he?"

"To all appearances, he is a trader."

"Meaning that appearances in this case could be deceptive?"

De La Rocque smiled. "Appearances generally are."

Chapter 13

His modest round hat gripped in both hands, his mind swirling with conjecture, Sir Henry Lovejoy followed a succession of clerks through the warren of damp, badly lit corridors that led to the Downing Street office of Sir Hyde Foley.

He found the Undersecretary of State for Foreign Affairs seated behind a broad, old-fashioned desk, its surface covered with what looked like dispatches and stacks of reports. The room was large and darkly paneled, with a massive mantel of carved sandstone and a window of diamond-paned, leaded glass overlooking a court below. As the somber clerk bowed himself out, Foley leaned back in his chair and breathed an exasperated sigh. "Well. It's about time. I expected you an hour or more ago."

Lovejoy gave a slight bow. "My apologies. I was in Bethnal Green, at the scene of a murder."

Foley grunted, obviously unimpressed. He did not invite Lovejoy to sit. "I called you here because I want to know what the devil is going on."

Lovejoy blinked. "I beg your pardon?"

"I'm referring to this business about Alexander Ross. The man died of natural causes. So what precisely is Bow Street doing, poking around and asking questions about his death? It presents a very odd appearance. Very odd indeed."

Lovejoy dredged up a faint recollection of reports of a young man attached to the Foreign Office who had died the previous week. "To my knowledge, we're not doing anything, Sir Hyde."

The Undersecretary's nostrils flared. "Don't even think of playing me for a fool, Sir Henry. I had Devlin questioning me this morning."

"Devlin? You mean, Viscount Devlin?"

"Of course I'm talking about Viscount Devlin. Who the bloody hell do you think I'm talking about?"

Lovejoy considered himself an even-tempered man. But he found he needed to draw a deep, steadying breath before he could trust himself to answer temperately. "Lord Devlin may have his own reasons for inquiring into the death of Mr. Ross. But if so, I am unaware of them. I can assure you that he is not doing so in cooperation with our office."

"You expect me to believe that?"

Lovejoy simply held the other man's cold stare and returned no answer.

Foley leaned forward. "Do you have any idea of the havoc that could be wrought if news of this were to leak out?"

"You mean, the news that Ross was murdered?"

"Good God, man; have you heard nothing I said? Ross was not murdered! I was referring to the turmoil that could result if rumors of some bizarre investigation into his *possible* murder were to be bandied about in the streets." Foley pushed to his feet and swung away to where the ancient mullioned window overlooked the flagged court below. "It's no secret that the situation on the Continent has reached a pivotal point. It would be difficult to overstate the importance of the diplomatic negotiations currently under way. The last thing we need is this sort of irresponsible nonsense mucking things up."

Lovejoy studied the other man's sharp-boned, tightly held profile. "I'll discuss your concerns with his lordship."

"See that you do," snapped Foley, turning back to his desk. "My clerk will escort you out. Good day, Sir Henry. It's to be hoped we won't meet again."

Chapter 14

Sebastian returned to Brook Street to find a response from Jarvis House awaiting him. He hesitated a moment, then broke the seal to spread open the single sheet with its terse message.

It is convenient.

He stared at the bold, almost masculine handwriting, aware of an odd, heavy sensation in his chest. He knew he should feel something. Relief, surely, combined perhaps with a pang of loss as the future he'd once envisioned slipped forever from his grasp. Instead, he felt dead inside.

He became aware of his majordomo, Morey, hovering nearby, and looked up.

Morey cleared his throat. "Tom has been awaiting your return, my lord."

"Ah." Sebastian thrust the note into his pocket. "In the library?"

"Actually, I believe I last saw him headed toward the kitchens. Shall I send him—"

A loud thump sounded from the depths of the house, followed by the clatter of running footsteps and a crash as the baize-covered door flew open. Tom catapulted into the hall. Morey hissed. The boy skidded to a halt, one hand coming up to straighten his hat.

"Beggin' yer pardon, gov'nor."

Sebastian's lips twitched. "Well? Any luck?"

"Aye, gov'nor. I swear, 'e never knowed I was behind 'im at all."

Sebastian turned toward the stairs. "So where did Sir Hyde go?"

"Carlton 'Ouse, my lord."

Sebastian paused with his foot on the first step. Since the institution of the Regency some eighteen months before, the center of power in the monarchy had naturally shifted from the Palace of St. James's to the residence of the Prince. There was no reason to assume—

"I 'ung around," Tom was saying, "'oping 'e'd come out again. And 'e did, not more'n ten minutes later. You'll never guess who was with 'im."

"Lord Jarvis?"

Tom's grin fell. "You already knew?"

Sebastian shook his head. "A lucky guess." He glanced at the tall clock that stood near the library door. "I've another assignment for you: I want you to discover what you can about a Swedish merchant named Carl Lindquist."

"A Swede?" Tom pulled a face. The tiger did not hold a high opinion of foreigners.

"A Swede. That's all I know about him."

Tom swallowed his revulsion. "I'll find 'im, gov'nor; ne'er you fear."

To Morey, Sebastian said, "Have Giles bring my grays around in half an hour. And Tom—"

The boy had started to run off. But at Sebastian's voice he turned, his head cocked in inquiry.

"Lindquist could well be something more than a mere merchant. Something considerably more . . . dangerous. Be careful."

Charles, Lord Jarvis was striding up Pall Mall when Sebastian came upon him.

Guiding his grays in close to the curb, Sebastian called out, "If I might have a word with you, my lord?"

The Baron kept walking. "If you wish to see me, make an appointment with my secretary."

"This won't wait."

"Unfortunate, since it will simply have to." Without breaking stride, Jarvis turned onto Cockspur Street.

Sebastian followed along beside him, the grays held to a walk. "What I have to tell you can be said here, if you insist. But I think you'll find it's not the sort of thing you'd care to have shouted in the streets."

Jarvis drew up abruptly and swung to face him.

Sebastian reined in and nodded to his middle-aged groom, Giles, who hopped off his rear perch and took a step back to await Sebastian on the footpath.

"My lord?" said Sebastian to Jarvis.

With unexpected agility, the big man leapt up into the curricle to take the seat beside Sebastian. "Very well. You may drop me at the Admiralty. Now, what the devil is it?"

Sebastian gave his horses the office to start, his attention all for the task of guiding the grays back out into traffic. "Miss Hero Jarvis has consented to become my wife."

Jarvis remained silent. Then he said, his voice calm, "I take it this is some sort of a jest. A vulgar wager, perhaps, or—"

"You know it is not," said Sebastian, turning onto Whitehall.

"You would have me believe that Hero has agreed to this? *Hero?*"

"Yes."

"Preposterous."

"Ask her."

Jarvis's large fist tightened around the seat's iron railing. "And if I refuse my consent?"

Glancing sideways, Sebastian studied the older man's florid, closed face. The thought of having Lord Jarvis as his father-in-law alarmed him almost as much as the concept of taking Hero Jarvis to wife. He said, "I assume you know your daughter better than that. She is determined to wed, with or without your approval."

Jarvis let out a sound somewhere between a grunt and a snort. "Why are you doing this?"

Sebastian met Jarvis's fierce stare. He tried to remind himself the man was a father, with a father's concerns. "Believe me when I say that my motives are nothing except honorable."

Jarvis turned his head away. "Pull up here."

Sebastian reined in his horses and waited while the Baron clambered down from the high seat. "The Archbishop's chapel in Lambeth. Thursday. Eleven o'clock. Be there or not, as you choose," he said, and drove off to retrieve his groom.

Chapter 15

*P*aul Gibson limped up Tower Hill, increasingly conscious of a faint but unmistakable stench of putrefying flesh that intensified as he drew closer to his small stone house and the adjoining surgery.

He was met at the entrance by his housekeeper, a square-faced, foul-tempered matron named Mrs. Federico. "I'm a housekeeper, I am," she squawked, flapping her stained apron at him. "A housekeeper! Not some bleedin' sexton."

"And a wonderful housekeeper you are, too, Mrs. Federico," lied Gibson, turning on the Irish and giving her a cajoling smile. "I don't know what I would do without you."

"*Hmph*," she said, stomping after him down the narrow hall. "I told them, 'I want nothin' to do with that thing.' But did they listen? No. 'Do you have a key to the buildin' out the back?' they ask me. 'Not bloody likely,' says I. 'Why, just keepin' his house and cookin' his meals is more than a Christian ought to be asked to do,' says I. 'Have you *seen* what he keeps in those jars of his?' says I."

Gibson poured a tankard of ale from the pitcher in the

kitchen and headed out the back door. The jars—or, more properly, their contents—were the excuse Mrs. Federico used to avoid cleaning most of the rooms in the house. He said, "I take it someone's brought me a body, have they?"

"If you want to call it that. 'Then we'll just have to wait for him,' they says, like the thing ain't smellin' bad enough to put the whole neighborhood off its dinner."

Gibson grunted.

She followed him out onto the back stoop. "I've already had Mel Jacobs here complainin'. And Mrs. Cummings too. Worse than a bloody charnel house, it is." She stopped at the top of the steps. "You don't pay me enough for this," she shouted after him as he cut across the unkempt yard. "You hear? You don't pay me enough!"

He found the constables waiting for him in the narrow strip of shade cast by the small outbuilding's stone walls. One was a gnarled, grizzled old codger who looked to be missing most of his teeth. The other, a burly, ruddy-faced man, pushed to his feet with a sympathetic grin as Gibson walked up to them.

"Present for ye," said the constable, nodding toward the canvas-covered shell at their feet. "From Bow Street. Sir Henry Lovejoy."

Hunkering down beside the shrouded form, Gibson flipped back the canvas. "Good God."

"Sorry. Guess I shoulda warned ye."

"The smell should have done that," said Gibson, his gaze riveted by the bloated, discolored, insect-ravaged face.

"Quite a sight, ain't he?"

"*Is* it a he?" asked Gibson. At this point, it was difficult to tell.

"Well, it's wearin' a gentleman's clothes, all right. Found him in a ditch in Bethnal Green, we did. Sir Henry wants to know what ye can tell him about how the gentleman died—and maybe a bit about who he is, while yer at it."

"Unidentified, is he?"

"'Fraid so." The constable gave him a concise outline of the body's discovery. Then he nodded to the outbuilding's padlocked door and said, "Want we should help ye move him inside?"

Gibson pushed to his feet. "Please. Just, ah . . . give me a moment first."

Unfastening the lock, he slipped through the partially open door and quickly pulled a sheet over what was left of Mr. Alexander Ross.

Lady Jarvis's reaction to the news of her daughter's approaching nuptials was at first incredulous, then hysterically joyous.

"*Married!*" she squealed, leaping up from her daybed to throw her arms around Hero. Since Hero stood over five foot ten and Lady Jarvis barely topped five feet, the embrace was somewhat awkward. "Oh, *Hero.*" She dragged Hero down onto the daybed beside her. "And here I'd no notion. Do tell me *everything.*"

Hero shifted uncomfortably. She loved her mother dearly, but this was not a tale she ever intended to divulge to anyone. "There isn't much to tell, actually."

"How can you say such a thing? When I must have heard you insist a thousand times or more that you were determined to end your days an old maid."

"Yes, well . . . There are certainly undeniable advantages to the married state." She searched her mind to come up with one. "This obligation to drag a maid with me wherever I go, for example; I find it beyond fatiguing."

Lady Jarvis looked puzzled for a moment, then gave a shaky laugh. "The things you do say, Hero." Her smile faded and she reached up to touch her fingertips to her daughter's cheek almost wistfully. "I do hope you will be happy, child."

Hero took her mother's dainty hand between her own larger,

more capable ones. "I'm quite certain that I shall be. Lord Devlin is above all else a gentleman."

"And so handsome! And *dashing*."

"Yes, he is certainly that," said Hero dryly. She felt her mother's hand tremble within hers and hastened to add, "And you mustn't worry about how you shall contrive to manage without me, for I intend to find a companion for you—someone who'll be able to see to your comfort as well as assist with the household affairs. And of course I shall be able to visit often. It's no great distance, after all, from Brook Street to Berkeley Square."

"Don't be silly. Now is not the time for you to be worrying about me."

"I shan't worry about you. But I have every intention of continuing to concern myself with your happiness and well-being."

Lady Jarvis tightened her grip on her daughter's fingers. "You know this is the answer to my prayers. For I don't scruple to tell you that I had quite given up hope of ever seeing you settled."

Hero sank her teeth into her lower lip and forced herself to keep silent.

"And *grandchildren*," gushed Lady Jarvis, her eyes shining. "I do hope we won't have long to wait."

"I trust not," said Hero.

It was some hours later, when Hero was gathering together her papers in the library, that she heard her father's heavy tread in the hall and turned to find him standing in the doorway.

"Is it true, then?" Lord Jarvis demanded without preamble, his gaze hard on his daughter's face. "What Devlin tells me?"

"It is." Hero went back to the task of assembling her papers. "I hope you mean to wish me happy, Papa. But I expect you know me well enough to realize that I shall marry, with or without your blessing."

"I could cut you off."

"You could," she acknowledged. Under the terms of her mother's marriage settlement, her father had obligated himself to provide any daughters born of their union with a portion of not less than ten thousand pounds. That Jarvis could not avoid. But as Jarvis's only surviving child, Hero stood to inherit a substantial chunk of all property not entailed to the male relative next in line to inherit the barony—in this instance a plump, vapid young man named Frederick Jarvis. It was well within Jarvis's power to change his will and leave everything to Frederick.

She said, "I've no doubt Cousin Frederick would be pleased."

Jarvis made a rude noise. "Cousin Frederick is a useless, addlebrained popinjay."

"True. I suppose you could always use your wealth to endow some charitable institution."

"Enough of this," said Jarvis. "I've no intention of cutting you off and you know it." He pointed a thick, steady finger at her. "But I intend to drive a hard bargain on the settlement, make no mistake about that."

"I should hope so."

He went to pour himself a glass of brandy from the carafe kept near the hearth. "The entire kingdom trembles with fear at the thought of displeasing me," he said. "But not my own daughter."

She smiled. "And you know you would have it no other way."

"Would I?" He set aside the carafe with a soft thump. "I assume you have your reasons for what you are doing."

"You're the one who is always pressing me to marry."

"But Devlin, Hero? *Devlin?*"

For more than thirty years, Jarvis had dedicated his life to safeguarding the stability of the British monarchy at home and expanding the nation's power and influence overseas. Few dared to stand against him for long. Working quietly and ruthlessly through a network of informants, spies, and assassins, he was the kind of man who valued order and stability above all else, who had nothing but contempt for such maudlin concepts as "fairness" and "justice." As far as Jarvis was concerned, the modern enthusiasm for "equality" constituted the greatest threat ever to confront civilization.

But Devlin was a man for whom power and authority were never sacred, whose values were justice and reason, not expediency and privilege. In the course of his murder investigations, he had not hesitated to probe into the murkiest corners of Jarvis's activities. Again and again, he had not only confronted the King's powerful cousin, but dared to thwart him.

And Hero had no doubt he would continue to do so in the future.

She said, "Can you think of another man brave enough to marry Lord Jarvis's daughter?"

At that, her father gave a reluctant laugh. He took a slow sip of his drink, his eyes narrowing as he studied her pensively. She thought she held up under his scrutiny with remarkable calm.

Then he said, "There's something you're not telling me."

Tucking her notes under one arm, she turned toward the door and simply ignored the comment, saying, "Do you go with Mama and me to the reception for the Russian Ambassador at St. James's Palace tonight? Or will you form one of the Prince's retinue?"

"I dine with the Prince. Which reminds me: Sir Hyde Foley tells me Devlin is investigating the possibility that the young man from the Foreign Office who died last week—Alexander Ross—was actually murdered. Do you know anything about that?"

She looked back at him in surprise. "Ross? Whatever gave Devlin that idea?"

"He hasn't mentioned anything to you about it?"

"No."

"Interesting," said Lord Jarvis, turning to pour himself another drink.

It didn't occur to Hero until she was mounting the stairs that he had not in fact wished her happy.

Chapter 16

"The first man up the stairs must be the one who killed Ross," said Gibson, his hands wrapped around a pewter tankard, his head resting against the high back of an old oak bench in the corner of the pub where he and Sebastian had met for a pint. "By the time the second man came and knocked on the door, Ross was dead. No one answered the door, so he left again right away, thinking no one was home."

Sebastian took a deep draught of his ale. "It's possible. The problem is, we've no way of knowing exactly when Ross was killed. It could have been long after Madame Champagne had retired for the night."

"Aye, there is that." Gibson blew out a long breath. "What about the mysterious veiled woman? Think she was this Miss Sabrina Cox?"

"Gently bred young ladies aren't generally in the habit of visiting gentlemen in their rooms—even if they are betrothed."

"Yet some still do," said Gibson with a wry smile.

"They do. If I could meet the lady, I might be able to judge the chances of that myself. Unfortunately, she's in mourning, which means she's gone into seclusion and the only visitors she's receiving are relatives or close friends."

"That does complicate things," said Gibson, draining his tankard.

"Considerably." Sebastian signaled the barmaid for two more tankards. "Although, frankly, I'm more inclined to suspect the veiled woman—whoever she was—is someone connected to Ross's activities with the Foreign Office."

"According to Dr. Astley Cooper, it was Sir Hyde Foley who called him in to examine Ross's body."

"Really? Now, that is interesting."

Gibson waited while the barmaid set the brimming new tankards on the boards before them. Then he said, "What about this French priest—de La Rocque? Sounds like a queer character."

"He is indeed. And whatever his dealings with Ross, I'll be surprised if they involved old books." Sebastian paused, listening to the tolling of the city's church bells, counting out the hour. He took a quick swallow of his ale and pushed to his feet. "Now you'll have to excuse me. I'm off to visit the Queen."

Gibson raised his tankard in a mock toast. "Give her my regards."

Returning to Brook Street, Sebastian donned the formal knee breeches and tails that were de rigueur for a gentleman attending an official function at the palace.

"I had occasion to ask around about your Mr. Ross," said Calhoun, holding out a fresh cravat.

Sebastian glanced over at him. "And?"

"I discovered nothing of interest, my lord. From all reports, Mr. Ross was a congenial, warmhearted young man well liked by all with whom he came into contact."

Sebastian wound the long, wide length of linen around his neck. "Except, apparently, by whoever killed him."

"So it would seem, my lord."

By the time Sebastian arrived at St. James's Palace, the parade of carriages lining up to pass through the ancient brick gatehouse and into the paved courtyard had dwindled and the crowds of curious onlookers were drifting away. The Season was rapidly winding its way to an end. Almack's had already closed; soon the Prince would remove to Brighton and the vast majority of the great noble families would depart for their country estates—if they hadn't done so already.

Sebastian could hear the soft strains of a chamber orchestra playing one of Handel's trio sonatas as he mounted the steps to the vast reception suite. Despite the heat of the summer, the rooms were still crowded, the leading members of society mingling with cabinet ministers, foreign ambassadors, and members of the royal family. The Queen herself, a stout, gray-haired matron splendid in blond satin trimmed in gold lace, presided over the evening from a richly carved and gilded arm-chair situated between the two main rooms. At her side sat her eldest son, the Prince Regent, and, standing beside him, the Prince's plump, gray-haired mistress, the Marchioness of Hertford.

Everyone else in the room stood.

"Viscount Devlin," intoned the powdered footman.

A tall woman in emerald silk who was conversing with a group that included the Foreign Secretary, Castlereagh, looked around at Sebastian's entrance. Their gazes met across the crowded room, and Sebastian saw his betrothed's eyes widen with surprise before narrowing speculatively.

"Well, this is unexpected," said Miss Hero Jarvis, separating herself from her circle and walking up to him. "Whatever are you doing here?"

If she felt any awkwardness at their meeting, she didn't show it. But then, in Sebastian's experience, her coolness and self-possession came close to rivaling her father's. Sebastian was only just beginning to realize that in her case, at least, all was not exactly as it seemed.

"I received an invitation," he said, accepting a glass of wine proffered on a tray by a circling waiter.

"London's hostesses are always sending you invitations. You only accept them when you have some ulterior motive."

Sebastian gave a soft laugh. From where he stood, he was able to watch the new Russian Ambassador, Count Christoph Heinrich von Lieven, bowing low over the Queen's hand. "Perhaps I've developed an interest in Russia."

She followed his gaze. "So it's true, is it? You are investigating the death of Alexander Ross."

"Word does get around, doesn't it?"

"When the topic of conversation is murder? What do you expect?" She stood beside him, her gaze, like his, drifting over the assembled company. "I must say, I am relieved to hear someone is looking into it. I personally found his sudden death beyond suspicious."

Sebastian glanced at her in surprise. "You knew him?"

"He was engaged to marry one of my cousins."

"Ah. The wellborn but impoverished gentlewoman sold off to the highest bidder by her gamester father. She's a relative of yours, is she?"

"She was. My mother's cousin Charlotte. Dreadful woman. I always thought old Peter Cox got far more than he bargained for with that match. Her son, Jasper, is just like her. But I rather like her daughter, Sabrina."

"And how is Miss Cox taking Ross's death?"

"She is dreadfully cut up about it, as one would expect. Why do you ask? Surely you aren't seriously considering *Sabrina* as a suspect?"

"At this point, I'm not ruling out anyone." He nodded across the room to where an animated young woman with dark hair and a long, graceful neck was charming the Prince Regent. "What can you tell me about the new Russian Ambassador?"

Miss Jarvis followed his gaze. "Well, I see you've already identified his beautiful and captivating wife."

"She is rather difficult to miss."

"There are those who say Countess Lieven is the Czar's real representative, that her husband is just a placeholder. But I think that's rather harsh. He's a shrewd man, ruthless on the battlefield and at the negotiating table. They make a good team."

"You've met them?"

"We had the senior members of the Russian delegation to dinner two nights ago."

Sebastian took another sip of his wine. "So which of the military-looking gentlemen accompanying the Count is Colonel Dimitri Ivanovich Chernishav?"

"There," said Miss Jarvis, nodding to a uniformed officer with a ceremonial sword buckled across a blue coat dripping with gold—gold sash, gold braid, gold plumes. "The blond gentleman with the mustache."

Sebastian studied the Colonel's broad, big-boned face. "You had him to dinner, as well?"

"Several times."

"Good," said Sebastian, setting aside his wine. "Then you can introduce us."

The Russian Colonel was studying a massive, full-length portrait of George II when they walked up to him.

"Devlin, is it? I have met your father, the Earl," said the Colonel, when Miss Jarvis had made the introductions. "He tells us he is a friend of Russia. Yet when it comes to Napoléon, all he is prepared to offer us is words of encouragement. No men."

"Our troops are rather busy these days," said Sebastian, "what with fighting the French in the peninsula and defending our interests in India and the New World."

The Colonel laughed. "You can't seriously consider the Americans a threat?"

"To Canada, yes."

"Excuse me, gentlemen," said Miss Jarvis, adroitly withdrawing.

The Russian watched her walk away. "A formidable woman, that one."

"Definitely," agreed Sebastian. He studied the Russian's cheerful, full-cheeked face, with its soft blue eyes and swooping cavalry mustache. He looked to be in his late twenties, his high rank obviously less an indication of experience on the battlefield than of wealth and birth. Britain and Russia were much alike in this sense, if not in others.

Sebastian said, "I understand you were acquainted with a friend of mine at the Foreign Office. Mr. Alexander Ross."

Chernishav's smile faded. "You knew Alexander?" He gave the name its Russian pronunciation, *Aleksandr*. "A shock, wasn't it? We were to meet at Cribb's Parlour the very evening he died."

"But you did not?"

The Russian shook his head. "No. He never showed up. I finally went round to his rooms and knocked at his door, but he didn't answer."

"What time was this?"

"Midnight? Perhaps a little earlier, perhaps a little later. I thought it strange at the time but wrote it off as a matter of miscommunication. Then I heard he'd been found dead in his bed, and it struck me as all the more peculiar. And now . . . Now you are asking me questions, and I have been in London long enough to know what that means."

He stared at Sebastian expectantly, but Sebastian only said, "You were friends?"

"For some years now, yes. We met in St. Petersburg when Alexander was with your embassy there. It's not easy, being a stranger in a strange land. This time, I am the one who's far from home. We would meet occasionally for a drink. Talk of Russia."

"When was the last time you saw him?"

The Russian looked thoughtful for a moment. "I suppose it must have been that Wednesday night, at Vauxhall. I formed part of the Ambassador's party, while Alexander was there with his fiancée and her brother. Lovely young woman—and fabulously wealthy, I understand." He gave a rueful smile. "I was quite jealous of my old friend's good fortune, you know. And then, just a few days later—" He kissed his bunched fingers and then flung them open in an ironic gesture. "Alexander is dead. Fate is a strange thing, is it not? Fickle and cruel."

"Know of anyone Ross had quarreled with recently? Anyone who might have wanted him dead?"

The Colonel's gaze shifted to the painting beside them. "It's a thought that naturally occurs to one, is it not?"

"And?"

He kept his gaze on the painting. "Alexander was a diplomat by profession. It can be a dangerous game, diplomacy. A dance of shadows in the darkness."

"Meaning?"

"Meaning, I know some of what Alexander was involved in. But not all."

"Yet you know something."

Chernishav hesitated, then said, "That night, at Vauxhall, I chanced to come upon Alexander in a heated conversation with Ambassador Ramadani."

"Ramadani?"

The Russian cast a significant glance toward the dark-eyed, dark-bearded man wearing long crimson robes, gold-embroidered slippers, and an elaborately wrapped turban, who was now engaged in conversation with the Marchioness of Hertford. "Mr. Antonaki Ramadani. The Ambassador from Constantinople."

Sebastian recognized the man. He'd frequently seen him—in different clothes—exercising a magnificent Turkoman in Hyde Park early in the morning. "Ross was involved with the Ottomans?"

"That, I do not know. But he was most certainly involved with Mr. Ramadani in some way."

"Any idea what the subject of their argument might have been?"

The Colonel shook his head. "Sorry. I only caught the last few words of their discussion. But what I heard was interesting, to say the least. I distinctly heard Ramadani say, 'Don't threaten me, you little English shit, or you will be the one to be sorry.'"

Chapter 17

"Threaten him about what?" asked Sebastian.

Chernishav shrugged. "I never discovered. They saw me then. Ramadani strode away, while Ross laughed and tried to pass the incident off as nothing. But I knew he was concerned."

Sebastian was silent for a moment.

Chernishav's light blue eyes glinted with quiet amusement. "You don't believe me, do you?"

"Russia and Turkey are well known to be age-old enemies."

"True," Chernishav acknowledged. "But since the recent Treaty of Bucharest, we are no longer at war." He shrugged. "Believe me or not, as you will. But if Alexander did not die peacefully in his sleep as we have been led to believe, you could do worse than to take a look at some of the more questionable activities of the Sultan's representative."

Placing one hand on the hilt of his ceremonial sword, the Russian gave a short bow and moved away.

Sebastian was watching the Colonel thread a path across the crowded room when Miss Jarvis walked up to him.

"Learn anything?" she asked.

He turned to look into her shrewd gray eyes. As Lord Jarvis's daughter, she probably knew more than almost anyone else in London about the delicate diplomatic maneuverings swirling around Ross's death. Yet the fact that she was Jarvis's daughter meant that Sebastian couldn't trust her. And it occurred to him that the implications of that lack of trust did not bode well for their future together.

"What?" she said, her gaze hard on his face.

He shook his head. "Nothing."

She raised one eyebrow. "Are you planning to tell me what makes you suspect that Alexander Ross did not, in fact, die peacefully in his sleep?"

Sebastian cast a meaningful glance about the glittering assembly. "This might not be the most appropriate setting for such a discussion."

"I will be spending tomorrow morning at the site of the old Grayfriar's Priory in Newgate. We can speak more freely there," she said, and withdrew.

He watched her walk away, torn between amusement and annoyance and the unsettling realization that his coming marriage would alter his life in more ways than he could begin to envision.

From the distance came the peal of the city's church bells, ringing out the half hour. Soon, it would be time to pay another, more surreptitious visit to Alexander Ross's rooms on St. James's Street. But first he had an important stop to make.

He ordered his carriage and set off for Covent Garden.

Auburn haired and beautiful, Kat Boleyn sat at her dressing table, the flickering candlelight casting a golden glow across her bare shoulders, her slender arms raised as she eased the pins from her dark hair. She looked up when he slipped into the room. Their eyes met in the mirror, and for one telling moment her breath caught.

She was the toast of the London stage, an actress famed for both her talent and her beauty. She was also the natural daughter of Alistair St. Cyr, the Fifth Earl of Hendon, and the love of Sebastian's life.

"Devlin," she whispered. She did not move.

He stood for a moment, his shoulders pressed against the closed door behind him. He had loved this woman for nearly a third of his life. Once, he'd sworn to make her his wife and to hell with the consequences. Then fate and a long, sordid tangle of lies had intervened. Now she was married to a man named Russell Yates, a dashing privateer whose secret sexual inclinations remained one of the few taboos still rigidly enforced by their otherwise lax society. While Sebastian . . .

Sebastian was about to marry the daughter of his worst enemy.

He said, "I'm sorry for coming here, but I had to see you."

She studied his face in the mirror. The effects of too many sleepless nights and too many brandies would be obvious to anyone who knew him as well as Kat. She said, "I'd heard you were wounded. Are you all right?"

He touched his arm, injured the week before in a fight to catch the killer of the Bishop of London. "It's stiff, but that is all." He drew a deep breath. "There's something I must tell you. I've asked Miss Hero Jarvis to be my wife."

"*Jarvis?*" She went white, the only sound the clatter of one of her hairpins hitting the surface of the dressing table. Once, Lord Jarvis had threatened her with torture and death. She had found a refuge of sorts through her marriage to Yates, but they both knew she would never really be safe from someone like Jarvis.

She let out a strange sound that might have been a shaky

laugh. "I suppose there must be a reason for this. But I can't at the moment imagine what it is."

"There is a reason." It was all he could say. He supposed the reason would be obvious enough in a few months' time, but it was not something he ever intended to confirm. He owed Miss Jarvis that.

"Does Hendon know?"

"Of the marriage? No."

"I think you should be the one to tell him."

When he didn't answer, she drew in a quick breath, and then another. Yet her voice was still a harsh whisper when she said, "You know I wish you happy, Sebastian." She hesitated, as if searching for something pleasant to say. "She . . . she does not seem overly much like her father."

"No. I don't believe she is." *Overly much*, he thought, although he didn't say it. He watched Kat remove the last pins from her hair to send it cascading about her shoulders. The urge to reach out and touch her, to run his fingers through that heavy auburn fall, to draw her into his arms, was so intense that he shuddered with it.

She said, "I hear you are investigating the death of Alexander Ross."

He was startled enough to smile. "Is there anyone in London who does not know of it at this point?"

"Probably not."

He studied the familiar contours of her face, the wide, sensual mouth and childlike nose, the intense blue eyes she had inherited from her father. He knew that once she had worked for the French, passing along secrets she hoped would aid her mother's people, the Irish. It had been more than a year now since she'd severed her connections to Napoléon's agents. But that had been before—when they'd still been lovers, the truth of the connection between them blissfully unknown. It was possible, he supposed, that her relationship with the French had been resumed. He knew that her husband, Yates, still maintained his contacts with the smugglers who plied the perilous waters between England and the Continent.

He said, "Have you heard anything about Ross's death?"

She shook her head. "No. But I can make some inquiries, if you'd like."

"It might be helpful to know more about his activities."

"I'll let you know if I learn anything."

She pushed up from her bench and turned to face him, her hands at her sides, her fingers curling around the edge of the table behind her. She wore only a petticoat, and a chemise beneath a short corset; he could see the heavy velvet folds of her costume thrown over a nearby chest. Her breasts were high and full, swelling above the confines of her corset. Her eyes shone wide and luminous in the candlelight, and for one dangerous moment out of time, he lost himself in looking at her.

She said, "I never would have married you. You know that, don't you? I've been saying it for nearly ten years now."

"If things had turned out differently, I could have made you change your mind. Eventually."

She laughed at that, a low, sad laugh rich with love and all the years they'd lost and all the years they'd shared. "Oh, Sebastian. Always so cocksure and arrogant, so certain that somehow the world can be put to right." Her smile faded and she gave a little shake of her head. "I realized long ago that if I truly loved you—and I do—that I couldn't ruin you by marrying you. The only way I could ever have married you is if I were to fall out of love with you, and that will never happen."

He felt an ache pull across his chest, but he managed to keep his own tone light. "Is this supposed to make me feel better?"

"It would, if you could ever be brought to believe it."

"I can't."

"Believe it, Sebastian. Believe it."

She came to him then, her skin soft beneath his touch, her hair sliding across his fingers as he drew her close, her lips yielding to his. It was a kiss of heartbreak and hopeless passion, of a wild, all-consuming yearning.

And a last good-bye.

She was the one who pulled away first. But still her lips came back to brush his, again and again, before she finally brought her fingers up to press them against his mouth. "I will always love you," she said, her forehead touching his, her breath mingling hard with his. "And I know you will always love me. But that doesn't mean you can't learn to love someone else."

He looked into her blue St. Cyr eyes. "And you, Kat? Have you learned to love Yates?"

She drew back then, her lips swollen from his kisses, her chest sill rising and falling with her rapid breathing. "That's different."

"Yet you think I can be happy, knowing you are not?"

"It is what I would wish."

He gave her a crooked smile. "And you say I am the one who likes to believe the world can somehow always be put to rights."

Chapter 18

$\mathcal{T}$he night was warm, the moon nearly half full and unusually bright.

Sebastian left his carriage on Piccadilly and strolled down St. James's Street, an evening cape thrown over his shoulders, the heels of his dress shoes clicking softly on the flagged paving. The windows of the gentlemen's clubs blazed with light. Music spilled from open doors; the laughter of ungenteel women carried on a soft breeze. Passing the Je Reviens coffee shop, he glanced in the oriel window. Despite the hour, the coffee room was still crowded, the burly, gray-bearded Frenchman at his station behind the counter.

Madame Champagne had obviously retired for the night.

Smiling softly at the thought of what she'd told him, Sebastian pulled his hat low and slipped in through the side door to quietly climb the steep, straight flights of steps. The stairwell was dark, with no telltale slivers of light showing beneath either of the doors on the first floor, the inhabitant of the one doubtless out on the town, the other asleep. The servants would long since have retired to their attic rooms.

On the second-floor landing, he paused and listened. Sebastian's hearing, like his eyesight, was acute. As a child he had simply assumed that everyone could see well enough to read in the dark and could hear whispered conversations from distant rooms. But in time he'd come to realize that his senses were so keen as to be considered uncanny by most. *Wolflike*, Kat used to call him. . . .

But he shut his mind to that.

He listened carefully but heard only the distant murmur of voices from the coffee shop and the clip-clop of hooves, the whirl of carriage wheels, the laughter and footsteps from the street below.

Reaching into his pocket, he drew out a ring with a cluster of small metal shafts, their tips bent at various angles. Selecting one of the shafts, he slid its tip into the door's keyhole. It was a thieves' tool, a picklock, and it took only a delicate touch and good hearing to slide the tip through the lock's gates and carefully press the levers aside. He heard the final click, and the lock sprang open.

Pocketing the tool, he slipped inside and quietly closed the door behind him.

The light filtering in through the drapes was dim but sufficient to enable him to see that the valet, Poole, had made little further progress in his assigned task. The comfortable clutter of a young gentleman's existence lay undisturbed, as if Ross had only just stepped out and was expected back at any moment.

Sebastian started in the bedroom, methodically searching through drawers, checking the pockets of the few coats left in the cupboard. But Poole's efforts were most apparent here. There was little left. He found a litter of stray buttons, a chit from Tattersall's, an enameled snuffbox that looked unused, as if it had been a gift. The framed profile shade—or silhouette, as the French called them—of a young woman, shadowy curls framing a winsome face, hung above the bedside table. One could imagine Ross pausing to gaze fondly upon it before retiring for the evening, never to wake again.

Except that Alexander Ross had not died peacefully in his sleep. He had been violently murdered, his body put to bed by his killer.

So where had the murder actually taken place? Here, in this room? Or somewhere else?

Sebastian went over the room carefully, looking for traces of blood. He found none.

Frustrated, he moved to the main chamber. He glanced through the invites on the mantel. In addition to the invitation to the Queen's reception for the Russian Ambassador, there were also cards for a function at the Swedish Embassy, a dinner with the American Consul, an assembly being given by the Portuguese Ambassador. Alexander Ross had been a handsome young man, a rising star at the Foreign Office, the heir to a barony betrothed to a wealthy and beautiful woman. The combination had obviously made him a popular guest in diplomatic circles.

Turning to a davenport desk standing near the hearth, Sebastian lifted the hinged top and sifted through the contents of the upper compartment. He found a few tradesmen's bills, but none of them excessive or overly extravagant. Beside the bills lay a sheet of parchment with what appeared to be a half-written letter addressed to Viscount Melville, First Lord of the Admiralty.

> *Sir:*
> *I am writing on behalf of a young American seaman, Mr. Nathan Bateman, impressed off the coast of New Bedford, Massachusetts, by the HMS Rodney in June of 1809. The citizenship of Mr. Bateman has been firmly established by documents presented by his father, namely a*

There the writing ended abruptly, as if Ross had been disturbed and set the letter aside to complete at a later time.

Thoughtfully tucking the letter into the pocket of his coat, Sebastian glanced quickly through the davenport's drawers, then went to stand in the middle of the room. He was acutely conscious of the passage of time. The longer he stayed, the greater the risk that one of the occupants of the rooms below would awaken or return to hear the sound of footsteps overhead, or that someone in the street might look up and catch a whisper of movement behind the drapes.

He shifted his attention to looking for those things Ross might have preferred to keep hidden. He turned over the clock on the mantel, the cushions on the chairs; he felt behind furniture. Inside the frontispiece of a worn copy of *The Meditations of Marcus Aurelius* he discovered a folded sheet of parchment. Opening the page, he found himself staring at a curious line of numbers:

7-10-12-14-17

Puzzled, he was thrusting the page into his pocket when he heard a faint sound. The brush of cloth against cloth. The scuff of quiet footsteps on bare stair treads.

Sebastian slipped the book back onto its shelf and moved to station himself beside the door. Whoever was creeping up the stairs had reached the first floor now and was coming around to the second flight of steps.

Dressed as he was, in formal knee breeches and low shoes, Sebastian had no weapon, not even the dagger he habitually kept sheathed in his boot. He held himself very still, listening as the footsteps reached the top of the stairs.

One man, only, Sebastian thought.

He could hear the man's quick breathing as he paused outside the door. Then Sebastian heard the soft click of metal against metal and recognized it for what it was: a picklock. He smiled into the darkness.

He heard the unseen intruder grunt, pleased but evidently not unduly surprised to find the door unlatched. There was a faint clatter of metal shafts clicking against their mates as the man put the thieves' tool away. Then, as Sebastian watched, the door latch slowly turned. The panel swung inward and the intruder stepped into the room.

He was carrying a horn lantern, its light carefully shielded so that it formed only a narrow slash. But this was no ordinary thief. Like Sebastian, he wore evening clothes: satin knee breeches, a black coat, silk stockings, and silver-buckled shoes. Sebastian waited until he had taken two steps into the room. Then Sebastian reached out, grabbed the man by the back of his coat, and shoved him forward, hard.

Caught by surprise, the man stumbled, off balance. Sebastian slammed his foot into the back of the man's right knee. With a startled cry, he crashed to his out-flung hands and knees; the lantern smashed and went out.

One hand still fisted in the back of the man's coat, Sebastian brought his right arm across the front of the man's throat and yanked him back, Sebastian's right hand bracing against his own left elbow as he shifted his other hand to press against the back of the man's head.

"*What the devil?*" exclaimed the man, flailing around with his arms, trying to reach the unknown and unseen assailant behind him.

"Who are you?" whispered Sebastian, his lips close to the man's ear. "What are you doing here?"

"Who the devil are *you?*" snarled the man, his nails raking across the back of Sebastian's head and sending his top hat flying.

Sebastian tightened his chokehold. "I ask the questions. You answer them."

"Bugger you," spat the man and threw himself violently to one side.

They went down together, pain exploding across Sebastian's ribs as he crashed into a small table that shattered beneath him. Sebastian lost his grip on the man's neck and caught a heel in his groin. His breath left his body in a whoosh, and he rolled reflexively to one side.

Scrambling up onto his hands and knees, the man lunged through the open door into the hall. Diving after him, Sebastian caught the man's foot and tried to yank him back. The shoe came off in Sebastian's hand as the man reared up and pivoted to face him. Sebastian saw the gleam of a knife in his hand.

"Whoever you are," sneered the man, "you just made your last mistake."

Sebastian surged to his feet, the leather dress shoe still in his hand, as the man slashed at Sebastian's eyes.

Sebastian jerked his head back, the knife whistling through the air. Then he stepped forward and slammed the shoe against the side of the man's head. The buckle bit deep, drawing blood.

Swearing, the man fell back, one hand swiping at the trickle of blood running down the side of his face. With a growl, he lunged at Sebastian, the knife clenched in his fist.

Sebastian sidestepped and felt his legs slam against the banister.

The man turned with a grin. "Got you, you bastard," he said and lunged again.

His back to the banister, Sebastian dropped. With his gaze on the other man's face, Sebastian knew the exact moment when the man realized what he'd done.

His lips twisted in a foul oath, the knife still clutched in his hand, he shot over the railing and plunged headfirst into the darkened stairwell.

Chapter 19

*S*ebastian rose slowly to his feet, his breath coming hard and fast. He started to close the door to Alexander Ross's rooms, only to pause and reach in to snatch up his hat from where it had fallen. Then he charged down the stairs.

He found the man sprawled near the base of the flight of steps, his eyes open and fixed, his neck bent back at an unnatural angle.

"Hell and the devil confound it," said Sebastian softly.

He realized he was still holding the man's shoe; a gentleman's shoe, barely worn, made of fine leather with a silver buckle. He dropped the shoe beside the body and eased the knife from the man's tight fist. It was always possible the man had friends waiting outside.

Descending the remaining flight of stairs, Sebastian carefully let himself out. A mist was rolling in from the river. Standing on the flagway, he threw a quick glance up and down the street.

Nothing.

He drew the night air deep into his lungs and felt a twinge

where the broken wood of the smashed table had raked across his side. Adjusting the set of his hat, he strode rapidly up the street toward Piccadilly. But when he reached the corner, he hesitated.

Since learning the bitter truth of his parentage, Sebastian had refused all attempts at communication from his father— from *the Earl of Hendon,* he corrected himself. But Kat was right. There was something he needed to do.

He turned his steps toward Grosvenor Square.

Once, the vast granite pile of the Earls of Hendon on Grosvenor Square had echoed with the shouts and laughter of a large, boisterous family. Now, all were alienated from one another, or dead, the house inhabited solely by one lonely old man and his servants.

Dismissing his father's butler with a silent nod, Sebastian paused in the doorway of the library, his gaze on the man who sat dozing in his habitual, comfortably worn chair beside the hearth. He was still a large man, despite his sixty-odd years, his features blunt, a shock of thick white hair fallen over his forehead. He had his head tipped back, his mouth slack with sleep, his eyes closed. A book—doubtless *The Orations of Cicero* or some such work—lay open on his lap.

Of the three young boys Hendon called son, only the youngest, Sebastian, had shared the Earl's love of classical literature. Sebastian's enthusiasm for the works of Homer and Caesar had delighted the Earl, even if Sebastian's reading tastes did range further afield than Hendon would have liked, to Catullus and Sappho and Petronius.

Yet the Earl's pleasure in this youngest child's precociousness had always been tinged with an element of odd perplexity that at times bordered on resentment. It was an attitude that both confused and hurt Sebastian, as a child. He'd never understood the sudden, icy aloofness that could tighten the Earl's jaw and cause him to turn away.

Now he did.

For a long moment Sebastian simply stood in the doorway, awash in a complex swirl of emotions—anger and resentment mingling with hurt and an unwanted but powerful upsurge of love that startled him by its intensity. Then the Earl's eyes fluttered open and the two men stared at each other from across the room.

Sebastian said stiffly, "I expected to find you abed."

"I would have been, soon." Hendon wiped one hand across his mouth but otherwise held himself quite still, as if afraid the least unstudied motion might cause his son—or, rather, the man he'd called son for nearly thirty years—to vanish from his sight. "Come in. Pour yourself a brandy."

Sebastian shook his head. "I'm here to tell you that the notice of my engagement will appear in Monday's *Post*." Even to his own ears, his voice sounded tight, stilted.

He saw the delight mingled with surprise and wariness that leapt in the old man's eyes. For years, Hendon had pressed Sebastian to marry, to beget the next St. Cyr heir. A supreme irony, given that the only St. Cyr blood flowing through Sebastian's veins had come to him from his mother, the errant Countess who had in that way of noble families married her own distant cousin.

Hendon cleared his throat. "Your betrothal?"

Sebastian nodded. "I will be marrying Miss Hero Jarvis on Thursday."

Hendon's breath came out in a long hiss. "*Jarvis?*"

"Yes."

"What madness is this?"

At that, Sebastian laughed. "The ceremony will take place

at eleven in the chapel of the Archbishop of Canterbury, at Lambeth."

Hendon stared back at him. "I am invited?"

"Yes." Sebastian turned to leave.

"Devlin—"

He paused to look back, one eyebrow raised in silent inquiry.

"Thank you," said Hendon.

But Sebastian found he did not trust himself to do more than nod.

Saturday, 25 July

The next morning dawned warm and clear.

Dressed in buckskin breeches, glossy black Hessians, and a drab olive riding coat, His Excellency Antonaki Ramadani, the Ambassador to the Court of St. James from the Sublime Porte, trotted sedately up Rotten Row. He might have been mistaken for any sun-darkened Englishman exercising his horse in Hyde Park. The only exotic touch came from the Ambassador's mount, a magnificent bay Turkoman with a high pointed saddle covered in crimson velvet.

"Good morning, Your Excellency," said Sebastian, bringing his own neat Arab mare in beside the Turk's bay. "I was sorry we didn't have the opportunity to meet at the Queen's reception last night. I am Devlin."

The Turk cast him a quick, speculative glance, then returned his gaze to the track before them. "I have heard of you." His English was unexpectedly good, with only a faint, barely perceptible trace of accent. "You're the peculiar English nobleman who enjoys solving murders. It's—what? A hobby of yours?"

"I don't know that I'd call it a hobby, exactly."

"Oh? What would you describe it as?"

"An interest, perhaps." *Maybe a compulsion*, Sebastian thought. Or a penance. But he didn't say it.

Ramadani raised one eyebrow. "You think that young gentleman from the Foreign Office who died last week—Mr. Alexander Ross—was murdered." It was a statement, not a question.
"And you think I did it."

Sebastian studied the Turk's hard, closed face, with its full
lips and light brown eyes. "You were seen arguing with him at
Vauxhall last— When was it? Wednesday or Thursday?"

"Wednesday." A faint smile crinkled the skin beside the
man's eyes. "As a diplomat, I am protected from prosecution in
your country. Even if I did kill Ross, your government could not
touch me."

"So, did you kill him?"

The Turk huffed a soft laugh. "And if I said no, would you
believe me?"

Sebastian smiled. "No."

"Then why bother to ask?"

"Conversely, if you have immunity from prosecution, then
why bother to deny it?"

"Because while I, personally, might not suffer from such an
accusation, the relations between your government and mine
would nevertheless be affected."

"If it were true," said Sebastian.

"If it were true," agreed Ramadani. They trotted together
in silence for a moment. Then the Turk said, "How was Ross
killed?"

Sebastian watched the Ambassador's face. "A stiletto thrust
to the base of the skull. Know anyone who uses that method to
dispose of his enemies?"

The Turk widened his eyes. "It's an assassin's trick."

"An assassin's trick common in the East, yes?"

Again, that faint hint of a smile. "I don't know if I'd say it's
exactly *common*. But it is known there, yes." He paused. "Personally, I prefer the garrote."

"I'll remember that," said Sebastian.

The Turk laughed out loud and turned his horse to trot back up the Row.

Sebastian fell in beside him again. "Your argument with Ross at Vauxhall; what was it about?"

Ramadani threw him a quick, sideways glance. The smile was still there, but it had hardened. "Perhaps you should ask Mr. Ross's superiors about that."

"Somehow I get the impression the Foreign Office is being less than forthcoming about the events surrounding Ross's death."

"And you're surprised?"

"No."

"You would be ill suited to diplomacy, my lord. You are far too blunt and direct." He gave Sebastian a sideways, appraising glance. "Although I think you can play a role when it suits you, yes?"

"Are you going to tell me the nature of your disagreement with Mr. Ross?"

"There is little to tell. Ross had approached me earlier, as the emissary of your Sir Hyde Foley. Let us just say that pressure is being brought to convince the Sultan to join the Czar of Russia in an alliance against Napoléon."

"The Russians and the Porte did recently sign a treaty of peace," said Sebastian.

"True. But a peace is not the same as an alliance. You must remember that the friendship between Paris and the Porte stretches back generations."

"Yet Napoléon has shown he has designs on Egypt."

"And the English do not?"

When Sebastian remained silent, the Ambassador said, "Who told you that I was seen arguing with Ross at Vauxhall?"

"I'm sorry; I can't say."

Ramadani nodded. "Yes. I can understand that." He drew up sharply, the glossy bay fidgeting beneath him. "It is always possible that your assassin does indeed lurk somewhere in the foreign diplomatic community, Lord Devlin. But if I were you, I would search for him closer to home." He inclined his head. "Good day, my lord."

Chapter 20

Sebastian arrived back at Brook Street to find Sir Henry Lovejoy awaiting him.

"Sir Henry," said Sebastian, clasping the magistrate's hand. "I hope you've not been waiting long?"

"Not long, no."

"Good. You're just in time for breakfast. Join me?"

Sir Henry cleared his throat uncomfortably. "Thank you, but I have already breakfasted."

"A cup of tea, then," said Sebastian, ushering the magistrate into the dining room and pouring him a cup. "I know better than to offer you ale."

"That's very kind of you."

Plate in hand, Sebastian surveyed the selection of dishes set out on his sideboard. "So, what brings you to Mayfair?"

Sir Henry cleared his throat again. He was a small man, barely five feet in his socks, with a squeaky, almost comically high-pitched voice. But his unprepossessing appearance disguised a sharp mind and a true dedication to justice. He had come to the magistracy in the middle years of his life, after achieving a modest success as a merchant. Once, he had hunted Sebastian as a murderer. But from those strange beginnings had grown respect and friendship.

Now the magistrate took a sip of his tea, then said, "I've just come from St. James's Street."

Sebastian paused in the act of spooning buttered eggs onto his plate. "Oh? Has something happened?"

"It's difficult to say, actually. You see, last night—at something like half past one in the morning—a young gentleman with rooms over the Je Reviens coffeehouse notified the watch that he'd come home to find a dead body lying on the stairs outside his door."

"A dead body?"

"Yes. A gentleman, dressed in evening clothes. With a broken neck."

"As if he'd taken a tumble down the stairs?" asked Sebastian, selecting a slice of bacon.

"One might suppose so, yes. Only, here's the odd part: When the constables arrived, there was no body to be found. Just a gentleman's shoe."

"One shoe?"

"One shoe."

Sebastian added grilled mushrooms and tomatoes to his plate. "Perhaps it was all a hum. I assume the gentleman who reported the body was foxed? He could have been seeing things."

"That was the assumption, naturally. I gather the constables were rather harsh on the young man. Only, when Mr. Alexander Ross's valet opened the door to his late master's rooms this morning—just above where the body was said to have been seen—he discovered signs of a struggle. A broken table. A smashed lantern." Sir Henry paused. "And a gentleman's hat."

"Indeed?" Sebastian came to sit at the table, thankful he had paused long enough to at least retrieve his own hat before leaving Ross's rooms. "How . . . puzzling. But I can't help wondering what all this has to do with me?"

The magistrate took a slow sip of his tea. "Sir Hyde Foley tells me you have been asking questions about Alexander Ross's death—that you believe he was murdered." He carefully set his cup back on its saucer, his attention all for the task. "Might I ask the reason for your suspicions?"

Sebastian shrugged. "A healthy young man attached to the Foreign Office is found dead. You don't find that suspicious?"

"I'm told Ross died of *morbus cordis.*"

"Yet no autopsy was ever performed."

Sir Henry nodded as if coming to a decision and pushed to his feet. "You're right. It does warrant looking into. I'll order the body exhumed."

Sebastian paused with a forkful of eggs halfway to his mouth. *"Exhumed?"*

"Yes. These things take time to arrange, of course. And we'll need to send word to notify Sir Gareth in Oxfordshire. So it won't be until Monday morning. We'll have the body sent to Paul Gibson, of course." Sir Henry turned toward the door. "I'll see myself out, my lord."

Half an hour later, Sebastian reined in his curricle before Paul Gibson's surgery. A skinny youth with a troubled complexion—a medical student, from the looks of him—was just emerging from the narrow passage that ran alongside the surgery. He was clutching something long and narrow wrapped in canvas, and, at the sight of Sebastian, he sidled over to the far side of the street and quickened his pace, throwing a nervous glance over his shoulder.

Sebastian watched the youth for a moment, then handed the reins to his tiger. "That sun's getting hot. Better water them."

Squeezing through the dank passage, he found Gibson in the small stone outbuilding at the base of the surgery's rear yard. He had the door thrown open wide, and as Sebastian approached through the unkempt garden, he could hear the buzzing of flies, smell the stench of rotting flesh.

"I wouldn't come too close, if I were you," said Gibson with a grin when he looked up and saw Sebastian.

Sebastian paused in the open doorway, his gaze on the nightmare laid out on the stone table in the center of the room. "Good God," he said softly.

"A delivery from Bow Street. Heat and water can do ugly things to the human body." Gibson dropped his scalpel in a tin basin and reached for a stained rag to wipe his hands. "Very quickly."

"How did he die?"

The surgeon walked around the end of the table and came to stand beside Sebastian, his gaze still on the cadaver. "I don't know yet. He wasn't shot. Wasn't strangled. Wasn't knifed. No blunt trauma that I can see."

"*Can* you see it, with the body that far gone?"

"Not always, but generally—when you know what you're looking for, yes."

Sebastian cast a quick glance around the room, looking for a different corpse. He said, "I've just had a rather troubling visit from Sir Henry Lovejoy. He's ordering Alexander Ross's body exhumed on Monday. We need to get Jumpin' Jack to put it back."

Gibson stared at him. "Put it back? You can't be serious."

Sebastian felt an unpleasant foreboding steal over him. "You do still have it, don't you? The body, I mean."

Gibson nodded to a truncated form lying beneath a tarp near the door. "Well . . . I've the torso and the head, yes."

"The torso and— *Bloody hell.* What happened to the rest of it?"

"It's not easy for medical students to get cadavers, you know; they're expensive. But they can afford . . . pieces."

"Are you telling me you've sold Ross's arms and legs to your students?"

"That's how it's done," said Gibson defensively.

Sebastian stared at his old friend. "Well, you'll just have to get the arms and legs back. Quickly."

"Yes, of course. It's just . . . You don't think that when they exhume Mr. Ross, they're going to notice that the body's already been carved up a wee bit?"

"There's not much we can do about it at this point, is there? At least they'll still be able to see—" He broke off as a new thought occurred to him. "The neck and head are still attached to the torso, aren't they?"

"Oh, yes. The lad who was to take the head isn't coming until this afternoon."

"Thank God for that."

"He's going to be disappointed, though."

"We'll get him another!"

"Right."

They turned to walk out of the dank, foul air of the mortuary into the hot sunshine. Gibson stood with his back resting against the rough wall of the outbuilding, one hand tugging at his earlobe. After a moment, he said, "I'm not certain Jumpin' Jack is going to like this. Putting a body back in its grave, I mean. Can't say I ever heard of such a thing being done before."

"Tell him it'll earn him a hundred quid. That should allay whatever qualms he may have."

Gibson nodded. "Any luck yet finding out who did for the poor devil?"

"At the moment my list of suspects seems to be in danger of expanding to include half the diplomatic community of London." Sebastian told Gibson about his discussions with the Russian Colonel and the Turkish Ambassador, and the mysterious disappearance of the body of the unknown intruder he'd encountered in Alexander Ross's rooms.

"That's a trick," said Gibson at the end of it. "How do you carry a dead body down the middle of St. James's Street?"

"Easy enough, I suppose, if you've two men. Simply support the body between the two of you, with its arms over your shoulders. Weave a bit as if you're all drunk, and no one's likely to give you a second thought—not at that time of night."

"Yes, you're right; that would work." Gibson pushed away from the wall. "You think this man's friends saw you?"

"If they were watching the front of the building, they must have seen me come out. Whether or not they recognized me is a different question."

"What do you suppose they were looking for?"

Sebastian blew out a long breath. The stink from the nearby cadaver was becoming overwhelming. "If I knew that, I might have a better idea who killed Alexander Ross."

Gibson looked thoughtful. "You say the man you fought was English?"

"He sounded it. But that doesn't mean he was. Members of the diplomatic corps can be surprisingly good with languages. And God knows there are plenty of Frenchmen who've been in this country long enough to sound as British as you or I."

"And then there's always the Americans," said Gibson. "They can certainly sound English."

"True," agreed Sebastian, remembering the half-written letter found in the davenport desk. He batted away a fly hovering near his eyes. "What do anatomists normally do with the bodies they dissect? Once they're finally through with them, I mean."

Gibson gave him a long, steady look. "Do you really want to know?"

"Yes."

"We-ell," said Gibson, drawing the word out into two syllables. "Some surgeons dump the bits in the Thames. But that's always dangerous. I mean, there's the chance of being seen, and it's never good to have stray pieces of cadavers washing up on the riverbanks. Tends to get people excited."

"I can imagine," said Sebastian dryly.

"More commonly, they'll dump them in the countryside, someplace where the wild pigs are likely to take care of the problem for them. Although I have heard of anatomists who bury them in the basements of their own houses."

Sebastian eyed his friend with mounting horror. "And you?"

"I usually don't have much to worry about, after I've passed on various body parts to my students. As for what does remain . . ." He stared off across the unkempt yard that stretched between the outbuilding and the house.

"Good God," said Sebastian, following his gaze.

Gibson grinned. "You did ask."

"Does Mrs. Federico know?"

Gibson cast his eyes heavenward. "The saints preserve us. She'd leave me for sure if she knew."

Sebastian laughed. "And that would be a bad thing?"

"Aye, it would. She's the devil of a housekeeper, but she cooks my dinner and washes my clothes. And the truth is that while she complains a lot, she's the only woman I've had who lasted beyond the arrival of the first cadaver sent by the magistrates for autopsy."

"Does she know about Jumpin' Jack?"

Gibson grinned. "He doesn't usually come around in daylight."

"But you do know how to contact him?"

"Ah, yes."

"Good. Offer him two hundred pounds if you must. Just get Alexander Ross back in his grave." Sebastian started to turn away, then paused. "I almost forgot; I've a favor to ask of you. I'm getting married at eleven o'clock Thursday morning and I'd like you to be my best man."

Gibson started to laugh, then broke off, his eyes narrowing as he searched Sebastian's face. "Good God," he said. "You're serious, aren't you?"

"Very."

Gibson swallowed hard. "Then I'll be honored. Who . . . who is the bride, if I may be so bold as to ask?"

"Miss Hero Jarvis," said Sebastian. Then he added, "And if you stand there like that with your mouth open, you're liable to get flies in it."

Chapter 21

Leaving Tom walking the chestnuts up and down Newgate, Sebastian found Miss Jarvis seated on a stool in the shade cast by a remnant of the long-vanished priory's old cloisters, a drawing pad on her lap. She wore a dusty pink walking dress trimmed with velvet, and a broad-brimmed straw hat with a matching pink velvet band and a tall feather that fluttered in the warm breeze when she turned her head to watch him walk up to her.

"Why, good morning, Miss Jarvis," he said, squinting down at her sketch. It was surprisingly good, a very accurate architectural rendering in bold strokes of black. "Fancy meeting you here."

"My lord," she said, wiping her hands on a cloth. "A surprise indeed." Pushing to her feet, she handed her sketch pad and drawing implements to her long-suffering maid. "Wait for me here, Marie," she told the woman.

"Yes, Miss Jarvis."

"I want to know what makes you think Alexander Ross was murdered," she said bluntly as they turned to walk together along the ancient, dilapidated cloister.

Sebastian had occupied himself on the drive from Tower Hill in deciding how much he could—and could not—tell Miss Jarvis. Now he said, "There was nothing wrong with Ross's heart. The attending physician missed the stiletto wound at the base of his skull."

She stared at him, hard. "How do you know this?"

"That, I'm afraid, I am not at liberty to say."

He saw a flash of something in her eyes, but she glanced away before he could be certain what it was. "A stiletto thrust to the base of the skull sounds like the work of an assassin," she said, their footsteps echoing along the stone arcade.

"It does, does it not?" Actually, it sounded like the work done by the sort of men her father typically employed, but he didn't say that.

She brought her gaze back to his face, her eyes narrowing, and he had the disconcerting realization that she knew exactly what he'd been thinking. But all she said was, "Have you a suspect?"

"At the moment? Everyone and no one. I keep getting dark hints about all sorts of shadowy diplomatic maneuverings, to the point that it's beginning to seem as if half the diplomatic community of London is somehow involved."

"And how exactly does Colonel Chernishav fit in?"

"Ross and Chernishav were to meet at Cribb's Parlor the night Ross died. When he didn't show up, Chernishav went to Ross's rooms in St. James's street, sometime around midnight. Ross didn't answer the door."

"So he says."

"Actually, in that, at least, I believe him. A man fitting the Colonel's description was seen climbing the stairs around midnight, only to come back down again immediately afterward."

She gave him a hard, thoughtful look. "You think Ross was dead by then?"

Sebastian chose his words carefully; he had no intention of

involving her in this murder investigation any more than he had to. "Another man was seen going up the stairs earlier that evening, somewhere around eight—and no, I haven't discovered yet who that might have been," he added before she could ask.

"So exactly what are you suggesting? That Ross was stabbed by this earlier visitor, then undressed and put into his bed so that it would appear as if he'd died naturally in his sleep?"

"It seems likely. Although it's also possible Ross was killed someplace else and his body brought back to his rooms in the predawn hours, when there was no one about to see it."

"Seems a risky thing to have done."

"It does, yes. Nevertheless, I can't rule it out." He was thinking about the body of the man with the broken neck that had disappeared from the stairwell of that same house just the night before. A ruse similar to the one used to carry that body *away* from St. James's Street could also have been used to return Ross's body to it.

They walked along in silence for a moment. Then she said, "I didn't know Ross well, but what I knew of him, I liked. He was a very open and engaging man. I can't imagine anyone having a reason to kill him."

"What about your cousin, Miss Cox; what is she like? Was she happy in her engagement, do you think?"

Miss Jarvis gave a sharp, incredulous laugh. "What are you suggesting? That Sabrina became disillusioned with her betrothal and hired an assassin to rid her of him?"

"The thought had occurred to me, yes." *Sabrina Cox, or her wealthy, disagreeable big brother.*

"That's because you don't know Sabrina."

"No, I don't. And unfortunately, her state of mourning makes it most difficult for me to approach her."

He was aware of Miss Jarvis giving him another of her long, steady looks. "So that is why you indulged my vulgar curiosity by coming here, is it? You'd like me to speak to Sabrina for you—ask if she knows of anyone Ross might have quarreled with lately, perhaps? See what other deep, dark secrets I can ferret out?"

Sebastian said, "Alexander Ross had another visitor the night he died. A woman wearing a veil."

"You think it was Sabrina?"

"I think it unlikely. But I don't know. Will you speak to her?" Sebastian asked.

Their perusal of the cloister's remnant had brought them back to her abigail. Miss Jarvis reached to take the sketchbook from the woman's hands. "I'll consider it," she said.

And he had to be satisfied with that.

After Devlin's departure, Paul Gibson went to stand again in the doorway of his small outbuilding, his hands on his hips, a niggling suspicion beginning to form in his mind.

It hadn't registered with him before, given the vastly different stages of decomposition exhibited by the two cadavers—or parts thereof—in the room. But it occurred to him now that Alexander Ross and this unknown man had both met their deaths at approximately the same time—late Saturday night or Sunday morning. The difference was that Alexander Ross had been kept on ice in a cool, darkened room while awaiting burial, whereas the unknown corpse from Bethnal Green had lain for days beneath a hot sun, half-submerged in water, the air around him swarming with insects.

His lower lip gripped between his teeth, Gibson went to carefully turn the cadaver on his table onto its side. Reaching for a probe, he shifted the fair hair at the base of the man's skull. Now that he knew what he was looking for, it took but a moment to find the slit. He watched the probe slide in, following the track left by an assassin's blade.

"Mother Mary and the saints preserve us," he whispered.

Chapter 22

$\mathcal{S}$ir Henry Lovejoy returned to the Bow Street Public Office after an early nuncheon to find the constable from Bethnal Green awaiting him, a wide grin splitting his ruddy face.

"Constable O'Neal," said Lovejoy, hanging his hat on a peg beside his door. "I take it you have something for me?"

"Aye, sir; that I do. We checked the pawnbrokers in Whitechapel and Half Nichols Street, the way you suggested. And look what young Jamie Durban sold just last Monday morning." The constable reached one meaty hand into his coat and drew out a gold pocket watch dangling from a short chain.

"Well, that's luck," said Lovejoy, reaching for it. "Is there an inscription?"

"Aye, sir; there is. And we've checked with the lad. He confessed to taking the watch from the body."

It was a rather plain timepiece, its case decorated with only a narrow band of ivy engraved around the outer edge. Flipping it open, Lovejoy read the inscription opposite the face. "For Ezekiel with love, Mahala." He looked up. "It's a promising start—assuming of course this Ezekiel is the man whose body we found lying in the ditch beside the green, and not his father or grandfather."

"It is an unusual name, sir. And here's the thing: I done some checking, and it seems there's an American by the name of Ezekiel Kinkaid disappeared from Rotherhithe just last week."

Lovejoy frowned. "Disappeared?"

"Aye, sir. Had a room at the Bow and Ox near the Surrey Docks, he did. Stepped out for a stroll last Saturday evening and never come back."

"Saturday, you say?"

"Aye, sir."

Lovejoy reached for his hat. "Collins," he said, calling to his clerk. "Cancel whatever appointments I have scheduled this afternoon." He glanced at the constable. "Interested in coming with me to the docks, Constable?"

The big constable turned a rosy hue. "I'd be honored, sir."

According to Tom's investigations, the Swedish trader Carl Lindquist operated mainly in the area of Wapping, where he was known as an importer of timber and furs.

After checking with the man's offices on Princes Square, Sebastian finally tracked Lindquist to a lumberyard on the banks of the Thames near the Prospect of Whitby at Pelican Stairs, where he was inspecting a new shipment of spruce and pine.

"I am a busy man, Lord Devlin," said Lindquist, striding along between two towering rows of timber. "Vat do you vant?"

The trader was younger than Sebastian had expected, no more than thirty or thirty-five at the most. Cleanly shaven, with full, flushed cheeks and a thick shock of straight golden hair, he was also quite tall. Too tall for his height to have gone unnoticed by Madame Champagne? Sebastian wondered. He wasn't sure.

"I understand you knew Alexander Ross," said Sebastian, keeping pace with him.

"I did, *ja.*"

"How exactly did you two meet?"

"I vas teaching him to speak Svedish."

"Swedish?"

"Dat's right." Lindquist drew up at the end of the row, his eyes blinking suddenly in the sunlight reflecting off the river. "Vat exactly are you suggesting, Lord Devlin?"

"I'm not suggesting anything. I'm just looking for a possible reason for why Ross was murdered."

Lindquist's face went slack. "He vas murdered? Ross? You are certain about dat?"

"Yes."

The Swede stared out over the crowded river, his nostrils flaring, his chest rising with his quickened breathing. "I vas told his death vas natural."

Sebastian watched him, curious. "Know anyone who might have wanted him dead?"

Lindquist glanced over at him, pale blue eyes narrowed. "Specifically? No. But . . ."

"But?" prompted Sebastian.

Lindquist shrugged. "I should expect suspicion to fall on the agents of England's enemies."

"Such as?"

"Why, the French, of course."

Sebastian smiled. It was, after all, Antoine de La Rocque who had given him Lindquist's name. He said, "Thinking of anyone in particular?"

"I've no dealings with the French, if dat's what you mean."

"All right. Who else besides the French?"

"The Danes, I suppose."

Inwardly, Sebastian groaned. The last thing he needed was

to find himself involved with yet another diplomatic mission. "How about the Austrians?" he said wryly. "Or the Prussians?"

Lindquist considered the suggestion, then shook his head. "Ross never had any dealings vith dem. At least, not dat I know of."

Thank God for that, thought Sebastian. "When was the last time you saw him?"

The Swede puffed out his cheeks. "Oh, probably not since the beginning of the month. I've been busy, you know. But I remember ve had a tankard of ale together at the Blind Beggar, in Whitechapel, a few veeks ago. Interesting old building; you know it?"

"I'm familiar with the place. Did Ross seem troubled by anything when you saw him?"

"Not so's I vas aware, no. He vas a cheery lad, you know. Not much could get him down for long."

"He never mentioned any problems he might have been having? In the Foreign Office, for instance?"

"No, no. He didn't talk to me about dat sort of thing."

"How about his fiancée, Miss Cox?"

The Swede started to shake his head, then hesitated.

Sebastian said, "What?"

"Vell, I don't think he got on de best vith her brother. But I vouldn't vant to make too much out of dat."

"He's a merchant, isn't he? Deals in timber and furs and wheat." Sebastian paused a moment, then added, "Like you."

The Swede chuckled. "Cox is one of the wealthiest men in London. Me? I'm yoost a small-time Swedish trader. My father's a vicar, in Uddevalla."

"But you know Cox well enough to know that you don't like him," Sebastian said.

"You'd be hard-pressed to find anyone along the vaterfront who doesn't have an opinion of Cox." Lindquist started to turn away. "Now you must excuse me, my lord. I have vork to do."

"Just one more question. Where were you the night Ross died?"

The Swede glanced back at him. "I vas home. Alone." His brows drew together in a frown.

"What is it?" said Sebastian.

"I vas yoost thinking . . . I know dat Ross had recently got himself mixed up vit something that had turned out to be more than what he'd bargained for. Some Americans—an older man and a young woman—who'd come here, to London. Something to do vit the impressment of the man's son. But I don't remember his name."

"You mean Nathan Bateman?"

"*Ja*, dat's it. Nathan Bateman."

Clad in an old-fashioned frock coat, breeches, and a long waist-coat stained with spilled snuff, the aged American sat on a bench in the churchyard of St. Pancras. His name was William Franklin, and he was an old man now, in his eighty-second year. Once, he'd been His Majesty's Governor for the Colony of New Jersey. Then had come revolution and imprisonment, followed by estrangement from his father, the death of his first wife, and endless decades of exile from the land of his birth. For years he had devoted much of his time to helping his fellow Loyalists in their struggles to receive compensation from His Majesty's government. That, and caring for his granddaughter, Ellen, a plain-faced child who grew to resemble her famous great-grandfather, Benjamin Franklin, more each day. Now William Franklin could usually be found here, near the grave of his beloved second wife, Mary.

Franklin looked up when Sebastian settled on the bench beside him, his head nodding in greeting. "I heard you'd been hurt. How is the arm?"

"Well enough that I hardly think of it, thank you. And you?"

"The warm weather is kind to old bones." Franklin glanced over to where Ellen was watching a line of ants marching between two moss-covered tombstones. "But I don't think you're here to talk about an old man's health, are you, my lord?"

Sebastian smiled. "I want to know what you can tell me about an American named Nathan Bateman. A seaman, impressed off the coast of New Bedford, Massachusetts, by the HMS *Rodney* back in June of 1809. Ever hear of him?"

"I have, actually." Franklin shifted his weight, both hands gripping the knob of the walking stick he held between his spread knees. "A nasty business, this impressment. Bad enough for a nation to essentially kidnap and enslave her own men, but to do it to the citizens of other countries?" He shook his head. "No wonder the United States complain. In fact, I'll be surprised if this high-handed behavior doesn't drive the Americans to declare war before the year is out."

"That, and their desire to take over Canada," said Sebastian wryly.

Franklin gave a laugh that turned into a cough. "That, too."

"Is Bateman an American?"

"Oh, yes. The Navy has impressed thousands of them, you know. As many as fourteen thousand, according to the previous U.S. Consul. The Admiralty says it's the Americans' own fault, because they allow deserters from His Majesty's Navy to sign up on American ships. They claim that when a British warship stops an American merchantman on the high seas, they're only looking for their own. The problem is, how the devil can you tell an American seaman from an Englishman? They look the same, sound the same. And the burden of proof always rests with the poor sod accused of being an Englishman. In other words, if he can't satisfy the boarding officer that he's *not* a British subject, then he is considered one. And if truth be told, when a warship needs men, they've been known to board an American ship and simply select the most able-bodied seamen, and to hell with any identity papers they might try to present."

"So tell me about Bateman."

"He was on a coastal schooner. The *Rodney* had run short of hands and stopped the schooner within sight of shore. Bateman was one of three men taken off, all Americans."

"He has proof of his American citizenship?"

"Oh, yes. His father has presented copies of his own commission from the days of the war, in addition to testimonials from the likes of President Madison and the current Governor of Massachusetts."

"So what's the problem? Why hasn't Bateman been released?"

"Some men are occasionally released by order of the Admiralty, on application of the American Consul." Franklin let out a huff of laughter that carried no amusement. "They send them on their way with nothing more than an apology to the effect that since Americans and Englishmen speak the same language and are of the same race, it's difficult to distinguish between them. Needless to say, few are mollified. Why the devil the Admiralty can't understand that if service in His Majesty's Navy weren't such a god-awful experience, they wouldn't have such a problem with desertion, is beyond my comprehension. When a sailor deserts his ship and turns around and signs with an American vessel, it should tell them something, now, shouldn't it?"

"What happened to Bateman's application?"

"Well, the original application was made by William Lyman, the previous American Consul. But then Lyman died last fall, and it took a while for his replacement to be posted. This new chap, Russell, renewed the application. But last I heard, it wasn't going anywhere. Bateman's father—a man named Jeremy Bateman—and the lad's sister finally made the journey over here themselves, hoping to have more success in person. But it doesn't seem to have helped."

"They're here, in London?"

"Last I heard, yes."

Sebastian stared off across the scattering of moss-covered gray tombstones. "What might any of this have to do with a man named Alexander Ross?"

Franklin shook his head. "Ross?"

"He used to be with the Foreign Office."

"Sorry. Never heard of him."

"Can you tell me where I might find this Jeremy Bateman?"

"No. But I can look into it, if you like."

"Thank you," said Sebastian, pushing to his feet. "That would be helpful."

Franklin looked up at him. "This Alexander Ross has been murdered, has he?"

"Yes."

"You think Jeremy Bateman and his daughter have something to do with it?"

"I don't see how they could, but I'd like to speak to them."

A gleam appeared in the old man's eyes. "If they thought you could put in a word for them at the Admiralty about Nathan, I suspect they might be more willing."

Sebastian smiled and dropped his hand on his friend's shoulder. "I'll see what I can do."

Chapter 23

*H*er curiosity thoroughly piqued by her morning's conversation with Devlin, Hero decided to pay a condolence call on
her kinswoman, Miss Sabrina Cox.

She found the girl seated in an elegant window embrasure
overlooking the expansive rear gardens of the Cox family's
lavish Bedford Square mansion. The room had been exquisitely decorated by Adams himself, with classically inspired
paneling picked out in sea green, pale pink, and gilt. Sabrina
had her head tilted to rest against the room's rich paneling,
her hands limp against the black crepe skirt of her mourning
gown.

Hero paused in the doorway, her gaze taking in the woman's
pale cheeks, the listless slump of her shoulders. She was a small,
slim thing of just eighteen, with a head of fashionable dark curls,
and the creamy complexion and delicate features that had come
to her from her mother's family. The two women were not particularly close, for the kinship between them was a distant one
and they were separated in age by some seven years. But Hero

had always had a fondness for Sabrina and liked her far better than she did her abrasive, arrogant brother, Jasper.

At that moment, Sabrina opened her eyes and turned her head, saw Hero, and said, "*Oh.*"

"I told the footman I'd announce myself," said Hero, going to embrace her in a gentle hug. "I hope you don't mind?"

"No, of course not," said Sabrina, pulling her down on the window seat beside her. "It was good of you to come."

Hero took the girl's hands between hers. "How are you holding up?"

"I'm trying to be brave," said Sabrina, her lips trembling slightly. "I know it's what Alexander would wish. But I miss him dreadfully. And when I realize I'll never see him again—" Her voice broke.

"I am so sorry. I wish I'd had the chance to know him better."

"Oh, Hero; he was such a wonderful person! So kind and generous. Always laughing and yet so fiercely honorable, so determined to stand up for what he believed in and do the right thing. What is it they say? 'He whom the gods love dies young'?" Her voice caught on a small sob.

"You'd no notion he wasn't well?"

She shook her head, her dark curls fluttering about her wet cheeks. "No. To tell the truth, when I heard he'd been found dead, my first thought was—" She broke off.

"Your first thought was—what?" prompted Hero.

Sabrina simply shook her head, her lips pressed tight.

"You thought someone might have killed him, didn't you?" said Hero.

Sabrina drew a quick, frightened breath. "It was just— Oh, I don't know. It's foolish of me to even think such a thing."

"Had Alexander quarreled with someone?"

What little color had been left in Sabrina's face now drained away. She pushed up from the seat to take a quick, agitated turn about the room. "I probably shouldn't even speak of it, but—" She swung back to face Hero. "You won't tell anyone, will you?"

"No, of course not," said Hero with earnest mendacity.

Sabrina came to sit beside her again, her voice dropping low. "He was involved with something important at the Foreign Office. Sir Hyde had him handling these *massive* amounts of gold. It made Alexander dreadfully anxious. Don't misunderstand me: He was excited about it, to be involved in something so important. But, well, who wouldn't be nervous, dealing with so much money?"

"Gold?" said Hero.

Sabrina nodded. "I don't know if it was a bribe or a payment or what, but it was being transferred in staged allotments to an agent of some foreign country."

"What country?"

"Alexander wouldn't say. He shouldn't have told me what he did, but I had . . . overheard some things. Things I wasn't meant to hear. He felt he needed to explain."

Hero searched the girl's delicate, grief-pinched face and wondered what she was hiding. "How was this transfer made?"

"I don't know exactly. All I know is that it was going on for weeks, with deliveries being made every few days."

"When was the last transfer?"

"Friday night." Sabrina gave a ragged sigh that shuddered her small frame. "I know because he was to go with us to my aunt's—Lady Dorsey's—ball that night. She's been sponsoring my come out, you see. Only, Alexander was so late we had to leave for the ball without him. When he finally did arrive, I . . . I'm afraid I wasn't as understanding as I might have been."

In other words, Hero thought, Sabrina had subjected her betrothed to an angry, emotional scene she would probably now regret for the rest of her life.

Aloud, Hero said, "Was that the last time you saw him?"

Sabrina dropped her gaze to her lap, where her fingers were

alternately pleating and smoothing the matte black cloth of her gown. "Yes."

The girl was a terrible liar.

Hero said, "How did Alexander get along with Sir Hyde Foley? Do you know?"

Sabrina looked up. "Sir Hyde? Why, he always had great respect for him. At least until . . ."

"Until?"

Sabrina's gaze darted away and she shook her head. "They quarreled about something recently. Alexander wouldn't say what."

"Was it the gold, do you think?"

She thought about it a moment, then shook her head again. "I really don't know."

Hero studied her averted profile. "When was this?"

"That they quarreled? Wednesday? Perhaps Thursday. I'm not—"

She broke off as a ponderous step sounded in the hall and her brother entered the room.

Jasper Cox was older than his sister by a decade or more, and little like her. Where his sister was dark, he was fair; where she was thin, he was already stout and would probably run to fat by middle age. The same small features that gave his sister such a winsome, appealing look were lost in his own full-cheeked face. Hero had never liked him; he reminded her too much of his mother.

"Cousin Hero," he said with boisterous heartiness, advancing on her with hand outstretched. "How good of you to come."

Sliding off the bench, Hero found her hand taken in a firm grip. "Jasper," she said.

He glanced over at his sister. "Shouldn't you be getting ready?" His lips were smiling, but his eyes were hard. "You've not forgotten we're to go to Lady Dorsey's?"

"I've time yet, Jasper."

Hero cast a deliberate glance at the mantel clock and withdrew her hand from Cox's grasp. "Goodness, look at how late it is." She turned to plant a kiss on Sabrina's cheek. "I'll see myself out."

"I'll walk you to the door," said Jasper, as if determined to see her off the premises and prevent her from having any further conversation with his sister.

Hero wondered why.

It took Paul Gibson the better part of the day, but he managed to get most of Alexander Ross back.

Then he ran into a snag with Jumpin' Jack Cochran.

"Cain't be done," said the resurrection man when Gibson met with him in the grassy fields of Green Park.

"I'm willing to pay two hundred pounds," said Gibson, then, "Three hundred!" when the resurrection man continued shaking his head.

Jumpin' Jack hawked up a mouthful of phlegm and spit it downwind. "'Taint a matter o' the money. I'd do it fer ye if I could, Doctor. The thing is, ye see, there was a wee young lass planted in St. George's Mount Street burial ground the very mornin' after we lifted yer Mr. Ross, and her grievin' parents have set a guard on the place."

Gibson stared at him. "Can the guard be bought, do you think?"

Jumpin' Jack scratched the several days' growth of beard under his chin. "Meybe. It's not like we're wantin' t' steal the tyke, after all. I'll see what I can do and get back with ye."

Chapter 24

*S*ebastian returned to Brook Street to find a note from Gibson awaiting him.

There's something I think you need to see, the surgeon had written.

Puzzled, Sebastian called for his curricle and headed back to Tower Hill.

By the time he reached the surgery, the sun was high in the sky, the heat intense, and the smell emanating from the small, stone-walled mortuary at the base of the yard so rank it made his eyes water.

"My God," he said, pausing in the doorway. "How do you stand it?"

Gibson glanced up with a grim smile. "After a while, you don't notice it so much."

"Is there a problem with Jumpin' Jack?"

"No, no; things are progressing nicely," he said a bit more airily than Sebastian would have liked.

He dropped his gaze to the bloated, discolored remnant of humanity that lay facedown on the slab between them. Six years of fighting across the battlefields of Europe, and the sight of raw, ugly death still unsettled him. "So what have you found?"

"Watch." Reaching for a probe, Gibson slid the thin metal rod into a small slit at the base of the cadaver's skull.

"Bloody hell," said Sebastian softly. "He and Ross were killed by the same man."

Gibson limped from behind the table. "Not just by the same man, but on the same night. The difference is, this one was left exposed to nearly a week's worth of sun and the rain before he was brought in."

"So who is he?" Sebastian asked, forcing himself to take a closer look at the wreck of a face.

"Last I heard, no one knows." He nodded to the clothing stacked neatly on a nearby bench. "Those are his clothes."

Sebastian went to study the coat, stained now with mud and vegetation and other things he didn't want to think about. It was a gentleman's coat, although far from the first stare of fashion. The breeches were a trifle worn, the linen fine but serviceable. He looked up. "No identification of any kind?"

"Nothing. Probably stripped off him when the body was dumped." Gibson rolled the body onto its back with an unpleasant *plop*. "As far as I can tell, he was a man in his thirties. Well formed, slightly above medium height. Good musculature. Sandy-colored hair." He pulled back the cadaver's lips to reveal a ghoulish grin. "This is probably his most prominent feature. Look at the size of those front teeth. They overshot his lower jaw in a way that must have been prominent."

"That's all we have to go on? He was a man in his thirties with blond hair and buckteeth?"

"Sorry."

Sebastian tossed the stained clothes aside. "Maybe Bow Street's had some luck with him."

"You could try them."

Sir Henry was eating a quiet dinner in the Brown Bear across the street from the Bow Street Public Office when Sebastian walked up to him.

"My lord," said the magistrate. "Please, sit down. You're looking for me?"

Sebastian slid onto the opposite bench and ordered a tankard of ale. "I'm interested in the gentleman whose body was dumped out at Bethnal Green last Saturday."

"You are?" said Sir Henry with obvious puzzlement. "Why?"

Sebastian leaned forward, his forearms on the table. "I think he was killed by the same man who killed Alexander Ross."

Sir Henry took a bite of his pasty, chewed slowly, and swallowed. "You have a reason for this belief, my lord?"

"I do. Only, I'm afraid I can't explain it to you just yet. Have you made any progress in identifying the body?"

"As a matter of fact, we have. It's difficult to confirm, given the state of the corpse in question, but we have reason to believe he may be a Mr. Ezekiel Kincaid, who disappeared from an inn called the Bow and Ox on the Blue Anchor Road, near the Surrey Docks."

"Ezekiel Kincaid?" Sebastian frowned. The name meant nothing to him. "Who was he?"

"As far as we can tell, he was an agent in the employ of the Rosehaven Trading Company."

"Rosehaven? Now, why does that sound familiar?"

"Perhaps because it is owned by Mr. Jasper Cox, brother of Miss Sabrina Cox, the young lady who was betrothed to the late Mr. Alexander Ross."

Sebastian stared at him. "The trading company reported Kincaid missing?"

"No, actually. They were under the impression he had sailed for the United States."

The United States again. Sebastian said, "So what makes you think Mr. Kincaid didn't sail?"

Sir Henry reached inside his coat. "It seems the young thatch-gallows who reported the body to the constables first helped himself to this—" He laid a plain gold pocket watch on the table between them.

Sebastian flipped open the watch and read the inscription. *To Ezekiel with love, Mahala.* "It's an uncommon name, I'll grant you that. But if Mr. Kincaid wasn't reported missing—"

"Ah, but you see, he was. He never retrieved his possessions from the Bow and Ox. I understand the ship he was set to sail on—the *Baltimore Mary*—waited as long as they dared. But they were finally forced to sail without him or miss the tide." Sir Henry rubbed the bridge of his nose. "I've had a look at the man's baggage; they were keeping it for him at the Bow and Ox. In it was a letter from his wife, Mahala."

Sebastian was aware of a suspicion forming on the edges of his thoughts. "A letter from where?"

"Baltimore."

"Kincaid was an American?"

"Oh, yes. Didn't I say?"

Chapter 25

The Surrey Docks lay on the south bank of the Thames, some two miles below London Bridge, in Rotherhithe. Once, this had been the center of the great Arctic whaling expeditions that set sail from London every April to return at the end of the season bearing blanket pieces of blubber that were then cut up and melted in vast iron pots. The stink of hot oil still permeated the district, mingling with the foul stench drifting downriver from the tanyards of nearby Bermondsey.

It was a squalid area of canals and basins lined with storehouses, of factories and artisans' shops and reeking tidal ditches. The air rang with the pounding of hammers, the *thwunk* of axes biting into wood. Wagons loaded with iron and hemp, canvas and squawking chickens, clogged the mean, narrow lanes. "Place always gives me the willies, it does," muttered Tom as they rattled over the uneven cobbles. "Too many foreigners, I s'pose."

Sebastian gave a soft laugh. "That must be it." He swung the chestnuts in through the arch of the Bow and Ox. "The inn at least appears respectable—and very English."

An ancient, half-timbered inn with a lichen-covered tile roof and cantilevered galleries, the Bow and Ox catered to the company agents and factors whose business required them to frequent the nearby docks and their less than savory environs. "Water them," said Sebastian, handing the horses' reins to his tiger. Despite the lengthening shadows that told of the coming of evening, the afternoon sun was still brutal. "Just don't let them get carried away. I shouldn't be long."

He found the landlady in the taproom. She was a short, rotund, grandmotherly-looking woman with a disarmingly beatific smile, who *tsked* sadly when asked about Ezekiel Kincaid.

"Aye, I remember Mr. Kincaid all right, poor lad," she said, drawing Sebastian a pint of ale. "Said he had a wife and two sons, back in America. I keep thinking of them so far away, waiting for him to come home and never knowing what happened to him."

"What do you think did happen to him?"

She set the tankard on the boards before him. "Footpads, if you ask me. Should've known better than to go off alone at night like that. And him so nervous, too."

"Nervous? In what way?"

"Oh, just ever so anxious, if you know what I mean?" She reached for a towel. "I kept his things for him, in case he came back for them. But that magistrate from Bow Street carried it all away with him."

Sebastian took a sip of the ale. "How many days was Mr. Kincaid here?"

"Never spent a night, poor man. Why, he'd only just docked that very morning. Took a room and ate a meat pie in the public room, he did, then went off for a good long while. If I recall, he said something about needing to see someone in the West End, but I could be wrong."

"He never came back?"

"Oh, no; he did." She ran the towel over the ancient dark wood of the bar. "Came back and had his dinner. But then he went off again, and that was the last anyone saw of him."

"No idea where he went?"

"Well, he did come and ask how to get to the St. Helena tea gardens. It's a lovely place, you know, with a brass band and dancing most every evening in summer."

"Where is it?"

She nodded downriver. "You follow the Halfpenny Hatch there, through the market gardens, to Deptford Road. 'Tisn't the best area to go walking through after dark, mind, seeing as how the top of Turndley's Lane is known as something of a resort for footpads. That's what we thought, when we realized he didn't ever come back—that he'd run afoul of footpads."

"You notified the constables?"

"The next day, yes. They checked along the pathway and all around St. Helena but never found a trace of him. No one at the tea gardens remembered seeing him, so we reckoned something must've happened to him before he got there."

"Tell me, what did Mr. Kincaid look like?"

"Hmm . . ." She paused, her face screwed up with thought. "He was in his thirties, I'd say. Hair the color of a haystack. Didn't notice his eyes, I'm afraid. He was a nice lad, to be sure, but it was hard when you were talking to him to notice anything but his teeth."

"His teeth?"

"Aye, poor lad. Could've eaten an apple through a picket fence, as the saying goes."

Sebastian drained his ale. "What ship did you say he came in on?"

"The *Baltimore Mary*. She was at the Greenland Dock." She gave him a considering look. "Going down there now, are you?"

"Yes. Why?"

She nodded toward the window, where the westering sun was casting long shadows across the road. "Best hurry, then. You don't want to be anywhere around there when it starts getting dark."

Chapter 26

Sebastian drove through long stretches of biscuit factories and anchor forges close built with sail lofts and tumbledown cottages. At the outskirts of the Greenland Dock, he left the curricle with Tom in the shade of a big brick storehouse on a quiet, cobbled lane and pushed on afoot through throngs of workmen in leather aprons and merchant seamen stinking of gin and old sweat.

The Surrey Docks were a jumble of harbors, canals, and timber ponds lined with warehouses and granaries and immense piles of timber or "deal wood." The vast whaling fleets of the previous century were almost gone now, their place taken by ships bearing timber from Scandinavia and the Baltic or wheat and cotton from North America. The air was thick with the stench of tar and dead fish and the raw sewage that scummed the water.

Sebastian had a double-barreled pistol in the pocket of his driving coat, primed and ready, and a knife in his boot. But he had every intention of heeding the landlady's warning to be gone from the waterfront before nightfall.

An army of quayside workers swarmed the docks, lighter-men and deal porters and the unskilled laborers who assembled every morning at area pubs like the King's Arms or the Green Man, where foremen selected their day's crews. A few carefully worded questions and the discreet distribution of largesse eventually brought him to a decrepit old wharf near the canal, where a big-boned, black-bearded Irishman named Patrick O'Brian was supervising the unloading of a cargo of Russian hemp from a sloop.

"Aye, we worked the *Baltimore Mary*, all right," he said, hands on his hips, eyes narrowed against the glare of the water as he watched his lads toiling on the ship's deck.

"She was from the United States?" asked Sebastian.

"That's right. Carryin' a load o' wheat."

"Landed last Saturday?"

O'Brian sucked on the plug of tobacco distending his cheek and grunted.

Sebastian stared out over the grease-skimmed waters of the basin, with its hundreds of crowded hulls, their bare masts stark against the blue sky. "Yet she sailed again on Tuesday? How is that possible?"

"Never seen anythin' like it, meself. Paid a premium, they did, to get that cargo off in a rush." He winked. "And ye can be sure the captain greased the palms o' the attendin' revenue officers, to get it through customs that fast."

"Why the hurry?"

"That I couldn't tell ye." He shot a mouthful of brown tobacco juice into the water. "I have meself a theory, though."

He paused to stare at Sebastian expectantly.

Sebastian obligingly passed him a coin. "And?"

"Normally, ye see, a ship's captain will unload. Then he'll go to the Virginia and Maryland Coffee House on Threadneedle Street, or maybe to the Antwerp Tavern. That's where all the traders go, lookin' to consign a cargo to some captain fittin' out fer the return voyage."

"But the captain of the *Baltimore Mary* didn't do that?"

"Nah. He unloaded his ship, took on a few supplies, then sailed out o' here with naught but ballast. Heard tell he was headin' for Copenhagen, plannin' to pick up a cargo and do his refittin' there. But I couldn't say for certain."

"Now, why would he do that?"

O'Brian laid a finger alongside his nose and grinned. "Only reason I can figure is that he had a powerful reason to get out o' London. Fast."

Sebastian studied the dock man's craggy, sun-darkened face. "What was this captain's name?"

"Pugh, I believe. Ian Pugh."

"Had you ever worked with him before?"

"A few times."

Sebastian handed over another coin. "So your theory is—?"

O'Brian glanced in both directions and dropped his voice. "There was this passenger aboard the *Baltimore Mary*, one Ezekiel Kincaid. He had quite a row with the captain, he did, just after they docked. And then, the next day, what do we hear but that Kincaid has turned up missin' and ain't never been found."

"So you're suggesting—what? That Captain Pugh murdered Ezekiel Kincaid?"

"Not sayin' he did; not sayin' he didn't. I'm just sayin', it makes you wonder." He looked at Sebastian expectantly. "Well, don't it? Don't it?"

Sebastian walked through darkening, empty streets echoing with the clashes of shutters as apprentices closed up their masters' shops. The evening breeze blowing off the water brought with it a welcome coolness but did little to alleviate the area's foul stench. He wondered if it was possible that the murderer he sought was indeed some American sea captain, at that moment organizing the refitting and loading of his ship in Copenhagen.

Possible? Yes. Except, what possible connection could exist between the unknown Captain Pugh and Alexander Ross? And how then to explain the intruder Sebastian had encountered at St. James's Street?

He was still pondering the possibilities when he turned into the quiet cobbled lane and saw his curricle standing empty before the looming warehouse, the chestnuts tossing their heads and sidling nervously. Two men loitered near the open doorway of the warehouse; rough men in black neck cloths, scruffy brown coats, and greasy breeches. One was chewing on a length of straw; the other, a younger man, held himself stiffly to one side.

Tom was nowhere in sight.

Sebastian became aware of the echo of his footfalls in the silent street, the steady beat of his own heart, the icy chill that coursed through him. There was no doubt in his mind that Tom would never abandon the chestnuts. Not willingly.

Slipping his hand into the pocket of his driving coat, Sebastian walked up to the man with the straw dangling out of the corner of his mouth. Of medium height and build, he had dark hair and a beard-grizzled face split by a provocative smirk.

"The groom who was with the curricle," Sebastian demanded, his voice tight. "A lad in a black and yellow striped waistcoat; where is he?"

The man cast a glance at his companion, then used his tongue to shift the straw from one side of his mouth to the other. "Nipped off to the gin shop up the lane there," he said, nodding toward the top of the hill.

"A gin shop?"

"Ye heard me."

Reaching out, Sebastian closed his fist around the front of the man's coat with his left hand as he whipped the pistol from his pocket. Drawing back the first hammer with an audible click, he shoved the barrel into the man's face. "I'll ask one more time. And you'd best give me an honest answer because I won't ask a third time. *Where is my tiger?*"

Out of the corner of his eye, Sebastian saw the other man shift his weight. A length of iron bar dropped out of his sleeve and into his hand. He took a step forward, the bar raised to strike.

Without losing his grip on the first man's coat, Sebastian pivoted, leveled the pistol over his outstretched arm, and fired.

The shot hit the ruffian at the base of his throat, the force of the blast slamming him back against the wall behind him. He slid down the wall slowly, his body crumpling sideways as he hit the earth.

"Jackson!" shouted the first man.

"Your friend was stupid," hissed Sebastian. Tightening his grasp on the man's coat, he pushed the ruffian back against the rough brick wall and shoved the hot muzzle of the gun up under the man's chin. "Let's hope you're smarter."

The smell of sizzling flesh filled the air and the man yelped, his eyes going wide.

"I want to know two things," said Sebastian, pulling back the second hammer. "Where is my tiger, and who sent you?"

The man licked his lips, his eyes darting toward the darkened entrance of the storehouse. "He's in there! He's not hurt. I swear it!"

"You'd best hope for your own sake that he is not." His finger on the trigger, one hand still fisted in the man's coat, Sebastian hauled him toward the open doorway. "You first."

Yanking him up short, Sebastian paused in the entrance to give his eyes time to adjust to the gloom. A vast cavernous space with a brick floor, the storeroom was filled with piles of crates and barrels and one small wriggling boy lying just to the right of the entrance.

It was Tom, his hands and feet bound, his mouth pried apart by a gag, his eyes open and alert. Sebastian felt a rush of relief, followed by a renewed upsurge of rage.

"Here's what we're going to do," Sebastian told the hireling, dragging him over to the wide-eyed tiger. "You're going to kneel right here"—he shoved the man to his knees—"and you're going to hold yourself very, very still. Do anything stupid and you're dead. Understand?"

The man nodded, his jaw set hard.

Hunkering down beside Tom, Sebastian transferred the gun to his left hand. Keeping the barrel trained on the man, he eased the knife from his boot. Quickly but carefully, he sawed through the ropes binding the lad's wrists. He was setting to work on the bindings at the boy's ankles when Tom yanked the gag from his mouth and yelled, *"Look out!"*

Chapter 27

*S*ebastian saw the man lunge up, the gleam of a knife blade in his hand.

Pivoting, Sebastian fired the remaining barrel of his pistol into the man's chest.

Within the confines of the warehouse, the report was deafening, the air filling with the stench of burnt powder. The man flopped backward, twitched once, then lay still.

"Gor," said Tom on an exhalation of breath.

Sebastian went to rest his fingers against the man's neck.

"Is he dead?" whispered Tom, struggling to sit up.

Rather than answer, Sebastian went to help the boy to his feet. Then he held him by the shoulders a moment longer than was strictly necessary, his gaze on the lad's pale, freckled face. "Are you all right?"

"Aye, gov'nor. They just roughed me up a bit. It was you they was lookin' to kill."

"They knew my name?" Sebastian caught the tiger's cap up off the brick floor and handed it to him.

"Aye. Who ye reckon set them on ye?" asked Tom, using the cap to whack the dust off his coat and breeches as he followed Sebastian out into the shadow-filled street.

"I'm not sure. But after we talk to the local magistrate, I think Mr. Jasper Cox has some explaining to do."

It was some hours later when he came upon Jasper Cox in the Cockpit Royal on Birdcage Walk, on the south side of St. James's Park.

The air in the small, theaterlike building was thick with the smell of dust and sweaty men and blood. Pushing through the outer ring of rougher men standing tightly packed around the curving walls, Sebastian found Cox sitting in the first tier of benches.

"Personally, I favor the black-gray," said Sebastian, squeezing in between Cox and a man in a drab coat who obligingly shifted over to make room for him. "How about you?"

Cox nodded to the bird being taken out of its bag by a whip-thin, sharp-nosed cocker. "My money's on the red pyle. Look at that size and girth."

Sebastian watched the setters move toward the stage in the center of the pit. Above them blazed a huge chandelier, its myriad flames adding to the heat of the close-packed room. "There's no doubt his spurs are long and sharp," said Sebastian.

Cox turned his head to give Sebastian a long, considering look. "I hear you think Alexander Ross's death was a murder."

"It was murder," said Sebastian, his gaze still on the stage below. "I assume by now that you've also heard of the death of one of your agents, an American by the name of Ezekiel Kincaid."

"I have. But I'll be damned if I see what the devil one has to do with the other."

"They both died on the same night. Did you know?"

"No, I did not. Yet what is that to the point?"

"You don't find it . . . suggestive?"

"Of what? Men die in London all the time."

"True." Sebastian watched the two birds ogle each other. "How well did you know Mr. Kincaid?"

Cox frowned. "Not well. He may have been in my employ, but I'd met him only a few times."

"I understand he had just arrived from America."

"That's right."

"In fact, his ship docked the very morning he died."

"Had it? I'm afraid I don't recall. It may seem significant to you, but my company deals with many such transactions on a daily basis. My personal involvement is minimal."

"That's unfortunate, because I was hoping you could enlighten me on something. You see, as I understand it, the *Baltimore Mary* dropped anchor and unloaded her cargo in near record time. She was supposed to undergo some repairs and negotiate a new cargo for the return journey. Instead, she weighed anchor and set sail just days later, leaving Mr. Kincaid behind."

"Yes, well; he was dead, wasn't he?"

"True. But the *Baltimore Mary* didn't know that. Or at least, I get the impression they didn't, since they seem to have made every effort to find him and nearly missed the tide waiting for him."

Jasper Cox narrowed his eyes against the haze as the birds circled each other in the ring below. "I really don't see what any of this has to do with me."

On the stage before them, the black-gray cock rushed in, feathers flying as the birds struck and slashed. The red pyle reeled back, bleeding.

Sebastian said, "Don't you? The thing is, you see, the only link I can find between Ezekiel Kincaid and Alexander Ross is you."

"You're assuming there is a link."

"Oh, there's a link, all right."

"I'll be damned if I see it."

The red pyle was down, dazed. Sebastian said, "Can you think of anyone who might have wanted to see Ross dead?"

Cox kept his gaze on the stage. His bird was finished. After a moment, he said, "Actually . . ." Then he shook his head. "No, it's absurd to even think of it."

"Think of what?"

Cox cast a quick glance around, then leaned in closer and dropped his voice. "I heard a rumor—don't ask me who from, because I won't tell you. But there are whispers that Yasmina Ramadani—the wife of the Turkish Ambassador—has made several conquests amongst the members of the diplomatic community, and that Ross was one of her paramours."

Sebastian studied the man's fleshy, sweaty face. It was the most preposterous suggestion he'd heard yet. "Are you seriously suggesting that Alexander Ross was conducting an illicit affair with the wife of the Turkish Ambassador?" Such an activity would have gone beyond mere folly and indiscretion to career straight into the realm of the suicidal.

Cox shrugged. "She is a very beautiful woman."

"You've seen her?"

"Oh, yes. She appears often in the park. She's not as retiring as you might suppose, given her position. I understand she's Greek. A Christian, in fact; from Corinth."

"And it didn't trouble you that your sister's fiancé was rumored to be involved with another man's wife?"

"Of course it troubled me. But I only just heard it, and before I had the opportunity to confront Ross with the accusation, he died. What was the point then in pursuing the matter further? Sabrina is cut up enough about his death as it is, poor girl. Leave her with her image of a noble beloved brought too early to his grave. Why tarnish the sweetness of her memories?"

"Why indeed?" said Sebastian dryly. "Although I fail to see how the Turkish Ambassador's wife could possibly have anything to do with Mr. Ezekiel Kincaid."

"You're the one who keeps insisting there's some link between Kincaid and Ross. Not I."

"So you're suggesting—what? That the Turkish Ambassador killed Ross in a fit of jealousy?"

"It's possible, isn't it?"

Sebastian huffed an incredulous laugh and pushed to his feet. "Incidentally, where were you the night Ross died?"

"Good God. You think I remember?"

"Are you saying you don't?"

Angry color flared in the other man's cheeks. "As a matter of fact, I do. I was attending a dinner at the home of the Lord Mayor, in Lombard Street."

"That should be easy enough to verify."

"Please," snapped Cox. "Be my guest."

Leaving the cockpit, Sebastian turned to stroll along Birdcage Walk, his gaze drifting out over the darkened park beside him.

His first inclination had been to dismiss out of hand the suggestion that Alexander Ross had taken the Turkish Ambassador's wife as his lover. Everything Sebastian had learned about Ross—his honor, his integrity—argued against it. And yet . . .

And yet, Sebastian had known otherwise honorable men who took mistresses. Hadn't the Earl of Hendon himself fathered Kat Boleyn by an actress he had in keeping? And then there was the legendary behavior of Sebastian's own beautiful, faithless mother.

But he jerked his mind away from that.

There was no denying that for a woman of Yasmina Ramadani's position and culture to welcome another man's advances would be dangerous; if Yasmina and Ross had in truth become lovers, then both had knowingly courted death. Was it improbable? Yes. But they would hardly have been the first to count the world well lost for love.

Sebastian's thoughts kept circling back to the inescapable fact that Cox's rumor fit rather tidily with what Sebastian had already been told. *Something* had obviously caused enmity between Ross and the Turkish Ambassador. Something Ross had preferred not to disclose to his Russian friend.

In the end, Sebastian decided that until he knew for certain what that "something" was, it behooved him to keep an open mind.

Arriving back at Brook Street, he found a scrawled note from Paul Gibson that read simply, *Complications.* The word was heavily underscored.

Throwing down a quick glass of wine, Sebastian called for his curricle to be brought round. Then he set off once more for Tower Hill.

Chapter 28

Sebastian was raising his fist to knock on Gibson's door when it opened to emit Mrs. Federico. She came bustling out, her shawl pulled up over her head against the cool breeze that had kicked up after dusk. Her habitual scowl was, if anything, fiercer than ever.

"The goings-on we've had here today!" she exclaimed, glaring at him. "I meant to be out of here hours ago, and more's the pity that I wasn't. *Havy cavy*, that's what I call them people. Havy cavy!" She tied the ends of her shawl in a knot and stomped off down the hill without looking back.

Letting himself in, Sebastian found Gibson sprawled in one of the ancient cracked-leather armchairs beside the parlor hearth, a brandy in one hand, the stump of his bad leg propped up on a stool.

"No, don't get up," Sebastian said when his friend struggled to do so.

Gibson sat back with a grunt. "Is that god-awful woman finally gone?"

"She is." Sebastian went to pour himself a glass of wine from the carafe near the window. "What havy-cavy 'goings-on' have you been subjecting poor Mrs. Federico to now?"

"Poor Mrs. Federico, indeed," said Gibson. "I've had Jumpin' Jack here today, is all."

"Came to collect the body, did he?"

"Uh . . . no."

Sebastian swung to face him. "No?"

"There's a wee catch, you see. Someone has set a guard over their loved one's new grave in St. George's burial ground."

Sebastian came to sit in the chair on the opposite side of the empty fireplace. "Well, that's the devil's own luck." He thought for a moment, then said, "Can we bribe the guard? I mean, it's not like we're wanting to steal—"

Gibson shook his head. "Jumpin' Jack looked into that. Seems the fellow's a high stickler. Some old Quaker or some such thing." He sighed. "The irony is, we came so close. The girl's body was held for more than two weeks in a funerary chapel before interment, which means it's so far gone, there's not much danger of anyone stealing it at this point. They've only paid the guard for two nights, and tonight is the last night."

"So what's the problem? The exhumation isn't scheduled until Monday."

"Jumpin' Jack leaves for Brighton tomorrow. It's his annual holiday."

Sebastian choked on his wine. "What the hell? He can't delay his departure for one more day?"

"Monday is his daughter Sarah's birthday. He says they always spend her birthday at the seashore, and he's not going to disappoint her."

"Not even for two hundred pounds?"

"I offered him three hundred. He says he wouldn't do it even for a thousand pounds." Gibson drained his glass. "Do you have any idea how much money a good resurrection man can pull in over the course of a year? I wouldn't be surprised if Jumpin' Jack is worth considerably more than Dr. Astley 'Have You Read My Article?' Cooper."

"Bloody hell," said Sebastian, pushing up to refill their glasses.

"He did offer to find someone to go along with him tonight and kosh the guard over the head," Gibson said. "He wasn't willing to do it personally, mind—not being a violent man himself. But he figured he could look the other way while someone else did it."

Sebastian glanced up from his task, his eyes narrowed with amusement. "He didn't actually say that?"

"He did. But when I told him I couldn't condone that sort of damage to one of my fellow men, he said there was nothing for it. If I was that particular about getting Ross back into his tomb, then I was just going to have to do it myself." Gibson's chest shook with his soft laughter.

Sebastian stared at him.

Gibson stared back, his smile fading. "Oh, no. Don't even think about it."

"Why not?'

"*Why not?* You can't be serious."

Sebastian poured a healthy measure of wine into their glasses. "Can you think of another way?"

The Irishman was silent a moment. "We-ell, I know some other sack-'em-up boys. But none I'd trust to actually do the deed. Doesn't do us any good to pay someone to put Ross back in his grave, only to have them tip the bits into the Thames."

"You did get all the bits back, didn't you?"

"Most of them."

"*Most* of them?"

"I'm working on it."

Sebastian handed his friend the refreshed drink. "We'll just have to put back what we have. If he's arranged artfully in his casket and Lovejoy sends the lot to you, there's no need for anyone to be the wiser."

Gibson stared up at him. "You can't seriously mean to do this?"

"If we've any hope of bringing Ross's murderer to justice, the authorities are going to need his body." Sebastian sank back into his chair. "I even have some experience in the resurrection trade, remember? I went with Jumpin' Jack last year."

"But you were *stealing* a body that time. This is going to be a wee bit different."

"How much different can it be?"

Gibson drained his glass again in one long pull. "I don't suppose you've forgotten that you're getting married in just a few days' time?"

Sebastian had forgotten, of course. But all he said was, "As long as we don't get taken up by the watch, that shouldn't be a problem."

That evening, Charles, Lord Jarvis, returned from a productive session with the Prince, Castlereagh, and Foley to find Hero seated beside the empty drawing room hearth, an open book lying neglected in her lap, her gaze lost in the distance.

"What's this?" he asked, pausing in the doorway. "No balls or routs? No boring but improving lecture at some learned society? No intellectually uplifting evening of rational conversation in the salon of a dreadfully unfashionable bluestocking?"

"No, just a quiet evening at home."

He went to take the seat opposite her, his gaze hard on her face. "You've been looking tired lately."

"Have I?" She gave him an affectionate smile. "What a dreadfully unflattering thing to say."

She wore a sprigged muslin gown with puffed sleeves and a simple scoop neckline filled with a fine fichu. But it was the bluestone and silver triskelion pendant around her neck that drew and held his attention. Said to have been worn by the Druid priestesses of Wales, the piece had a long, troubled history that included a mistress of the last Stewart king of England and a bizarre legend to which Jarvis gave no credence whatsoever.

He had given it to her on a whim, some twelve months before. Once, the necklace had belonged to the errant Countess of Hendon, Viscount Devlin's mother. But Hero didn't know that. And it struck Jarvis now, looking at her, that if he were a superstitious man he would find the pendant's history unsettling.

He frowned. "Why are you wearing that?"

She touched her fingertips to the bluestone disk. "I like it," she said simply. "Why?"

He shook his head. "Are you still determined to wed Devlin?"

"Of course. Why do you ask?"

There were things he could tell her, about Devlin's birth and about the errant Countess of Hendon; things that even Devlin himself did not know. But Jarvis had learned long ago that knowledge could be power, and he understood his daughter well enough to realize that none of these old, ugly secrets would have the effect of dissuading her if her mind was made up.

He said, "You almost—almost, mind you—make me wish I'd encouraged your scheme to travel the world."

She rose to her feet with a soft laugh, her book clasped in one hand, and kissed his cheek. "Good night, Papa."

He watched her walk away, his frown deepening.

He was feared from one end of the country to the other, his network of spies and the eerie omniscience it gave him legendary. Yet there was something going on here, something that involved his own daughter, and somehow the truth of its nature eluded him.

Pushing to his feet, he went to yank the bellpull beside the fireplace.

"Yes, my lord?" said Grisham, appearing in the doorway.

"As soon as she is free, send Miss Jarvis's abigail to me."

Chapter 29

*T*he next morning, Sebastian received a note from His Excellency Antonaki Ramadani, the Ambassador to the Court of St. James from the Sublime Port, inviting him for coffee at the Ambassador's residence that afternoon.

Sebastian stood for a moment, the elegant cream card in his hand, a thoughtful frown crinkling his forehead. Then he wrote out a short, gracious reply, accepting the Ambassador's invitation.

After that, he spent some time at the Mount Street burial ground, studying the lay of the land and the exact location of Alexander Ross's empty grave. He was heading home again when he heard himself hailed by a breathless, aged voice.

"Devlin?"

Turning, he saw William Franklin shuffling up the street toward him, his walking stick tap-tapping on the flagstones of the footpath.

"Sir," said Sebastian, going to meet him. "Are you looking for me? There was no need to put yourself to such exertion. If you'd sent round a note I would have been more than happy to come to you."

"Poo," said the aged American Loyalist, pausing to catch his breath. "When a man stops moving he might as well be dead."

Sebastian smiled and nodded to the tavern beside them. "May I buy you some refreshment?"

The old man's eyes twinkled. "Now, that I will allow."

They sat in a nook near the empty hearth, each fortified with a tankard of ale. Franklin took a deep drought, wiped the back of one hand across his mouth, and said, "You asked about Jeremy Bateman, father of Nathan Bateman."

"Yes," said Sebastian, sitting forward.

"He and his daughter Elizabeth have taken rooms at the Ship and Pilot, on Wapping High Street, in Stepney." Franklin slid a piece of paper with the name and direction across the table. "I haven't told them the details of your interest in them. But I must confess I did suggest you might be able to do something to help their son, for they were at first somewhat reluctant to speak to you."

"I'm certainly more than willing to try," said Sebastian. "Although my acquaintance with the First Lord of the Admiralty is slight." He frowned down at the address. "Seems strange for someone at the Foreign Office like Ross to have become personally involved in an affair of this nature."

"I've no notion how it came about. Perhaps Bateman can enlighten you."

Before he left for Wapping, Sebastian called the various members of his household together in the servants' hall. The official notice of his forthcoming nuptials was due to appear in the next morning's papers, and it had occurred to him that it might be a good idea to warn his staff first.

He waited while they filed into the room, whispering amongst themselves and throwing him curious, furtive looks as they took their seats. He raised his voice. "I won't keep you long."

The room instantly quieted as all eyes trained upon him.

He said, "I've called you together because I have an announcement to make. This household will soon have a mistress: Miss Hero Jarvis has consented to become my wife. We will be wed this Thursday."

A moment's stunned incredulity greeted his words. Then Tom blurted out, "Gov'nor! No!"

Morey clamped a warning hand on the boy's shoulder, silencing him, as Calhoun leapt to his feet with a hearty hurrah. "Congratulations, my lord!"

The others quickly chimed in, although in some instances Sebastian suspected he detected a forced note to their good wishes. A few, no doubt, anticipated more work as Sebastian's carefree bachelor ways came to an end; others perhaps feared their new mistress might be unduly critical or even demand a change in staff. But only Tom sat with his arms crossed and a black scowl on his face.

Tom was not fond of Miss Hero Jarvis.

When the majordomo leaned down to whisper something in the boy's ear, Tom squirmed from his grasp and fled the room.

"He'll come around soon enough," said Calhoun later, as Giles was putting in the chestnuts.

Sebastian tossed his driving coat over his shoulders and reached for his gloves. He hesitated a moment. Then he went in search of his tiger.

He found the boy in the hayloft, a forlorn, prostrate figure with his face buried in the crook of one elbow and bits of straw plastered to his livery. "Go away," he wailed in a gross breach of etiquette when Sebastian crouched down beside him. But then, their relationship had always been more than a simple one of lord and servant. Once, the boy had saved Sebastian from the gallows, while Sebastian in turn had given Tom a new life away from the brutal dangers of the streets.

Sebastian said, "You are aware, of course, that I could by rights have you thrashed for that?"

A ragged sob shook the boy's thin frame, and he mumbled something incoherent.

Sebastian said, "I beg your pardon, but I didn't quite catch that."

Tom twisted sideways, showing him a tear-streaked face. "I said, why are you *doing* this?"

Sebastian rubbed the side of his nose with the back of his knuckles. "It's quite a common thing, you know—for a man to marry."

"But why *her*? She tricked me. And she's—" Tom broke off. But Sebastian knew what he'd been about to say. *She's Jarvis's daughter.* And, *She's not Kat.*

Sebastian said, "She is quite an accomplished horsewoman, you know. And no mean whip."

Tom sniffed, unimpressed. "Everything's gonna change."

"Some things will undoubtedly change, yes. But not every-thing. I shall still have need of a tiger." Sebastian paused. "If you're willing to continue in that position."

Tom sniffed again and hung his head. "*Oh, yes, sir.* I am. Please." He gulped. "And I am very sorry, my lord."

Sebastian pushed to his feet and began to draw on his driving gloves. "I'm off to the East End. Must I take Giles as my groom?"

"The chestnuts don't like Giles," said Tom, dragging his sleeve across his eyes as he scrambled up beside him.

"Then, come along," said Sebastian.

. . .

Sebastian could remember his father—or rather, the man he'd thought of at the time as his father—taking him to Wapping as a boy of four or five, to view a famous pirate hanging in chains on the banks of the Thames. It was the custom to hang the pirates at the low-water mark and leave them there until "three tides had overflowed them." Sebastian had a particularly vivid memory of a crow perched on the dead pirate's shoulder, its shiny black head jerking up and down as it pecked through the iron netting that enclosed the body.

He found himself shadowed by that long-ago day as he drove through the crowded streets of Stepney. Like Rotherhithe on the opposite bank, this was an area focused on the river and its maritime trade, the narrow lanes and alleys crammed with ship and boat makers, biscuit bakers and rope makers, mast makers and anchor smiths, its taverns and alehouses overflowing with drunken seamen. Thanks to the long decades of war with the French, the settlement around the Wapping Docks had expanded and expanded again. They didn't hang pirates here anymore.

The Ship and Pilot proved to be a modest but respectable establishment. Leaving Tom with the curricle in the inn's yard, Sebastian tracked Bateman to the Shadwell Spa in Sun Tavern Fields.

The day was sunny but not excessively hot, the sky arcing above the open fields a pale blue scattered with puffs of high white clouds. The fine weather had brought out a score of the area's aged, lame, and otherwise afflicted to drink the Shadwell mineral waters, whose sulfurous content was reputed to assist all manner of ills. The American was seated, alone, on a rustic bench in the shade of one of the ancient elms ringing the springs.

"Mr. Bateman?" said Sebastian, walking up to him and holding out his card. "I'm Devlin."

Bateman squinted up against the bright sun, his hair white and sparse, the lines on his face dug deep by the passage of the years and the ravages of a life lived in the sun and weather. He took the card, but he did not glance at it.

"You're a viscount?" he said incredulously.

Sebastian laughed and pulled up a nearby chair. "I am indeed. Don't I look like one?"

"I suppose. But . . . You're *walking*. And alone."

"Ah, I see. I left my carriage and retinue at the inn."

"Oh." The man still didn't sound convinced.

He looked to be somewhere in his sixties, of medium height with slightly stooped shoulders and a ponderous belly that hung over his sticklike legs. His worn, old-fashioned clothes were those of an honest shopkeeper or tradesman down on his luck. Sebastian suspected that the desperate struggle to save his son from the horrors of the British Navy, topped off with a voyage to London and the extended stay here, had essentially bankrupted him.

Sebastian said, "Mr. Franklin tells me you're attempting to secure the release of your son, Nathan."

"That's right." The old man rubbed one hand over his swollen right knee. "Been in London near two months now, for all the good it's done us. Seems to me we spend most of our time at this spa, drinking these nasty-tasting waters. My Elizabeth insists on it—says it's good for my rheumatism." He nodded over Sebastian's shoulder. "There she comes now."

Pushing to his feet again, Sebastian turned to see a tall, dark-haired young woman walking toward them, a glass of the spa's famous curative waters in her hands. She wore a simple cambric gown made high at the neck. It was neither stylish nor new, but she wore it with an unconscious grace. Unlike her father, she scrutinized Sebastian's card with care, then looked at him speculatively.

"Mr. Franklin tells us you may be able to speak to the Admiralty about Nathan."

"I trust he didn't raise your hopes too high. But I'll do what I can, yes."

She was attractive if not exactly beautiful, with a long nose and widely set brown eyes and a generous mouth. She was not the woman whose silhouette Alexander Ross had framed and hung above his bed. But she might well be the mysterious woman who had visited his rooms the night of his death.

Sebastian watched her settle on the bench beside her father. "Tell me about your brother."

"He was originally taken by the HMS *Rodney*. But we understand now he's been transferred to the *Swiftshore*."

"And where is the *Swiftshore?*"

"With the British fleet, off Toulon. At first we tried sending his documents to Sir Edmond Pellew, the Commander in Chief of the squadron. They were hand delivered to Pellew, in person. We expected the Navy to release Nathan within days, but nothing happened. Nothing! They know he's an American. They knew that when they kidnapped him! But it doesn't matter. Nathan says there's Swedes and Portuguese on board with him, all impressed, just like him."

"You've heard from your brother?"

She nodded. "He's managed to get several letters through to us."

"Who have you spoken to here in London?"

It was her father who answered. "We've been to the Admiralty on any number of occasions. But we've only been allowed to speak to low-level functionaries. Our efforts to meet with Viscount Melville have been repeatedly rebuffed."

"So what did you do then?"

"The American Chargé d'Affaires—Mr. Jonathan Russell—

got us a meeting with the Undersecretary for Foreign Affairs. A Sir Hyde Foley."

Something of Sebastian's reaction must have shown on his face, because Miss Bateman said, "You know Sir Hyde?"

"I do. And I suspect my opinion of the gentleman matches your own. What happened?"

"Condescending twit," muttered Bateman. He took a sip of his waters and shuddered. "Prattled on and on about how as 'provincials' we obviously didn't understand the workings of the British government, since the Foreign Office had nothing to do with the Admiralty. I said, 'Well, I may not know anything about that, but I do know something about war, and that's what you lot are going to have on your hands if you keep kidnapping honest American men."

Sebastian hid a smile. "So what did Sir Hyde do then?"

Bateman's brows lowered. "Kicked us out, he did."

"Is that when you met Mr. Alexander Ross?"

The old man nodded. "We were coming out of the Foreign Office just as he was going in. Elizabeth here was somewhat distressed by the encounter—"

"I was in a towering rage," she added darkly.

"And Mr. Ross kindly paused to see if he could offer any assistance."

"So you told him about Nathan?"

"Yes. And he said he knew this bigwig at the Admiralty and offered to write him on our behalf."

"When was this?" Sebastian asked. "That you encountered him, I mean."

"A couple of weeks ago, I suppose. I can't say for certain."

"Did you ever meet with him again?"

Miss Bateman nodded. "Yes. He came to see us here—or rather, at the Ship and Pilot—several days later. In order to look at our supporting documents and confirm his understanding of the events before he actually wrote the letter. Unfortunately, I suspect he died before he was able to finish the letter, for he was to send it with our documents, and he never did."

"So you never saw him again after that?"

Father and daughter exchanged guarded glances.

"Well, did you?" prompted Sebastian.

"Not exactly."

Sebastian shook his head. "What does that mean?"

She said, "We *saw* him—last Friday evening, here, in Stepney. But he didn't speak to us."

Sebastian studied her pale, strained face. "Where was this?"

"Not far from here. Papa had been drinking a glass of the waters, and we were walking back toward the Ship and Pilot. Mr. Ross came out of one of the houses on Market Street, but he turned and walked away very quickly. As I said, I don't think he saw us."

"You're certain it was him?"

"Oh, yes," said Bateman. "It stays light quite late these days. I may be old, but there's nothing wrong with my eyesight."

"Do you remember the house? Would you be able to show it to me?"

"Gladly," said Bateman, setting aside his glass and making a move to get up.

His daughter put out her hand, stopping him. "Not until you've finished your waters, Papa."

He made a face but dutifully drank it all down.

They walked together across the field, past a vast rope walk where sweating men were turning cables nearly a foot in girth. The air was thick with the scent of sun-warmed grass and tar and the smells of the river. Just beyond the field they came to a lane bounded on one side by modest but well-kept houses, and Miss Bateman drew up.

"This one," she said, nodding to the small, tidy house with

whitewashed bricks and yellow trim and shutters that stood near the corner. She turned to look at Sebastian, her brows drawing together with thought. "It's Ross you're really interested in, isn't it? This all has something to do with his death."

Sebastian saw no reason to deny it. "Yes. But if there is any way I can help your brother, I will."

Her nostrils flared. "You English. You like to talk about justice and personal freedom. But the truth is, they're just meaningless, hollow phrases that only serve to make you feel good about yourselves. The only thing that matters to you is maintaining the maritime supremacy you've enjoyed since Trafalgar."

There was something about this woman—her obvious intelligence, or perhaps it was simply her passion—that reminded Sebastian of Hero Jarvis. She might lack Miss Jarvis's polish and inbred acumen, but the two women shared a similar inner strength and determination and calm resourcefulness.

"That may well be," he said. "But somehow I doubt that expressing those sentiments to the Admiralty will do much to advance your brother's cause."

She colored. "No; you're right, of course. I do beg your pardon. It's just . . ."

"I understand your frustration. I promise, I'll do what I can."

"Thank you," she said.

He stood for a moment, watching her support her father down the flagway, toward the Ship and Pilot. Then he turned to walk up the short path to the front door.

He was just reaching the front step when the door opened. Mr. Carl Lindquist came bustling out onto the front stoop, then drew up sharply, his eyes widening at the sight of Sebastian.

Chapter 30

"My Lord Devlin," exclaimed the Swedish trader. "*Herregud*, you startled me. I vas not expecting you."

"To be frank, I wasn't expecting you, either." Sebastian squinted up at the house's simple facade. "You live here?"

Lindquist hesitated, as if tempted to deny it. Then he obviously realized the folly of the effort, for he said, "*Ja*. It is hopelessly unfashionable, I know. But very near the docks." He stared owlishly at Sebastian.

Conscious of standing on the doorstep, Sebastian said, "I wonder if I might have a word with you?"

Rather than invite Sebastian inside, Lindquist pulled the door closed behind him and nodded briskly. "If you vish, my lord. I am on my vay to visit one of my storehouses."

They walked through increasingly mean streets crowded with blue-smocked men and lolling seamen. Sebastian said, "I understand Alexander Ross visited you last Friday evening."

"Friday? No, no."

"He was seen coming out your door."

The Swede put on a great show of remembrance. "Ah, now dat you mention it, I do recall he came to see me. *Ja, ja.*"

"Cut line," said Sebastian dryly. "You lied to me. Why?"

The trader's lips tightened. "I do not see how it is any concern of yours."

"Ross is dead. Someone killed him. Would you rather talk to Bow Street? That can be arranged."

"No, no," said Lindquist quickly. "It's yoost . . ." His voice trailed off.

"Yes?"

The man gave a nervous laugh. "It is yoost a touch embarrassing, you see. Ross and I, uh, ve shared an interest in spiritualism. Ve met together from time to time vith other like-minded individuals in an attempt to contact the spirits of the dead."

Sebastian stared at him. "Are you telling me Ross came to your house for a *séance?*"

Lindquist stared back, as if daring Sebastian to disbelieve him. "*Ja.*"

"I see. And precisely who were you attempting to contact?"

"My vife. She died two years ago, in childbirth."

"I am sorry for your loss," said Sebastian.

Lindquist nodded solemnly in acknowledgment. "And Mr. Ross, he vas interested in contacting his father."

"Were either of you successful?"

"Unfortunately, no."

"And who else was at this, er, séance?"

Lindquist ran the fingers of his right hand up and down his watch chain. "I am sorry, but you must understand dat I cannot betray the confidentiality of the other participants." He drew up before a vast brick warehouse with a massive overhead iron catwalk that joined it to its twin across the street. "But I can tell you dis: Mr. Ross was obviously disturbed dat night. He apologized for it aftervards. Agitation of one of the participants can sometimes interfere with one's ability to make contact, you know."

"No, I didn't know. Do you have any idea what had 'agitated' him?"

"All I know is dat someone had come to his rooms, yoost as he vas preparing to leave. I gather they had quite a confrontation. But what the argument vas about or who vas involved, I am afraid I cannot tell you. I did not feel it vas my place to press him."

Sebastian studied the Swede's watery blue eyes. He had no doubt it was all a hum. But it occurred to him that he could do worse than ask Madame Champagne about the visitors to Alexander Ross's rooms the Friday before his death.

Angelina Champagne's seat beside the window in the Je Reviens coffee shop was empty.

Following the directions of the burly Frenchman behind the counter, he found her on a rustic bench overlooking the reservoir in Green Park. Despite the fierceness of the afternoon sun, she wore a hat with only a short brim and held no parasol. An assortment of ducks and pigeons and sparrows fluttered around her. She smiled as she watched him walk up to her.

"So. How progresses your investigation, Monsieur le Vicomte?"

"Not as well as one might wish," admitted Sebastian, settling on the bench beside her. He watched her crumple a piece of stale bread and toss it to her feathered friends, who fluttered, cooed, and quacked around her. "You come here often, I take it?"

"Every afternoon." She broke off another chunk of bread. "They abuse me dreadfully if I am late."

They sat side by side for a moment in companionable silence, watching the birds. She said, "On the southern tip of the island of Pellestrina, near Venice, is a beach known as Ca' Roman. It's a lovely, quiet spot, famous for its birds. Your mother used to go there often. She especially liked the colonies of little terns and Kentish plovers. During the migration periods, you could sometimes see hoopoes and nightingales, too."

Sebastian watched a mallard drake waddle off toward the water's edge. This was a side of his mother he had never known. In his memories, her enthusiasms had all been for silks and ribbons, masquerades and routs. He wondered whether she missed England, when she watched those Kentish plovers dip and glide over a foreign lagoon.

He wondered whether she missed him.

His voice quiet, he said, "Was she happy, do you think?"

"Happiness comes in spurts, does it not? Especially when one has lost so many of those one holds most dear." She was referring to his mother, of course. But he knew she spoke, also, of herself.

He studied her flawless profile, the still-smooth line of her cheek, the sensuous curve of her generous mouth, the softly fading fair hair that hid much of the slender silk tie that held her eye patch in place. Then she turned her head to look directly at him, and he experienced again the visceral shock that came with the reminder of that hidden, ruined eye. He realized that for her it must be a constant, inescapable reminder of all that she had suffered, all that she had lost.

He said, "Do you miss France?"

She glanced away again to gaze out over the sun-sparkled water. "I miss the France that once was. I miss the life I lived there, those I loved." A shadow of a smile fluttered across her features, then was gone. "Perhaps what I really miss is the past, which they say is a sign of growing old, yes? To mourn for all that once was and is now gone is to stop looking forward and prefer the past."

Her words reminded him of something. He said, "Would you know if Alexander Ross had an interest in spiritualism?"

"Spiritualism?"

"Séances. Mediums. Contacting the spirits of the dead. That sort of thing."

"Ah." She shook her head. "No. I never heard him speak of such things. But that is not to say he had no interest in them. Those who do rarely speak of their beliefs openly." She tipped her head, her remaining eye narrowing as she studied Sebastian's face. "You think that is what's involved here? Spiritualism?"

"Frankly? No. I suspect it's more than likely a cover for something else. But I'm also told Ross quarreled violently with someone who came to his rooms the Friday evening before he died. Would you know anything about that?"

"As a matter of fact, I heard them." Her lip curled. "His father may have been a nobleman, but Antoine de La Rocque has the manners and breeding of a peasant."

"Ross's argument was with de La Rocque?"

"Yes. I told you he visited Ross frequently. I believe he came that Wednesday, and then he returned again, on the Friday before Alexander's death."

"Do you know what the argument was about?"

"I didn't hear most of what was said. Only de La Rocque's parting shot, which he delivered as he was descending the stairs so that it echoed through the stairwell."

"Which was?"

"I don't recall the exact words, only that de La Rocque evidently believed his life was in danger and he wanted Ross to give him more money because of it. Ross refused."

"Why didn't you tell me this before?"

She gave him a crooked smile. "You didn't ask."

He found himself returning her smile. "What else do you know that you're not telling me?"

She looked troubled at that and seemed to withdraw into herself. Scattering the last crumbs of her bread, she pushed to her feet and turned toward the path. "I know nothing more. Nothing."

After she left, Sebastian stayed for a time, his elbows propped on his knees, his chin resting on his hands as he gazed thoughtfully out over the wind-ruffled surface of the pool.

Then he returned to St. James's Street.

Glancing in the oriel window, he saw that she had still not resumed her accustomed seat. He entered the side door and ran up the stairs to Ross's rooms.

His knock was answered by the valet, Poole, who blanched at the sight of him. "My lord! I was . . ." He looked like a frightened rabbit seeking a place to hide. "I was just going out."

"I won't be long," said Sebastian, brushing past him into the room.

All traces of the broken table that had once stood beside the door were gone. The valet had made surprising progress in his efforts, boxing up some items to be sent to Charlbury Priory, disposing of others. The plump little man had obviously managed to secure a new position and was now eager to move on.

"Just a few questions," said Sebastian. "I've been wondering about the clothing Ross was wearing the night he died."

Poole looked confused. "My lord?"

"His coat, shirt, breeches, stockings, cravat—everything he had on when last you saw him. Where was he in the habit of leaving the clothing he removed at night? On a chair? The floor?"

"His linens he dropped on the floor, my lord, to be washed. If his coat, waistcoat, or breeches required attention, he would place them on the daybed. Otherwise, he frequently put them away himself." Poole paused. "Unless he was foxed, of course."

"And when you found Mr. Ross dead on Sunday morning, were his clothes from the previous night on the floor?"

"His linens, yes, my lord."

"You're certain?"

"Yes, my lord."

"Nothing was missing?"

"No, my lord."

Sebastian frowned. A stiletto thrust to the base of the skull would have caused considerable bleeding. The killer would have needed to strip off Ross's bloodstained clothing, stop the bleeding, manhandle the body into a nightshirt, dump it into the bed, then remove the bloody clothes. But the missing clothes would have presented a problem, for a valet would notice immediately if his master's clothing was not lying in its habitual place the next morning.

Sebastian supposed it was possible the killer had substituted items from Ross's cupboards—a shirt and cravat deliberately crumpled, perhaps, as if worn. But . . .

"His coat and breeches were in the cupboard?"

Both of Poole's chins disappeared back into his neck. "To be honest, my lord, I did not check immediately. But I have now done a complete inventory."

"And?"

"As I said. Nothing was missing, my lord. Nothing."

Chapter 31

$\mathcal{A}$ntoine de La Rocque was straightening the towering shelves of his dusty, overcrowded collection on Great Russell Street when Sebastian walked in the front door and closed it behind him with a soft click. "I should perhaps have warned you," he said, "that I don't appreciate being lied to."

De La Rocque turned, eyes widening. "Lied to, my lord? But . . . I don't understand."

"Allow me to refresh your memory. You said you'd last seen Alexander Ross the Wednesday before he died. Now I discover you had a spectacular set-to with Ross at his rooms that Friday. I want to know what it was about."

The émigré's nostrils quivered. "I cannot conceive who would have told you such a thing, for in truth—"

Sebastian advanced on him, backing the émigré up until he was flattened against the towering stacks of books. "I should also warn you," said Sebastian, "that when it comes to murder, I tend to be a trifle impatient. I'll ask you one last time: What was the subject of your argument with Alexander Ross?"

De La Rocque licked his lips. "I told you that from time to time I provided Ross with old books I thought might be of interest to him."

"Yes," said Sebastian when the Frenchman hesitated.

"Well . . . Along with books, I did sometimes provide Mr. Ross with information. Nothing important, you understand—just the sort of rumors and innuendos one overhears in the émigré community. But passing information can be dangerous. I thought it not unreasonable that the British government should increase the remuneration I receive in light of the . . . danger involved."

"You mean, because you felt the danger had recently increased?"

"Yes."

"But Mr. Ross didn't agree?"

"Unfortunately, no."

"And what precisely led you to believe that the danger you face is rising?"

De La Rocque pushed out his upper lip. "Don't you feel it? It's . . . in the air. Things are happening this summer. Momentous things."

"Such as?"

De La Rocque's gaze shifted away. "I prefer not to say."

Sebastian brought up his left arm and pressed it against de La Rocque's throat, pinning him to the bookshelves. "I'll keep your preferences in mind. Now, tell me: This danger you feel threatens you; did it also threaten Mr. Ross?"

"One would assume so," said the Frenchman dryly. "Seeing as how he is dead."

"But you didn't kill him?"

"*Mon Dieu!* What a ridiculous notion."

"Is it? Then why lie to me?"

The émigré's lips curled in derision. "If you'd had heated

words with a man shortly before he was murdered, would you volunteer the information?"

"That is one explanation. On the other hand, you could have kept quiet because you killed him."

"What possible reason would I have to kill Alexander Ross?"

"I don't know. To be frank, I haven't found a believable reason for anyone to kill him."

"You haven't?" He said it as if he were truly astonished. "Would you like a list?"

Sebastian huffed a soft laugh and took a step back, releasing him. "Please. Be my guest."

De La Rocque straightened his cravat and smoothed the lapels of his worn old-fashioned coat. "*Ah, bien*. To begin, there are the French—by which naturally I do not mean Royalists such as myself. I refer to the agents of the usurper." His face contorted with the violence of his hatred. "Napoléon."

"Why would Napoléon's agents want to kill Ross?"

De La Rocque cast a quick glance around and dropped his voice, although they were completely alone. "Presumably because Ross was instrumental in the transfer of some rather sensitive information to the British Foreign Office."

"A minute ago, you claimed your information was mere rumor and innuendo; now you say it's 'sensitive.' It can't be both."

"No, no! I speak not of the information he received from *me*. I meant information from *other* channels."

"Why not simply kill the sources of information?"

The Frenchman blanched. "That danger also exists. Hence my request for an increase in my remuneration."

"Are we talking about anyone in particular here, or just some nameless, faceless French 'agents' and 'channels'?"

"Believe me, *monsieur*, if I had names, I would give them to you."

Sebastian laughed. "Of course you would. Please continue. Who's next on your list? The Americans?"

De La Rocque looked genuinely confused. "Why would the Americans want to kill Alexander Ross? I was thinking of the Mohammedans. Specifically, that Turk."

"By whom I take it you mean the Ambassador from the Sublime Porte, His Excellency Antonaki Ramadani?"

De La Rocque gave a small bow. "Precisely."

Sebastian studied the other man's hollow-cheeked, narrow face. "Are you referring to the rumor that Ross was involved with Ambassador Ramadani's wife?"

"So you have heard, have you?" De La Rocque tittered. "Although, somehow, I doubt any of us has actually seen His Excellency's *true* wife. Or should I say, perhaps, wives? Constantinople is full of courtesans and concubines, and the Turks know as well as any the value of a beautiful woman when it comes to acquiring information from weak men."

Here was a new slant that Sebastian had yet to consider. If what de La Rocque suggested was true—if Yasmina was indeed a woman well practiced in the arts of seduction—then it made her conquest of Ross all the more probable. He said, "Was Ross weak?"

De La Rocque's lids drooped, half hiding his eyes. "All men are weak, each in his own fashion."

"Now you sound like a priest."

"One's early training is sometimes difficult to walk away from."

"Is it?"

The émigré gave Sebastian an appraising look. "As well you know."

Sebastian ignored the jibe. "I can see Ramadani killing a man he believed had dishonored his wife. But if Yasmina is in reality a beautiful courtesan sent here to coax information from the men she seduces, then why would Ramadani kill one of her sources?"

De La Rocque smiled. "I can think of several reasons. The target could have become jealous of her other lovers."

"Were there others?"

"One hears rumors. It is conceivable, is it not, that Ross might have heard the rumors, as well? Perhaps he became remorseful. Or frightened."

"All right," said Sebastian. "We'll make Ramadani Suspect Number Two. Who's Number Three?"

"The Swede, of course. You have looked into Mr. Carl Lindquist, as I suggested?"

"I have." Sebastian studied the ex-priest's sallow, foxlike face. "I wonder: You wouldn't happen to know if Lindquist has an interest in spiritualism and séances, would you? An interest he perhaps shared with Ross?"

De La Rocque laughed out loud. "Spiritualism? Is that what he told you?"

"He did. He also claims to be nothing more than a simple trader."

"Lindquist is a trader, yes. But he is also an agent of the Swedish Court."

"Ah," said Sebastian. "Now, that he failed to mention."

"Well, he would, wouldn't he?"

"True. But I fail to see why the Swedes would have any more reason to kill Ross than the Americans."

De La Rocque shrugged. "The British and the Swedes were, until quite recently, at war."

"And now they are at peace. On the other hand, the Americans and the British may soon be at war. Yet I can't see that as a reason for the subjects of either nation to start killing one another in the streets . . . or in their beds."

"True. But then, Ross was not exactly a mere innocent spectator to all of this, was he?"

"No. Yet you could use the same argument to indict the Russians. After all, Britain and Russia were also until recently at war."

"Except that, by invading Russia, Napoléon now has made the two countries close friends indeed."

"So that's your list?" said Sebastian. "Some nameless French agent, Lindquist, and the Turkish Ambassador?"

"Is that not enough?"

"You've left off one rather significant figure."

De La Rocque opened his eyes wide as if in astonishment. "I have? And who is that?"

"Sir Hyde Foley."

The Frenchman gave a disbelieving huff of laughter. "What possible reason could Sir Hyde have to murder one of his own men?"

"You don't think Ross's weakness for dark-eyed, exotic women might be a reason for the Foreign Office to quietly dispose of him?"

De La Rocque pursed his lips and tilted his head, as if considering this as a new possibility. "Perhaps."

"I can think of another reason," said Sebastian.

"Oh?"

"If Yasmina's lover from the Foreign Office was not in truth Ross but someone else—say, Sir Hyde himself—and Ross found out about it, I can see Sir Hyde killing Ross to keep his indiscretion quiet."

"Ridiculous. Sir Hyde has a most beautiful young wife. Have you not seen her?"

"Since when did the possession of a beautiful wife keep a man from straying? Ross was betrothed to a beautiful young woman himself, remember?"

"Betrothed. Not wed," said de La Rocque with a sly smile. "It makes a difference. Does it not, Monsieur le Vicomte?"

"To some men. Not to others."

"And which sort of man was Alexander Ross? Hmm? Perhaps that is the question you need to answer before all others."

. . .

Sebastian stood on the flagway of Great Russell Street, his eyes narrowed against the glare of the hot sun. *What sort of man was Alexander Ross, really?* He had spent the better part of three days trying to find the answer to that question, yet he still felt as if the truth were eluding him.

Alexander Ross was either a warmhearted, generous man, honorable, decent, and kind, or he was a weak, self-indulgent traitor who had betrayed both his country and the woman he loved. He couldn't be both.

Unfortunately, it would be difficult to either confirm or disprove the allegations against the Turkish Ambassador and his lady. One could not, after all, simply come right out and ask an ambassador if the woman he claimed as his wife was in truth a beautiful courtesan sent by his government to seduce the powerful men of his host country. Nor was a blunt question directed to the likes of Sir Hyde Foley likely to elicit an honest response.

Sebastian could think of only one person who might—just might—both know the truth and be willing to talk about it. It was not exactly the type of thing a man normally discussed with his gently bred future wife. But then, Miss Hero Jarvis was an unusual gentlewoman.

He stepped off the flagway and went in search of his betrothed.

Chapter 32

*H*ero spent the early hours of the afternoon in Duke's Place, in that part of London known as Aldgate.

Once, a century ago, Duke's Place had been a fashionable address. But as the cream of London society moved steadily westward, the place had grown increasingly seedy. Now the open square was crowded with rickety market stalls thronged by pale, gaunt-faced women in ragged shawls and tattered skirts; the once-grand houses overlooking the market had long since fallen into a state of disrepair. Hero was careful to keep her carriage—and two stout, wooden-faced footmen—nearby, the high-bred team of blood bays sidling restlessly and flinging up their heads at every ragged urchin who ventured too close. Her abigail stood at her elbow, nervously clutching Hero's sketchbooks, drawing implements, and parasol.

Hero herself had her hands full, with a notebook tucked under one arm and a large folio of maps balanced against her hip. She was studying a bricked-up, arched doorway in an old stone wall when a man's shadow fell across her. Looking up, she found Lord Devlin studying her with an indecipherable expression on his lean, handsome face.

"Devlin," she said in surprise. "Whatever are you doing here?"

"Looking for you." He transferred his gaze to the wall beside her. "What exactly are you peering at with such fascination?"

"It's my belief that Duke's Place follows exactly the outline of the cloisters of the old Holy Trinity Priory, pulled down after the dissolution of the monasteries under Henry the Eighth." She gestured toward the ancient stonework beside them. "Look at this. I think it may once have been the entrance to the original chapter house."

He looked instead at her. "I didn't know you were interested in this sort of thing."

She handed the maps to her maid and retrieved her parasol. "Dr. Littleton is compiling a volume on the surviving remnants of medieval London, and I've offered to contribute a section on the traces of the city's monastic houses. I'm finding it fascinating. It is astonishing how much is still here, if one only knows where to look. Unfortunately, it is disappearing far too quickly."

His strange amber eyes narrowed with amusement. "And here I thought you an advocate of modern science and technology."

"I am excited by the possibilities inherent in today's scientific advances, yes. But I also believe it is important to preserve the memories and relics of the past." They turned to walk along the edge of the square, away from the squalid racket of the market. "There must be things you're passionate about— besides the usual male fascination with guns, horses, hounds, and wine."

He laughed. "I do enjoy poetry and music. Does that redeem me? And the theater," he added, then looked as if he wished he hadn't.

She decided that under the circumstance it was probably best to ignore that. "And murder," she said. "You enjoy murder."

"I would hardly say I *enjoy* it. But I am passionate about seeing justice done, yes."

"And are you any closer to finding justice for Alexander Ross?"

His lips compressed to a tight, frustrated line. She was beginning to realize just how much of himself this man invested in what he was doing. "I don't feel as if I am," he said. "I know more about Ross's activities in the days before his death, but that is all."

They entered a narrow, shadowy passage that led toward the looming bulk of the church of St. James. It was cool here, the ancient stones filling the space with a dank closeness. Behind them, Hero's abigail shivered.

Hero said, "So what precisely was Ross doing in his last days?"

"Well, on Wednesday he met with a certain defrocked French priest with a passion for old books."

"You mean, Antoine de La Rocque?"

"You know him?"

She nodded. "He's a regular at the salons of the city's bluestockings, particularly Miss Hershey and the Misses Berry."

He opened his eyes wide, as if in astonishment. "Are you?"

She gave a soft laugh. "I wouldn't describe myself as a 'regular.' But I do sometimes attend, yes. Who told you about de La Rocque?"

"The owner of the Je Reviens coffeehouse."

"Ah, Angelina Champagne."

"Don't tell me you know her, as well?"

"She also attends the salons of Miss Hershey and the Misses Berry—although not, of course, in the company of de La Rocque."

He said, "Yes, I had the distinct impression Madame Champagne is not excessively fond of de La Rocque."

"One could say that."

"Do you know why?"

"Possibly because he's such a ridiculously affected person. Although I suspect there's more to it than that. I think she may have known him before, in Paris."

"I understand her husband was Baron Champagne."

Hero nodded. "He was killed in the September Massacres of 1792." She kept her gaze on the ancient, soot-stained tower of the church before them. "They were imprisoned in La Force, with the Princess de Lamballe. The mobs broke in and dragged them out into the courtyard. Champagne was killed before his wife's eyes, while she herself was . . . used harshly by the men. She lost her eye as a result of the beatings and abuse she endured."

Devlin was silent for a moment. Then he said, "What happened to her after that?"

"When they realized she was still alive, they threw her back in prison. She kept expecting to be sent to the guillotine, but they never came for her. She was released after something like four years."

"Hence her fondness for the sun," said Devlin quietly.

Hero nodded. "She rarely speaks of those years. But I have heard she had a child—a small boy—who was with her when she was first thrown into prison. He didn't survive long."

"It certainly explains the fierceness of her hatred for the Revolution. But then, de La Rocque claims to despise the current regime, as well."

"You know that he is in all likelihood a smuggler?"

"No, although I'm not surprised." He cast her an assessing look. "Are you certain?"

"He's either a smuggler or on very good terms with one. It's how he endears himself to the Misses Berry. He brings them things like lace collars from Bruges and Sèvres porcelain snuffboxes—pretty little trinkets that are not currently allowed to enter the country through the proper channels."

"Ah," said Devlin.

"You find that significant. Why?"

He stared back at her blandly. "Just, *ah*."

"Right." She transferred her gaze to the soot-grimed walls of the church before them. "So what happened after Ross met with de La Rocque on Wednesday?"

"That night, he went to Vauxhall in the company of his betrothed and her brother."

"That sounds innocuous enough."

"It does. Except that while there, he had a rather heated confrontation with His Excellency Antonaki Ramadani, the distinguished Ambassador from the Sublime Porte."

"Really? About what?"

"Actually, I was hoping you might be able to tell me that."

"Me?"

"I'm curious about Ramadani's wife, Yasmina. Have you met her?"

"I have."

She was aware of him watching her intently. "And?"

"She is a very beautiful, intelligent, remarkably well-educated woman."

"That's all you know about her?"

"Why do you ask?"

"It's been suggested that Ross might have been having an affair with her."

They'd reached the iron fence bordering the narrow old burial ground around the church. Hero stopped and swung to face him. "You can't be serious."

"You don't know anything about that?"

"Good heavens, no. It's ridiculous."

"Is it? Because of what you know of Yasmina Ramadani? Or because of Ross?"

"I don't know Yasmina that well. But I can't believe Alexander Ross would ever have been unfaithful to Sabrina."

They began to walk along the churchyard. Devlin said, "I think you might be surprised at some of the men—both married and betrothed—who succumb to the lure of an illicit affair."

She cast him a quick sideways glance. She was aware of an odd, uncharacteristic compulsion to ask, *Would you?* Instead, she said, "What happened on Thursday?"

For a moment, he looked puzzled, as if his thoughts, too, had strayed in a different direction entirely. "Thursday?"

"The Thursday before Ross died. You said that on Wednesday he met with de La Rocque, then went with Sabrina and her brother to Vauxhall. What happened on Thursday?"

"Nothing that I am aware of. The next significant event appears to have been a second meeting with de La Rocque on Friday evening, during which the two men argued so loudly they were overheard by Angelina Champagne. De La Rocque claims he was merely attempting to secure an increase in his remuneration."

He paused, as if expecting her to ask, *Remuneration for what?* But Hero suspected she actually had a clearer grasp of the émigré's activities than Devlin. She said, "You don't believe him?"

"Let's just say there is something about Monsieur de La Rocque that does not inspire confidence in his veracity."

"That I can understand," she said dryly. "And after Ross's meeting with de La Rocque? Then what?"

"Ross left to attend a séance at the home of a Swedish trader by the name of Carl Lindquist, who may or may not be an agent of the Swedish government."

"A *séance?*"

"Are you insinuating you don't believe Mr. Lindquist either?"

"Hardly. This is obviously where the gold comes in."

It was Devlin's turn to stop abruptly. "The gold?"

"Ah. Didn't know about that, did you?"

"No."

"According to Sabrina, at the time of his death, Ross was involved in the transfer of gold to a foreign state. She didn't know to which state, or for what reason. But from the sound of things, I'd say the state is Sweden."

"How much gold are we talking about?"

"A considerable sum, I think. The payments were being delivered in staged transfers."

"Do you know the dates of these transfers?"

She shook her head. "All I know is that one occurred the Friday night before Ross died."

He cast her a steady, assessing look. "How long have you known about this?"

"Since I visited my cousin yesterday afternoon."

"And when, precisely, were you planning to tell me about it?"

"I am telling you now." She returned his accusatory gaze with unruffled serenity. "You aren't going to claim you've told me everything, are you?"

Rather than respond, he turned to walk along the churchyard again. He said, "When was the last time your cousin saw him?"

"She claims Friday night. They quarreled when he was late for Lady Dorsey's ball."

Her use of the word "claims" did not escape him. He said, "But you don't believe her?"

"I think she's hiding something, but I don't know what. She also says Ross recently had a serious quarrel with Sir Hyde. She doesn't know exactly when it occurred, but I had the impression it was only a day or two before he was found dead."

"For an easygoing man, Alexander Ross seems to have quarreled with an unusual number of people his final week."

"He does, does he not?" Hero stared out over the crowded array of gray, moss-covered tombstones beside them. "In my experience, most male quarrels are over two subjects: money and women."

"And honor. We also fight over honor."

"True. But not nearly as often as over money and women." She paused, then said, "You are right, you know. I do know things that I haven't told you. But before I tell you more, there's someone I must discuss it with, first."

"You mean, your father."

Turning, she took the folio of maps and her notebook from her maid. "I go to dinner tonight at the Spanish Ambassador's residence, then to the theater and Lady Weston's ball. I should be able to tell you more at that time."

"I'll look for you at Lady Weston's, then." He sketched a bow. "Miss Jarvis."

She watched him walk toward his waiting curricle, a tall, elegant figure with broad shoulders and a languid way of moving that for some reason brought to mind that fateful afternoon in the ruined gardens of Somerset House. Horrified by the direction of her thoughts, she opened the folio of maps and gave all appearance of studying it intently.

It was a full minute before she realized she held the maps upside down.

Chapter 33

A few discreet inquiries led Sebastian to the fashionable promenade in the park, where he found Sir Hyde Foley strolling along the crowded pathway in the company of his young wife and an even younger lady who looked as if she had only recently emerged from the schoolroom.

Charmingly gowned in sprigged muslin and a primrose satin spencer, Lady Foley looked to be half a dozen or more years her husband's junior, with short, dark curly hair, large blue eyes, and a rosebud complexion. Sebastian recalled meeting her in her husband's company at one of his father's dinners.

At one of Hendon's *dinners*, he reminded himself.

"Lord Devlin," she said, extending her gloved hand with an unaffected smile when she saw him. "What a pleasure to see you again! Have you met my younger sister, Miss Eastlake?"

He stood talking politely to the two ladies for some moments, then turned to say to Sir Hyde, "If I might have a word with you for a moment, sir?"

The Undersecretary fixed him with a dark glare. "You aren't still going on about Ross, are you?"

"I am, actually."

They continued along the pathway, pointedly falling back a few steps behind the ladies. Foley said, "I checked with Bow Street. There is no investigation into the murder of Alexander Ross. And do you know why? Because Alexander Ross was not murdered! So what is the purpose of this nonsense?"

Sebastian let his gaze rove over the fashionable crush of curricles, coaches, and hacks filling the carriageway beside them. "I'm curious about Ross's dealings with the Sultan's Ambassador, Mr. Antonaki Ramadani."

Foley drew up short. "What dealings? I don't know who you've been speaking to, but Ross was not in any way involved in our negotiations with the Sublime Porte."

"No? My mistake."

Foley said, "Just so," and continued on his way.

Sebastian fell into step beside him again. "Am I to take it, then, that the shipments of gold Ross was handling were not intended for Constantinople?"

Foley let out a warning hiss and pointedly lowered his voice. "Where the devil did you hear about that?"

Rather than answer him, Sebastian said, "I understand one of the transfers took place a week ago last Friday night, barely twenty-four hours before Ross . . . died."

"How came you to know this?"

"Does is matter?"

"Of course it matters. Good God! The security of the realm is at stake."

Sebastian studied the other man's flushed, pointed face. "Exactly how much gold are we talking about here?"

"That is none of your affair. You hear me? None of this is."

"Ross's death is my affair."

"Oh? And who made it so? Hmm? You tell me that. Who made it so?"

"'And whatsoever you do unto the least of my brothers, you do unto me,'" Sebastian quoted softly.

"Oh, please," said Foley with a scornful huff.

Sebastian said, "I'm curious: Was your argument with Ross over the gold? Or over something else entirely?"

"What argument? I had no argument with Ross."

"The Thursday before he died. Perhaps the Wednesday. Or the Friday. But there was definitely an argument. There's no point in denying it. Ross was troubled enough to mention it to a friend."

Foley's pale gray eyes narrowed. "All right; we did disagree. But over a diplomatic affair; that is all. Not the sort of thing that would lead to—" He broke off.

"To murder?" suggested Sebastian.

"Go to the devil," snapped Foley, and strode off after his wife and sister-in-law.

This time, Sebastian let him go.

Charles, Lord Jarvis, was in his dressing room adjusting the final set of his coat when Hero came to knock on the door.

"Could I speak with you for a moment, Papa?"

"You look lovely this evening," he said, dismissing his valet. "I like the way you've started doing your hair."

"Thank you." She closed the door behind the departing valet, then said without preamble, "Did you kill Alexander Ross?"

"I did not."

"Did you have him killed?"

He gave her a hard, searching look, but she simply stared back at him steadily. He said, "Are you here as Devlin's emissary?"

"He has spoken to me, yes. But that is not why I am here."

"Then I will answer your question. No, I did not have Ross killed. On the contrary, I find his death troubling. Very troubling."

"Why is that?"

He tucked an enameled snuffbox into his pocket, then turned to face her. "Some of what I am about to tell you, you may pass on to Devlin. But not all of it. Is that clear?"

She met his gaze and held it. "Yes."

Before he could confront Lindquist with tales of mysterious gold transfers, Sebastian had an appointement to keep at the Turkish Ambassador's residence in Portman Square. He was met by a wooden-faced English butler who bowed and said, "The Ambassador is expecting you, my lord."

At that moment, Ramadani himself appeared in the vast hall. He was dressed as was his habit in the doeskin breeches, carelessly tied cravat, and riding coat of a country gentleman. "Lord Devlin," he said. "*Hoşgeldiniz.* Welcome."

"*Hoş bulduk.*" Sebastian handed his hat and walking stick to the butler, who gave another dignified bow and withdrew.

Ramadani's teeth flashed in a delighted smile. "You speak Turkish!"

"No. Just, *boş bulduk.*"

"Please, this way." Ramadani led Sebastian to a small salon draped floor to ceiling with endless yards of red gauze, so that the effect was something like that of a Turkish tent. A low banquette piled with cushions surrounded three walls, with round tables of dark carved wood and figured brass scattered across the thick, colorful carpets. "You will join me for coffee? Ours is much thicker than yours, and sweet. But you will like it, I think."

"Thank you," said Sebastian, settling back against the cushions.

A dark-haired boy of perhaps fifteen, dressed in baggy trousers, a loose white shirt, and a sleeveless vest, brought coffee and sweetmeats, then disappeared.

The cups were delicate, of glass painted with a gold arabesque pattern. Sebastian took a cautious sip of the thick, hot brew. Ramadani watched him closely. "If it is not to your taste, I do have brandy."

"I find it pleasant, thank you. I remember your coffee well."

"You have visited the Ottoman world, Lord Devlin?"

"I was in Egypt, once; that is all."

"With the Army, yes?"

"Yes." Sebastian found it significant that the Turk had obviously gone to the trouble of looking into his background. "I would someday like to see more. My future wife is very keen to travel."

"I have heard of your betrothal to Miss Jarvis. Please accept my felicitations."

"Thank you."

Ramadani sipped his coffee, his eyes alert and watchful behind half-lowered lids. "How does your investigation into the death of Mr. Ross progress?"

Sebastian kept his own expression bland. "Why do you ask?"

"Curiosity only."

Sebastian raised one eyebrow. "Really?"

"You don't believe me?"

"No."

Ramadani gave a sharp bark of laughter. "Very well. Let's cut to the chase, as you English say, shall we? I am curious, yes, but with a purpose. Incidents of this nature can be dangerous. There are those who might seek to use this unfortunate young man's death to drive a wedge between our two nations."

"Such as?"

The Ambassador reached for the tall glass and silver water

pipe that stood beside him and began to prepare it, loading the bowl with tobacco and covering the tobacco with a fine metal screen. "For me to answer that question would not be diplomatic, now, would it?"

Sebastian chose his words carefully. "If you have some knowledge of the circumstances which led to Ross's death, I would be interested to hear of it."

"If I learn anything, you will of course be the first to know." From a perforated covered brass box, the Turk extracted glowing coals and carefully placed them atop the screen.

"You have smoked the *narguileh?*" asked the Ambassador, handing him one of the pipe's two hoses. "In northern Africa I believe they call it the *shisha.*"

"I have, yes." The wooden mouthpiece was decorated with smoothly polished nuggets of aquamarine and garnet. Holding it between his lips, Sebastian inhaled, the charcoal flaring as the air was pulled through the tobacco and down to bubble up through the water. The smoke was cool and faintly flavored with mint.

"It is a vice, I am told," said Ramadani, sucking on his own hose. "But then, some of life's greatest pleasures are so labeled; is this not true?"

The soft patter of footsteps and a faint waft of jasmine drew Sebastian's attention to the door. Small and delicate and breathtakingly lovely, a woman slipped into the room.

Unlike her husband, Yasmina Ramadani was dressed in the style of her homeland, with a short fitted jacket of dark purple velvet worn over a white, filmy silk blouse and a brocade divided skirt that Sebastian suspected Miss Jarvis would love. A necklace of gold coins draped her long, thin neck; on her head she wore a purple velvet cap edged with more small gold coins. But her hair flowed loose, a glorious cascade of auburn-tinted dark waves. She looked to be somewhere in her twenties, with almond-shaped eyes, a long nose, and full, sensuous lips that broke into a wide smile.

"I believe you have not yet met my wife, Yasmina," said the Ambassador.

Rising to his feet, Sebastian swept her a gracious bow. "Madame Ramadani. How do you do?"

He found himself looking into a pair of thickly lashed, piercingly intelligent green eyes. "Lord Devlin," she said, extending a tiny, almost childlike hand. "My husband has told me much about you. Welcome to our home."

Her English was good, exotically accented yet very clear. But then, a woman sent to seduce some of England's finest would need to speak the language well.

"You like the *narguileh?*" she asked, coming to lounge gracefully on the carpet beside them. Rather than take her husband's hose, she reached for Sebastian's, her eyes on his as she took the mouthpiece between her full lips and sucked. Still holding his gaze, she pursed her lips and blew out a soft stream of mint-scented smoke.

"It's certainly more pleasant than sniffing snuff."

She gave a delighted laugh. "It does not shock you to see a woman smoke?"

"I've seen it before, in Egypt."

"So you know our lands."

"Not well, no." He took the hose as she handed it back to him, her fingertips brushing his ever so discreetly. He said, "Do you miss Stanboul? Life is very different here, is it not?"

"It is, but not unpleasantly so—especially now that summer is here. I am very fond of your city's parks. It is wonderful to be able to ride out every morning, even though we live in the middle of London. The Ambassador is an early riser, in the saddle always with the dawn. But me, I prefer to wait until the sun has chased away the mist." She paused, her head tilting prettily to one side. "Do you ride in the park, my lord?"

"Sometimes, yes," said Sebastian, once more drawing the sweetly scented tobacco deep into his lungs.

Her gaze holding his, her smile a warm secret that beckoned and tantalized, she reached once more to take the water pipe's hose from his hand. "Then perhaps I shall see you there."

His visit to the Turkish Ambassador's residence left Sebastian with much food for thought as he turned his horses once more toward the east, to Stepney.

Until now, he'd given little credence to the rumors that Alexander Ross had been romantically entangled with the wife of the Turkish Ambassador. Not only did it fly in the face of everything he thought he had come to know about the man, but the logistics of such a liaison had seemed too fantastic to be credible.

Now he understood only too well how such a relationship could have come about. And yet he still found himself unwilling to believe it—although he also recognized that he could simply be allowing his sympathy for the dead man to cloud his judgment. There was certainly no doubt in his mind that Yasmina was a beautiful, brilliant young woman well versed in the arts of seduction—and that her "husband" had attempted to set her to work her wiles on Sebastian himself.

Why? Sebastian wondered. To discover what he might have learned about Ross? Or to lure Sebastian to his own death?

By the time he drew up before the Swedish trader's neat white brick house with the yellow shutters, the setting sun was throwing long shadows across the narrow, cobbled streets. The house's shiny black door stood open wide. A red-faced, sweating constable on the footpath out front was shooing away a gawking crowd of half-grown boys. A hackney carriage waited nearby, the bay between the poles twitching its dark tail against the buzzing flies.

"What the devil?" said Sebastian, handing Tom the reins.

A small man in a modest top hat and with a pair of spectacles perched on the end of his nose came out of the house to walk down the short path. "My lord," said Sir Henry Lovejoy, pausing beside the curricle, his head tipped back so he could look up at Sebastian. "I gather you've come to see Mr. Lindquist?"

"I have, yes. Why?" asked Sebastian, hopping down to the flagway.

Lovejoy scratched the side of his nose. "Interesting. You see, he's just been found dead."

Chapter 34

"Murdered?" asked Sebastian as they walked together toward the house.

"I'd say so, yes. Unless you think he somehow bashed in his own head with a cudgel."

Sebastian suppressed a smile. The magistrate was obviously becoming seriously aggrieved by Sebastian's inability to be entirely forthcoming about his interest in the death of Alexander Ross. "Who found him?"

"The woman who comes in daily and does for him. She'd nipped down to the shops for some onions. By the time she came back, he was dead."

Sebastian paused on the threshold. The house was small, with just a narrow hall and two rooms—a parlor and a dining room—on the ground floor. A steep staircase led up to the bedrooms and down to the kitchen. Carl Lindquist lay sprawled in a pool of blood just inside the parlor door, the back of his head a gruesome, crimson pulp. A gore-stained cudgel lay beside him.

"Nasty," said Sebastian, hunkering down to study the dead

man's pale, blood-streaked face. No neat dagger thrust to the base of the skull here.

"Very," said Sir Henry, stepping around the body to enter the parlor.

Sebastian let his gaze wander the room. It was simply furnished with a settee and several chairs, a tea table, and a small writing desk near the front window. But one of the chairs had been knocked over; the carpet was bunched, as if Lindquist had realized he was in danger and sought to resist. "One wonders why the killer didn't wait until the housekeeper had left for the evening. Or even break in later tonight. Much less chance of being discovered that way."

"True. Perhaps the murder was a spur-of-the-moment decision. Or a crime of passion."

"It certainly was passionate." Pushing to his feet, Sebastian went to take a look at the writing table. A quill lay on the floor; a bottle of ink had been tipped over, the stain on the blotter still wet to his touch. He glanced around. No sign of any letter, journal, or notebook entry that Lindquist could have been writing.

Sir Henry said, "It's possible Lindquist knew his assailant. He let the man in."

"If so, that could explain the timing."

The magistrate cleared his throat. "May I venture to ask your interest in Mr. Lindquist, my lord?"

"Alexander Ross came here, the Friday before he died."

"I see. And do you know the purpose of his visit?"

"A séance, according to Mr. Lindquist."

"A séance?"

"So said Mr. Lindquist. He claims Ross was interested in spiritualism."

"You can't be serious."

"I only know what—"

Sebastian broke off as a loud tread clattered down the stairs from the upper floor. "Sir Henry!" A gangly young constable burst into the room. "Sir Henry!"

Sir Henry frowned. "Yes, Constable? What is it?"

"You gotta come see this, sir! Upstairs!"

"Constable Starke, you forget yourself."

"But it's gold, Sir Henry! Gold! A whole trunk full of it!"

Divided into small, sturdy canvas pouches, the gold almost filled an iron-banded wooden trunk shoved into a corner of a disused back bedroom littered with boxes and crates.

"Interesting," said Sebastian, hunkering down to heft one of the bags and assess its contents. It weighed something like twenty pounds. Unknotting the string, he tipped its coins out onto the floor. Gold sovereigns, as shiny and new as if they'd come fresh from the mint, spilled across the bare floorboards.

He glanced up to find the magistrate staring at him, hard. "You know what this means," said Sir Henry. It was more of an accusation than a question.

"Not exactly."

"Yet you don't appear at all surprised to find it here."

Sebastian rose to his feet. "I'd heard Alexander Ross was involved in a transfer of gold and that the transaction was causing him some nervousness. But I didn't know for certain the gold was going to Carl Lindquist. And I can't begin to hazard a guess as to its purpose."

Sir Henry frowned down at the open trunk. It represented a staggering sum, and it would be his responsibility to keep it secure. He nodded to the young constable. "I want a heavy chain and a padlock brought here, at once. Then I will personally be escorting this to Bow Street."

"Yes, sir," said the constable, dashing off.

Sir Henry shifted his gaze to Sebastian. "I assume you'll be attending the exhumation of Ross's body? It's scheduled for eight tomorrow morning."

"I'll be there," said Sebastian, turning toward the door.

Hopefully, Alexander Ross would be, too.

"I trust all is set for tonight?" Sebastian asked sometime later as he prepared for Lady Weston's ball.

"It is, my lord," said Calhoun, smoothing the set of Sebastian's evening coat across his shoulders. "I've arranged to borrow a wagon and a dark mule from my mother, and before he left for Brighton, Jumpin' Jack kindly lent Dr. Gibson his wooden spades and various other tools of the trade. He also bribed the sexton of the churchyard to oil the gate's hinges and leave it unlocked."

Sebastian adjusted the snowy white folds of his cravat. "What time does Jumpin' Jack suggest?"

"Half past two, my lord, as most residents of Mayfair will have found their way home by then. Sunrise is at six. We ought to have a good three hours before the humbler residents of the city begin to stir again."

Sebastian cast a glance out the window. Thick clouds had come roiling in shortly after nightfall, obscuring moon and stars. "Let's hope the rain holds off."

"At least it will be dark, my lord."

"That it will." Sebastian slipped his watch into his pocket. "You and Tom take the wagon and collect Gibson and Mr. Ross. I should be back here by two. But if by some chance I'm not, I'll meet you at the burial ground."

Chapter 35

$\mathscr{S}$ebastian arrived at Lady Weston's ball at the unfashionably early hour of a quarter past twelve. Miss Jarvis, looking splendid in gossamer-fine silk of the palest pink with rosette-and-pearl-trimmed swags around the hem, did not put in an appearance until long past one.

"I was beginning to think you must have changed your mind," he said, walking up to her. It came out considerably less gallant and more impatient than he'd intended.

She held a painted silk fan trimmed with fine lace and had a strand of pearls woven through her hair, but there was nothing either fragile or frivolous about the way she assessed him through narrowed eyes. "Why? Have you a pressing engagement elsewhere?" she said with an insight he found unsettling.

"At this hour?" He let his gaze rove casually over the glittering rooms, the bejeweled ladies and exquisitely tailored gentlemen, and lowered his voice. "I'm hoping to hear why His Majesty's government is transferring vast sums of gold to the Swedes."

She made a show of fanning her face, the delicate ivory and

silk confection stirring up a useless eddy heated by hundreds of dancing candles and the hot press of fashionable bodies. "It's quite warm in here, don't you think?" she said for the benefit of anyone who might be listening. "Perhaps you would be so good as to escort me out to the terrace for a breath of fresh air."

He smiled and gave a short bow. "With pleasure, Miss Jarvis."

The terrace overlooking the darkened gardens was largely deserted, thanks to a gusty wind that had blown out most of the festive hanging lanterns. Heedless of the threat to her carefully curled locks, she walked to the stone balustrade at the edge of the terrace and drew a deep breath. "Smells like rain."

"I sincerely hope not," said Sebastian.

She glanced over at him in surprise. "Why? We need a good rain to clean the air of dust and wash down the streets."

"True," he agreed. Unfortunately, rain would also make St. George's burial ground a muddy mess.

She was silent for a moment, as if collecting her thoughts. Then she said, "I am not betraying my father's confidence in what I am about to tell you. It is known in certain circles, yet the fewer who know, the better."

"I understand."

"Two weeks ago, at Örebro, Britain signed a treaty with both Sweden and Russia. It is a peace treaty without any alliance obligations, which represents something of a failure for Russian diplomacy, since the Czar has been pushing for more."

It was difficult sometimes to remember, but Russia had officially been at war with Britain for the past five years. He said, "Go on."

"The war between us was never vigorously pursued by either side, and had been largely maintained by the Czar in order to placate Napoléon. But by invading Russia last month, Napoléon effectively ended the need for that fiction."

"Hence the Treaty of Örebro," said Sebastian.

She nodded. "Likewise, the Anglo-Swedish War has essentially been a paper war for the last two years. The Swedes' main argument is with the Russians, who seized Finland."

"Losing the entire eastern half of your kingdom is rather difficult to swallow with equanimity," said Sebastian.

"True. But the Swedes have now let it be known that they would be willing to allow Russia to keep Finland if they could receive some sort of compensation."

"Meaning?"

"Norway."

"But Norway is part of Denmark."

"Exactly. And Denmark is an ally of France."

"Denmark is an ally of France because we attacked Copenhagen and sank the Danish fleet," said Sebastian dryly.

She shrugged. "Such is the price of neutrality."

"Well, they're certainly not neutral anymore."

She turned to face him, so that she was leaning back against the balustrade, the wind blowing the short curls around her face. She put up a hand to push them back. "Your perspective is certainly unusual, I'll give you that."

Sebastian said, "Napoléon has been unhappy with Sweden because, despite being officially at war with us, the Swedes still allowed us to station our troops in the Swedish port of Hano and trade with the Baltic states. In fact, as I understand it, Sweden has remained our largest trading partner. In other words, Napoléon's recent attack on Sweden was driven by exactly the same motive as our attack on Denmark."

"And now Sweden is also willing to attack Denmark."

"In exchange for Norway."

"And certain subsidies," she said.

"Ah. Define subsidies."

"Gold. Transferred from the British Treasury to the Swedish Embassy here in London."

"So that's how it all comes together," said Sebastian softly. He stared out over the shadowy shrubbery below. "Tell me, how are these transfers usually effected? I find myself woefully ignorant in the niceties of such details."

"It isn't as if you can simply appropriate the payments from the Treasury, drive a wagon up to the Swedish Embassy, and offload trunks of gold. That sort of activity would be bound to attract unwanted attention and speculation. Generally, deliveries are made in incremental amounts—"

"Say, twenty-pound bags of gold sovereigns, delivered every few days?" He was remembering the list of numbers he'd found in Ross's copy of *Marcus Aurelius*. He thought he knew now what they meant: They were the dates of Ross's deliveries of gold to Lindquist.

"Something like that. The gold is typically passed by someone attached to the Foreign Office—"

"Meaning Alexander Ross?"

"Evidently. The gold is delivered to an agent of the recipient government."

"Carl Lindquist," said Sebastian.

"Has Mr. Lindquist been discovered in possession of an inexplicably large number of gold sovereigns?"

"Mr. Lindquist is, unfortunately, dead."

"Good heavens. When did this happen?"

"This afternoon."

She looked thoughtful a moment. Then she said, "Did you kill him?"

"I did not. But he most certainly had a large trunk of gold in his possession."

"How was he killed? In the same method as Ross?"

"Nothing anywhere near so tidy. Someone bashed in his head."

She fixed him with a steady stare. "You say Alexander Ross

died from a dagger thrust at the base of his skull. Yet you have not told me how you came to know that."

One of the tall French doors from the drawing room burst open behind them, disgorging a tangle of laughing young women bedecked in white muslin, satin ribbons, and pearls, and trailed by a clutch of clucking mothers. In the distance, the church towers began to strike the hour.

Two o'clock.

Sebastian cast the chattering women a significant glance. "Now is perhaps not the time. May I call upon you tomorrow? There are a number of things we really must discuss—and I don't mean simply about the death of Alexander Ross."

She got that harried look on her face, the one that stole over her every time he attempted to bring the conversation around to their looming marriage. "Not tomorrow," she said vaguely. "I already have several previous engagements."

"Tuesday morning, then."

He thought for a moment she meant to refuse him. Then she said, "Very well. Tuesday. At half past eleven?"

"Half past eleven," he said, just as the first drops of rain splattered the stone flagging of the terrace.

Chapter 36

$\mathcal{A}$ fine, misty rain was falling by the time Calhoun reined in his mother's mule on South Audley Street. Sebastian was waiting for them on the footpath. There'd been no time to return to Brook Street or to change out of his evening dress into something more appropriate for digging up graves.

"Ah, there you are, my lord," said Calhoun, handing the reins to Tom. "I was thinking we were going to have to do this without you."

The Church of St. George, Hanover, famous as the scene of so many fashionable Mayfair weddings, stood in a narrow triangle of land formed by the confluence of George and Conduit streets. As a result, the parish's two burial grounds had to be located farther afield. The largest lay to the north of Hyde Park, beyond Edgeware Road. The older and more crowded was situated here, just off Mount Street and South Audley, its side entrance a narrow cobbled passage that ran beside the South Audley Chapel and what was known as the Mount Street dead house.

"Seems a dead giveaway, so to speak," said Tom in a loud whisper, "t'ave the wagon sittin' right outside the churchyard gate. I mean, what's the watch t'think, if'n 'e 'appens to see me 'ere? This t'aint exactly a gentleman's carriage."

"Good point," said Sebastian, unloading the shovels and coils of stout rope. Between them, he and Calhoun eased the heavy sack containing Alexander Ross off the back of the wagon. Then he nodded to the tiger, who wore a simple dark coat and trousers in place of his usual, distinctive striped waistcoat and livery. "Wait for us in Grosvenor Square. We'll catch up with you there."

"Aye, gov'nor," said Tom, spanking the reins against the mule's back. The wagon moved off noiselessly, the axles well greased.

"Ready?" said Sebastian, shifting his grip on the burlap bag.

Gibson shouldered the shovels, their ends wrapped in burlap so they wouldn't clatter when they knocked against each another. "Fine lot of sack-'em-up boys we make—a one-legged Irishman, a lord dressed like he's going to the opera, and a gentleman's gentleman."

Calhoun laughed.

They plunged between the high walls of the narrow passageway. The wind gusted up, driving the cool rain against their faces and rustling the leaves of the half-dead trees in the graveyard. "Devilish dark back here," said Calhoun, nearly dropping his end of the burlap sack as he stumbled over the uneven cobbles. "How the blazes are we supposed to see what we're doing?"

"A lantern would be asking for trouble," said Sebastian. "Too many houses with windows nearby."

"Easy for you to say," grunted Gibson, bringing up the rear. "You've got the eyes of a bloody owl."

The burial ground opened up before them, a vast enclosed square filled with moss-covered gravestones and rusty iron railings overrun with tangled vines and weeds. "It's here," said Sebastian, leading the way to a mound of sodden dark earth in the lea of the dead house.

"Lord save us," said Calhoun, burying his nose in the crook of his arm. "What's that smell?"

"It's coming from the dead house," answered Gibson. "A couple of watermen fished a body out of the river yesterday. I understand it was pretty ripe." Despite the exclusivity of its neighborhood, the Mount Street mortuary was the destination of all unidentified bodies pulled from the Thames between the bridge and Chelsea.

Calhoun gazed up at the elegant row of houses that backed onto the burial ground. "Imagine being a fine lord, living in one of those great big places, and having to smell *that* every time they pulled somebody out of the river."

"Maybe they get used to it," suggested Sebastian, easing Alexander Ross down onto the wet grass beside his empty grave.

Calhoun studied the dark mound of recently turned earth before them. "You don't think the sexton will notice the grave's been disturbed when he comes to dig it up in the morning?"

Sebastian spread a tarp to catch the soft dirt. "It hasn't been that long since he was buried, and the rain will help cover any traces we leave."

They went to work with the shovels, the rain pattering softly as they threw aside a growing mound of sodden earth. The resurrection men had refined their technique so that they typically dug down only at the head of a coffin, then broke the lid with a pry bar and pulled the body out of its grave with ropes. But since their aim now was to put Alexander Ross back into his grave, they would need to expose the entire casket.

The shovels bit into the wet earth quietly. They were made of wood rather than metal in order to avoid the telltale, ringing clang that could come from a metal spade unexpectedly striking a rock or hitting wood. They were just scraping the dirt off the top of Ross's smashed coffin lid when Sebastian raised his head, his acute hearing catching the muffled clop of a horse's hoof, the scuff of furtive footsteps.

"What is it?" asked Gibson, watching him. "Company?"

"Actually, I think we may have competition." Sebastian slipped the loaded double-barreled flintlock from his pocket. "I'll take care of them. Just get Ross back where he belongs as quickly as you can."

Moving soundlessly, he slipped between the tumbled tomb-stones, toward the mouth of the narrow passage, and flattened himself behind the coarse stone wall of the dead house.

"I tell ye," he heard a man say in a harsh whisper, moving stealthily toward him along the passageway. "I don't like the looks o' that wagon sittin' in the square. I tell ye, somebody's poachin' on our territ'ry, they are."

"Yer always lookin' t' borrow trouble, Finch. That's yer problem."

Sebastian could see them now; two men, one small and gently rounded, the other bigger, burlier. They were loaded down with the burlap-wrapped shovels, the pry bar, the rope, the crumpled muddy sack of their trade. Sebastian stepped from behind the mortuary wall and said softly, "Good evening, gentlemen."

The first body snatcher—the smaller, rounder one—let out a muffled shriek. "'Oly 'ell!" He staggered back, his eyes widen-ing until the whites caught the gleam of light from the distant windows. "Ye near scared the shit out o' me."

His companion—older, bigger, tougher—took a belligerent step forward but drew up abruptly when Sebastian pulled back the right hammer on his pistol with an audible *click*.

"This is our territ'ry, ye hear?" said the man, his jaw jutting out mulishly. "Ours."

"Actually," said Sebastian, casually leaning one shoulder

against the wall of the dead house, "if I'm not mistaken, this is Jumpin' Jack's lay."

"Be that as it may, ev'rybody knows Jumpin' Jack goes to Brighton at the end o' July. And when he goes, *we* take over."

Sebastian used the muzzle of his gun to tip back the brim of his hat. "Bad time of year for the resurrection trade, I hear. Bodies don't last long in the heat. And then, with the medical schools closed, there can't be much of a market."

"The prices drop in summer; ain't no doubt about it," said the other resurrection man soulfully. "But a man's got to eat." He winked. "And support 'is other 'abits, if ye know what I mean."

Sebastian glanced back toward Alexander Ross's grave. Between them, Calhoun and Gibson had worked the ropes beneath the empty coffin and lifted it from the grave. Now Calhoun was busy clothing the corpse with his inimitable skill and arranging it in the casket. Bringing his gaze back to the resurrection men, Sebastian said, "The thing of it is, gentlemen, we're not here to encroach upon your trade."

"Get on wit' ye," said Finch. "What else would ye be doing here?" He squinted at Sebastian through the darkness. "Although ye must be a regular green 'un, dressin' like that fer this kinda work."

Sebastian could hear the scrape of ropes, the thump of the now laden casket being lowered back into its grave. "Actually, we're looking for a skull."

"A skull?"

The soft thud of quickly tossed shovelfuls of wet earth hitting the top of the casket drifted across the churchyard.

Sebastian said, "Just a skull. For Lady Lennox's masquerade. You see, I rather fancy the notion of going as the angel of death."

"The what?"

"The grim reaper. Death personified."

The two resurrection men exchanged guarded glances. The

elder one squinted at Sebastian through the misty rain. "Ye must be foxed—or mad. What are ye, then? Some kind o' bloody lord?"

"Would a lord be robbing a burial ground?" asked Sebastian, pushing away from the wall as Calhoun and Gibson came up beside him. "Now, if you'll excuse us, gentlemen, we'll be on our way."

"Lord love us, I need a drink," said Calhoun, looking faintly green around the gills as he paused on the flagway in front of the chapel to draw in a deep breath of fresh air. "I've dressed many a gentleman in my career—sober, drunk, and even dead. But I must say, this is the first time I've ever been called upon to dress one who was *in bits.*"

Monday, 27 July

By the next morning, the rain had settled into a steady downpour.

Arriving at the Mount Street burial ground just after eight, Sebastian found Sir Henry Lovejoy standing beside Alexander Ross's half-opened grave. He had his hat pulled low, his shoulders hunched as he watched a sexton and his young helper struggle to shift the wet, heavy mud.

"Nasty day for it," said Sebastian, coming up beside him.

"Nasty work, full stop," said the magistrate.

They stood together in silence, watching the gravediggers. There was a loud scratching as the shovels scraped along wood. One of the men exclaimed, "It don't look good, Sir 'Enry."

Lovejoy peered through the pounding rain. "What does that mean?"

"The lid o' the coffin's all busted up."

With a rare oath, Sir Henry ventured closer to the edge of the open grave. "Are you telling me the resurrection men got him?"

The sexton clambered down into the hole with his ropes. "That's what I was thinkin' when I first seen it, sir. 'Cept the coffin's mighty heavy, for all that."

The sexton's face turned red as, between them, the two men slipped their ropes beneath the shattered casket and heaved. The coffin came up out of the ground with a sucking plop, the lid bouncing and clattering loosely as it hit the wet grass, hard.

Lovejoy held a thickly folded handkerchief to his nose. "Well?"

"Something's in here," said the sexton, cautiously sliding the lid to one side. "Course, it could jist be rocks. I've seen 'em do that."

The lid fell away to reveal Alexander Ross lying nestled in the mud-streaked satin liner of his casket, his death-swollen face now turned a ghastly shade of reddish green, his body clothed with rare skill by one of London's finest, who'd risen admirably to the occasion despite the considerable handicaps imposed by darkness, the need for speed, and the disjointed nature of the gentleman involved.

"Don't understand it, sir. 'E's 'ere, all right. But 'is shroud's been cut off and left in a muddy wad at 'is feet."

"Perhaps the sack-'em-up boys were interrupted at their work," suggested Sir Henry.

"Could be, sir. 'Cept why then was the grave filled back in?"

Sir Henry nodded toward the shell borrowed from the nearby dead house. "The important thing is, he's here. Move the body to the shell."

"Why not simply transfer him in his own coffin?" suggested Sebastian.

"We use shells," said Sir Henry. He turned to the sexton. "Get him out of there."

"Yes, sir."

The sexton positioned himself at the body's feet. He and his young helper had a minor argument over the best way to effect the transfer. Then the younger man grasped the body's shoulders and the sexton seized his ankles.

Sebastian clasped his hands behind his back.

And waited.

Chapter 37

"On the count of three," said the sexton. "One, two—"

The men heaved. The body's limbs, held together by nothing more than Calhoun's artistry, separated from the torso. The sexton, finding himself grasping two loose legs, landed on his backside in the mud. One of the corpse's arms flopped back into the open grave; the other—formed of wadded cloth owing to Gibson's inability to retrieve the original—dangled at a disjointed angle.

"What the bloody 'ell?" howled the sexton.

Sir Henry stood quite still. Around them, the rain poured. After a moment, he said quite calmly, "Collect what is left of Mr. Ross and convey the body to Paul Gibson on Tower Hill." He turned a wooden countenance toward Sebastian. "Or should I perhaps say, convey the body *back* to Mr. Gibson?"

Hero devoted several hours that morning to the task of interviewing the impoverished distant relative she hoped might serve as companion to Lady Jarvis.

Once, Mrs. Emma Knight had been young, pretty, and head-strong, but those days were behind her. The spirited daughter of a country vicar, she had eloped at the age of nineteen with a dashing but penniless lieutenant. Her father immediately disowned her, and he had never relented, even when the dashing lieutenant got himself blown to pieces by a badly aimed artillery barrage in India.

A hardscrabble life and the need to constantly defer to others had left Emma a little too timid for Hero's taste. Still, she would do until Hero was able to find someone more suitable.

After that, she spent some time with her mother, who was blissfully consumed by the heady task of deciding What to Wear for the Wedding. Then, her duties as a daughter satisfied, Hero ordered her carriage. Her conversation with Devlin had left her with a number of questions, not all of which her father had been able to resolve.

But Hero knew where to look for some of the answers.

Her first destination was Montagu House on Portman Square. Once the home of the eighteenth-century queen of the blue-stockings, the house now served as the residence of the Turkish Ambassador to the Court of St. James. The Ambassador's wife, Yasmina Ramadani, received her in an exotic kiosk in the residence's extensive, high-walled rear gardens. By now the morning's rain had cleared, leaving the deep blue sky clean and fresh.

"Miss Jarvis," said Yasmina, taking Hero's hand to draw her toward the kiosk's array of plump cushions and exquisite silk carpets. "I've been hoping you would visit me again. Please, come join me."

She was a beautiful woman, fine boned and dusky skinned and green eyed, with a heavy fall of dark hair and a wide, red-lipped mouth. She had a way of moving that fascinated Hero—

not just graceful but sinuous, each gesture one of fluid beauty. It occurred to Hero that she was utterly at ease in her own body in a way few Englishwomen were. Like a dancer, perhaps.

Or a courtesan.

"The clouds didn't last long, did they?" said Hero, opening her parasol and positioning it carefully to shade her face from the sunlight.

Watching her, Yasmina leaned back against her cushions and gave a melodious laugh. "Believe me, Miss Jarvis, the English sun is not strong enough to require such vigorous measures to hold it at bay."

Hero tugged at her skirts. There was obviously a talent to lolling gracefully on cushions, and she didn't have it. "Easy for you to say. You don't have a tendency to freckle."

"Ah. For that you must use . . . crushed strawberries, is it not? I was reading something about it just the other day." Her English was enviably fluent, with only a light, deliciously lilting accent. Hero had learned that in addition to Turkish and English, the woman also spoke Greek, Arabic, French, and what she called a "smattering" of Farsi.

Hero said, "I don't think even a gallon of strawberries would help my freckles after a day in the sun."

Laughing again softly, Yasmina reached out to idly run her fingers over the strings of an *ude*, a wooden instrument similar to a guitar that lay on a nearby cushion. "You are to be married soon, is this not so?"

The question took Hero by surprise.

Yasmina's smile widened. "I saw the announcement in this morning's papers."

"Oh, yes; I'd quite forgotten the notice was to appear this morning."

Casting Hero an enigmatic sideways glance, Yasmina picked up the *ude* and began to play it softly. "I have met your Lord

Devlin. He is a wild one, yet clever, too. I understand he likes solving puzzles."

"He enjoys mysteries," said Hero, wondering when and how the Viscount had managed to meet the reclusive Turkish woman. "Murder mysteries."

Yasmina's fingers moved across the strings of the *ude*, the strange melody floating over the English garden, the soft smile on her lips never faltering. "He is involved in a murder investigation now, yes?"

Hero kept her gaze on the other woman's delicate features. "He is. A gentleman who used to work with the Foreign Office named Alexander Ross. Did you know him?"

"Ross?" She shook her dusky hair. "No. But then, I meet few men. Our culture is not like yours. The sexes do not mix freely outside the family."

To Hero's knowledge, Yasmina was the first wife of a Turkish ambassador to ever accompany her husband to London. She had never appeared in society in the way of other ambassadors' wives. But Hero had heard she did sometimes serve as hostess at the small, intimate dinners given by her husband. Hero said, "You have met some Englishmen, have you not?"

Yasmina threw her a sideways glance. "Some, yes."

"What about the Swede, Carl Lindquist? Are you familiar with him?"

"I don't believe so, no. He is with the Swedish Embassy?"

"Not officially. But he was affiliated with them in some way. Now he's dead."

"Murdered as well?"

"Yes."

Yasmina tsked softly. "It is a dangerous place, London. I'd no notion."

"More dangerous than Constantinople?"

Yasmina's eyes crinkled with amusement. "Perhaps not." For

a moment she seemed to give all her attention to her instrument. Then she said, "I hear that Englishwomen often fear their wedding nights; that they know not what to expect. Is this true?"

Hero felt herself grow hot with embarrassment. The last thing she wanted was to find herself discussing her looming wedding night with this exotic, sensual woman. Devlin had assured her that he was prepared for their marriage to be one of name only. The problem was, she herself wasn't exactly certain that was what she wanted. She had discovered it was possible to be both leery of a man and physically attracted to him at the same time.

"It is true of some, I suppose," Hero said slowly.

The Turkish woman's intelligent green eyes narrowed thoughtfully, and Hero wondered what she saw—and understood. "But not you," said Yasmina. "That is good."

The conversation shifted then to other topics, to the latest sleeves and the Eastern use of henna and the new China roses Yasmina was having planted in the residence's gardens. It wasn't until later, when Hero was leaving, that Yasmina said casually, "You didn't tell me: Is Lord Devlin close, you think, to finding this killer he is looking for?"

"I think so, yes," Hero lied.

"That is a relief."

It was said with an intense, heartfelt sincerity that would have fooled most. But Hero was Jarvis's daughter. He had taught her from an early age how to know when someone was telling the truth and when they weren't.

And there was no doubt in her mind that Yasmina Ramadani was lying.

"That certainly answers the question of how you knew Ross had been murdered," said Sir Henry Lovejoy, his hands wrapped around a hot cup of coffee.

Sebastian started to say something, but the magistrate held up one hand. "It might be better if I remain in official ignorance of the facts."

"I thought so."

They sat in a snug little coffeehouse on Mount Street. A fire crackled on the hearth, filling the room with a pleasant warmth and the smell of wet wool. Sir Henry said, "So we have two men killed in the same unusual manner on the same night, one a gentleman at the Foreign Office, the other a newly arrived American. What possible connection can there be between the two?"

"If there is a connection other than the Cox family, I have yet to find it."

Sir Henry frowned. "Kincaid's body was dumped in Bethnal Green at three in the morning. But he disappeared from Southwark much earlier, around eleven that night. You think Ross was killed before then?"

"I think Ross was dead by the time Colonel Chernishav knocked on his door at midnight."

Sir Henry nodded. "So you're suggesting—what? Ross was murdered, then stripped of his clothes and put in bed so he'd be found there by his manservant in the morning?"

"Unless Ross was naked when he was killed."

Sir Henry looked confused. "But why would a man be naked—" His voice trailed off as understanding dawned. He cleared his throat uncomfortably. "Ah, yes; the woman." The magistrate shifted in his seat. "It would be highly unusual, although still possible, I suppose."

"Alternatively, the killer could have taken clean linen from Ross's cupboard, crumpled it, and dropped it on the floor for the valet to find. He would then have needed to carry the bloodstained items away with him, had them cleaned, and surreptitiously returned them to Ross's rooms at a later date, since according to the valet, no items were missing."

"Yes, I suppose that's possible, as well. It shows an attention to detail, a thoroughness and calm clearheadedness that is disturbing." Sir Henry shivered and fortified himself with another sip of his coffee. "You've suspects?"

Sebastian gave him a quick rundown of what he'd discovered, leaving out only the diplomatically sensitive information given him by Miss Jarvis.

Sir Henry said, "Any of these men have alibis for the evening in question?"

"Jasper Cox was at a dinner given by the Lord Mayor. Others claim to have been home. But if we're dealing with a hired professional, it doesn't really matter, does it?"

"No, I suppose not." Lovejoy sipped his coffee in silence for a moment. Then he said, "We're obviously missing something."

Sebastian pushed to his feet. "I think this French émigré, de La Rocque, may have played a larger role than he's admitting. I have some questions I'd like him to answer."

Sir Henry nodded. "Let me know if you discover anything." He hesitated, then said, "I understand congratulations are in order, my lord."

Sebastian shook his head, not understanding. "I beg your pardon?"

"I read the notice of your coming nuptials in the paper this morning."

"Oh, yes; of course. Thank you, Sir Henry."

"A splendid young woman, Miss Jarvis. Splendid."

Sebastian said, "The ceremony is this Thursday morning, at Lambeth Palace, at eleven. I would be honored if you could attend."

The little magistrate turned pink and gave one of his peculiar little bows. "Why, thank you, my lord. I assure you the honor is mine."

Chapter 38

*A*fter leaving the Turkish Ambassador's residence, Hero made a brief stop in Bond Street to pick out a pair of pale blue satin slippers for the wedding. Then she directed her coachman to Great Russell Street.

"Monsieur de La Rocque?" she called, pushing open the heavy door to his establishment.

Her voice echoed through the empty cluster of interconnected rooms lined floor to ceiling with shelf after shelf of moldering books.

"Oh, Miss Jarvis," whispered Marie, hovering close beside her, her face pale as she followed Hero from one overcrowded room to the next. "Should we even be here? I mean—"

"Don't be absurd, Marie," said Hero firmly. "There is nothing the least—" She broke off, her gaze fixed on the single, worn brown shoe poking out at an odd angle from beneath the curtain of a nearby archway.

"Stay here," she ordered the maid and thrust aside the curtain.

The defrocked priest lay sprawled on his back, arms flung

wide, his swollen tongue protruding from a discolored, puffy face, his bloodshot eyes wide and staring. A wire had been wrapped so tightly around his neck that it cut into the flesh.

She heard a soft sigh behind her and turned in time to see her abigail's eyes roll back in her head as the woman collapsed in an insensate heap.

Ignoring her, Hero went to crouch beside the Frenchman's body. Reaching out, she pressed her fingertips to one out-flung wrist. He was still faintly warm.

She heard the creak of a hinge and a light tread on the old floorboards at the front of the shop. Spinning around, she saw Devlin draw up in the curtained archway. His gaze traveled from her to de La Rocque and back again.

"Good God," he said. "What are you doing here?"

She spread an expressive hand toward the corpse. "I came to speak to Monsieur de La Rocque. Unfortunately, as you can see, he is dead."

Devlin's gaze shifted to the crumpled maid. "And your abigail?"

"Tiresome woman. She's gone off in a faint."

"Imagine that," he said dryly, hunkering down beside the maid. "Have you a vinaigrette in your reticule?"

"No. I never faint."

"Of course not," he said, gently tapping the woman's pale cheeks.

"If you wake her up, she's liable to start screaming," Hero warned.

"True. But it must be done."

The abigail stirred, her eyelids fluttering open. She drew in a shaky gasp and looked confused, her gaze focusing on Devlin's face. Then she turned her head, saw de La Rocque's awful purple countenance, and started screaming.

"Now, now; enough of that," said Hero briskly, going to help Devlin coax the woman to her feet.

The screaming continued. Over the woman's head, Devlin's gaze met Hero's. "There's an inn several doors down. Perhaps you can entrust her to the care of the landlord's wife?"

Hero nodded. "Come, Marie," she said, grasping the maid's arm in a firm grip and suppressing the impulse to box the silly creature's ears as she steered her toward the door. "Hush, now; there's nothing to be afraid of."

"Hang on a minute," said Devlin, scrounging around in a nearby desk for paper, a quill, and ink. He dashed off a quick note, folded it and affixed a wafer, then wrote, *Sir Henry Lovejoy* across the front. "Have the landlord send one of his lads with this to Bow Street."

Leaving Devlin hunkered down beside the dead body, Hero hectored and bullied the now hysterical abigail to the nearby inn, where she consigned her to the gentle ministrations of the clucking landlady. On her return, she found Devlin systematically going through drawers and cupboards in a rear office. "Discover anything?" she asked.

He moved on to one of the towering bookcases. "Not yet."

"Like some help?"

He looked over at her in surprise. "Please."

She started on the lower shelf. "What precisely are we looking for?"

"You'll know when you find it."

But at the end of another twenty minutes, she was hot, dusty, and empty-handed.

"It would take days to go through all these books," she said, shoving a tooled copy of *Plutarch's Lives* back onto a shelf.

"At least," agreed Devlin, moving on to the next case.

Pushing the hair off her forehead with the back of one gloved hand, Hero went to crouch again beside the dead Frenchman. "Fascinating," she said, studying the purple spots on his face, the deep scratches on his neck—left, she now realized, by his own fingernails as he clawed frantically at the constricting ligature. "I've never seen someone who was strangled."

Devlin glanced over at her. "Have you no sensibility, Miss Jarvis?"

She looked up. "None at all, I'm afraid. Why? Does that disturb you?"

"Actually, it relieves me."

She bent to have a closer look at the wire wrapped around de La Rocque's neck.

"What is it?" asked Devlin, watching her.

"This wire. It's not ordinary wire. It's silver wrapped around silk."

"What the hell?" He left the shelves to come hunker down beside her.

She looked up at him. "I believe it's a harp wire."

"A *harp* wire?"

"Mmm. Which suggests your murderer may be the husband of a woman who plays the harp—or the woman herself."

Devlin looked doubtful. "*Could* a woman strangle a man?"

"If she were tall enough and strong enough, I don't see why not." Hero nodded to the bloated-faced corpse beside them. "De La Rocque was not an excessively large man."

"True."

She said, "Harp players typically develop calluses on their fingertips. Did you happen to notice the hands of any of the females implicated in your investigation?"

"Actually, there aren't that many women involved in this."

"But there are some."

"There's your cousin, Miss Sabrina Cox. Does she play the harp?"

"Sabrina? You can't be serious. She's a tiny woman. And full of sensibility."

"Her brother is not." He regarded her steadily. When she remained silent, he said, "Well? Does Miss Cox play the harp?"

Hero stared back at him. It had been only days since she visited her young cousin and held Sabrina's hands in hers. Yet to her chagrin, she could not recall noticing either if the girl's fingertips were calloused or even if there had been a harp in the room. She said, "To be honest, I don't know; but I can find out. What about some of the other females involved?"

"I've met the Turkish Ambassador's wife, but I confess I didn't pay a great deal of attention to her fingertips."

Hero decided to keep her own recent visit to the Ambassador's residence to herself. She said, "*Would* a Turkish woman be likely to play the harp?"

"Why not? Do you think they don't have harps in the seraglios of the East?"

"I wouldn't know," said Hero, "not having ever been in a seraglio." She studied him thoughtfully. "Have you?"

"I have not."

"Besides," she added, "Yasmina plays the *ude*. And she is also very tiny."

"Ramadani is not. And I have it on the best authority—his own—that he's partial to the garrote."

"He told you that?"

"He did. He also—" He broke off as the sounds of a carriage and men's voices carried from the front of the building.

"Ah," said Hero, pushing to her feet. "Bow Street has arrived."

She was aware of him studying her with an inscrutable expression on his face. He said, "Your father isn't going to like this—your involving yourself in another murder, I mean."

She gave her skirts a businesslike twitch that released a small cloud of dust. "Considering that we are soon to be wed, he's going to have to get used to it, isn't he?"

At that, Devlin gave a surprised huff of laughter. "You do have a point."

His smile faded, their gazes meeting as awareness of all that their coming marriage would mean settled on them both.

Then Sir Henry Lovejoy drew up in the doorway, his gaze riveted on the corpse's swollen purple countenance as he said with a gasp, "Merciful heavens!"

Chapter 39

"What can you tell me?" asked Sebastian, watching Paul Gibson study the body laid out on his slab.

The Irishman wiped his hands on a stained rag. "Right now? I can tell you Antoine de La Rocque was strangled. If you want more, you're going to have to wait."

Sebastian blew out a harsh breath, his gaze on the dead Frenchman's waxy profile. "For some reason, I feel as if we're running out of time."

Gibson grunted. "From what you've told me about Monsieur de La Rocque, his murder may not be related to the death of Alexander Ross at all. Those mixed up in the trade between France and England do tend to be a pretty rough lot."

"The deaths are related," said Sebastian, his gaze drifting to the shelf that ran along the far wall, where another silent form hidden by a sheet lay awaiting collection by the authorities. "Did you discover anything when you looked at Carl Lindquist?"

"Nothing of note. The cudgel found beside the body was definitely the murder weapon. He was hit from behind. In all likelihood he was dead within a few minutes; I doubt he even knew what happened." Gibson reached for a scalpel and held it aloft. "Now, are you certain you want to stay for this?"

Sebastian beat a hasty retreat to the unkempt yard.

He stood for a moment, the afternoon sun beating down hot and golden on his shoulders. He was aware of the buzzing of flies, the distant cry of some street hawker, the faint but inescapable scent of death that haunted this place. A new idea was beginning to take shape in his mind, hazy still, but tantalizing in its promise.

The time had come, he decided, for him to pay a visit to the charming young Lady Foley.

Hero was in the library of the house on Berkeley Square, an ancient tome on the dissolution of the monasteries lying open on the table before her, when she heard the distant peal of the front bell. A moment later, Grisham appeared in the doorway.

"Excuse me, Miss Jarvis, but the Earl of Hendon is here to see you. I have taken the liberty of showing him to the drawing room."

"Yes, thank you, Grisham," she said, curiosity mingling with wariness as she rose to her feet and hurried up the stairs. She paused just outside the drawing room door to smooth her skirts, then entered with her hand outstretched. "Lord Hendon. I'm so sorry to have kept you waiting. May I offer you some tea? Or would you prefer a glass of wine?"

He arose from his seat near the fireplace, a big, barrel-chested man with a shock of white hair and the famous blue eyes so noticeably lacking in his heir. For years she had known him as one of Jarvis's fiercest and most determined rivals; it struck her suddenly that she would need to begin to think of him as the father of the man who would be her husband.

"No, nothing, thank you," he said gruffly. "I won't keep you long." He clasped her hand, and she was aware of his gaze hard on her face, as if he were searching there for something that might make sense of the incomprehensible. Then he released her and cleared his throat. "It's no secret that your father and I have had our differences in the past, and I've no doubt we will continue to do so in the future. But, well, I'm here to assure you this coming marriage has my blessing, for all that."

"Thank you, my lord," she said, unexpectedly touched.

"I won't deny it comes as something of a surprise," he continued. "In fact—well, never mind that. The truth is, it's long been my wish to see my son and heir settled in life before I die, and I am grateful that it has come to pass."

Hero found herself smiling. "Even if you can't help but wish he might have chosen to ally himself with a different house."

An answering gleam shone in the Earl's blue St. Cyr eyes. "I won't deny that, no! But it doesn't alter the fact that I wish you well, and I just wanted you to know that."

Even if I don't understand what the bloody hell it's all about. The unsaid words hovered in the air between them.

She said, "Won't you please reconsider and have a glass of wine?"

"No, no; I've a meeting with Castlereagh at the Foreign Office." He reached into an inner pocket and drew forth a small trinket box. "I also wanted to give you this. It's not much, but it belonged to my great-grandmother."

Hero found herself holding an exquisite relic from a previous century, its enameled top worked in a style she'd never seen before. "Thank you," she said quietly. "I shall treasure it."

"Yes, well . . ." He tightened his grip on his hat. "Until Thursday, then."

After he had gone, she went to lean against the window frame, her gaze on the square below. She was still standing there, her thoughts far away, when she saw her father alight from his carriage and enter the house.

She was fully expecting him to seek her out and express his displeasure at her involvement in one of Devlin's murder investigations. But when he entered the parlor a few moments later, his attention was obviously elsewhere.

"Ah, there you are," he said, a sheaf of papers in one hand. "I've just come from a meeting with our man of business. I think you'll be pleased with the provisions of the settlement. Not only has Devlin agreed to an annual jointure set at fifteen percent of your portion rather than the usual ten percent, but he has also insisted on including a number of provisions that are highly irregular, to say the least."

"Such as?"

"Listen to this." He flipped open the document. "'It is hereby agreed between the parties that all the property of the said Miss Hero Jarvis shall be always and entirely at her own sole disposal and command the same as if she were still unmarried, and that she may, as often as she pleases, sell or dispose of the same or reinvest the money in any manner she pleases without any consent or concurrence being necessary or required from her husband.'"

Jarvis tossed the document on the table between them. "You have obviously treated him to one of your diatribes on the inequities of our marriage laws."

"I have," she said, her voice not quite steady. "May I see that?"

"Be my guest." He watched as she read through the terms. It was not the usual thing, for a young woman to be encouraged to interest herself in her own marriage settlement. But then, he knew well that Hero was not like most women.

By the time she reached the end, she found herself prey to a variety of conflicting emotions. Devlin had told her, of course, that he intended to honor her wishes. But she had never expected him to be either so thorough or so generous. In that, she realized, she had underestimated him. It occurred to her that it was a habit she had with him, and she was honest enough to wonder why.

"Well," she said, handing the papers back to her father with a composure she was far from feeling. "That is reassuring."

"Reassuring? It's madness. It's only my confidence in your intelligence and strength of character that inspires me to agree to this." He turned toward the door. "Although when I hear of your presence at a certain murder scene on Great Russell Street, I almost—almost, mind you—begin to doubt my wisdom."

But Hero only laughed.

While not excessively large, the Undersecretary's house on Half Moon Street was tastefully appointed, with gently aging Turkish carpets, gleaming rosewood furniture, and endless yards of lush silks, satins, and brocades. As expected, Sebastian found the Undersecretary not at home. He then asked for and was received by Lady Foley.

"Lord Devlin," she said, greeting him with a charming smile. "Sir Hyde will be sorry he missed you. How may I help you?"

His gaze was so riveted by the harp positioned between the drawing room's two front windows that it was a moment before he answered. "I was wondering if you're familiar with a gentleman named Antoine de La Rocque," said Sebastian, taking the delicate satin-covered chair she indicated.

"De La Rocque?" Lady Foley's forehead crinkled with thought as she settled back on the sofa. "No, I don't believe so. Is he an associate of Sir Hyde's?"

"He may have been."

"*May have been?*" Her smile faltered. "Dear me; has something happened to him?"

"I'm afraid so. You never heard Sir Hyde mention him?"

A wary look crept across her features. She might be relatively new to the diplomatic world, but she had evidently learned enough to know that all was frequently not as it seemed and that she had need to tread carefully. "Not that I recall," she said, the calloused fingers of one hand repeatedly smoothing the cloth of her muslin gown where it lay across the damask upholstery of her chair.

"But you did know Alexander Ross."

"Oh, yes." She gave a sad sigh. "Such a charming man. And so young to die. We often had him to dinner, you know. He was quite a favorite of Sir Hyde's."

"I'm curious: Would you happen to know Mr. Ross's opinion of the proposed alliance between Russia and Great Britain?"

Foley might not confide his affairs to his young wife, but she obviously paid attention to dinner table conversation. "Why, yes," she said. "He was most anxious to see us enter into an active alliance with the Czar. I gather the time he'd spent in St. Petersburg had left him with a sincere fondness for the country and its people. I remember that he was quite concerned that without such an alliance to stop him, Napoléon might even reach Moscow."

"I believe Sir Foley too is an advocate of such an alliance."

"But of course!" exclaimed Sir Foley's wife. "It is very important."

"Do you know if Ross had any dealings with Ambassador Ramadani?"

The sudden shift in topic seemed to confuse her. She looked at him blankly. "You mean, the representative from the Sublime Porte? I shouldn't think so, no. I was under the impression Ross dealt mainly with the Baltic states and Russia."

"And France, of course."

"Yes." Her head turned toward the door as a woman's voice sounded from the hall.

"Just look at this charming cap!" said Lady Foley's younger sister, appearing in the doorway with a pattern book in her hands. "I am determined to make it for my new nephew. And it's no use saying he won't be a nephew, because I just know— Oh." She broke off, coloring fiercely at the sight of Sebastian. "I do beg your pardon! I'd no notion you had a visitor."

Sebastian stretched to his feet. "Please, don't mind me. I was just on the point of taking my leave."

Lady Foley rose gracefully from her seat, one hand cupped tellingly over the gentle swell of her belly. "It isn't well-known yet," she said shyly, "but Sir Hyde and I will be welcoming a new member to our family in the spring."

"Then let me be one of the first to congratulate you," said Sebastian, bowing. "No, don't bother to ring; I'll see myself out." He bowed again. "Ladies."

His next stop was the Public Offices in Bow Street, where Sir Henry's clerk, Collins, met him with wide, startled eyes.

"But . . . Sir Henry's not here, my lord. He sent you a message, not more than an hour ago. Did you not receive it?"

"No," said Sebastian. "Regarding what?"

"There's been *another* murder, my lord. Some foreign diplomat's wife."

Sebastian knew a rising coil of anger and frustration and something that felt much like helplessness. "You can't mean Yasmina Ramadani?"

"Yes, that's it; Madame Ramadani."

Chapter 40

Sebastian found Sir Henry Lovejoy in the private parlor of a small but respectable hotel on Queen Ann Street. The room was neat and clean but not particularly stylish, with a scattering of old-fashioned tables and chairs and a fading, slightly threadbare carpet on the floor. Near the heavy round table in the center of the room lay a still form covered by a sheet.

"May I?" asked Sebastian, going to crouch down beside the body.

"Please." Sir Henry's voice sounded strained. "I would more than welcome any assistance you can provide in making sense of all this. I've already been informed by the offices of both the Prime Minister and the Foreign Minister that to have the wife of an ambassador to the Court of St. James meet with foul play in our city—particularly an ambassador from a state as strategically located as Ottoman Turkey—is not only diplomatically sensitive but also a profound national embarrassment."

"Not to mention a personal tragedy."

Sir Henry watched Sebastian draw back the sheet. "That aspect of the situation appears oddly irrelevant."

The woman known as Yasmina Ramadani lay curled on her side, her thick-lashed hazel eyes wide and staring, her mouth parted, her head twisted back at an unnatural angle. Even in death, she was beautiful, her flesh as pearly and smooth as a statue. In contrast to her dress the day he saw her, she wore a cream silk walking gown caught up with a scarlet ribbon; a gold pendant nestled between her breasts; a reticule embroidered with red poppies rested near her hip, its ties still wrapped around her delicate wrist.

"Her neck is broken?" asked Sebastian softly.

"It appears to be, yes."

Sebastian reached out to touch her pale cheek. She was already growing cold.

He pushed to his feet. "Who found her?"

"A maid. She chanced to notice that the door stood slightly ajar and went to close it. I'm told the latch is faulty and frequently fails to catch unless the door is firmly shut. Otherwise I doubt the poor woman would have been discovered until morning."

Sebastian let his gaze drift around the small parlor. A tapestry-covered footstool lay overturned near the hearth; otherwise, the room appeared undisturbed. "What the devil was she doing here?"

"That I do not know. According to the landlord, Madame arrived alone just after two o'clock this afternoon and requested a private parlor. As far as we can tell, no one besides the Ambassador's wife was seen entering or leaving the room."

"What does her husband say?"

"He is devastated, naturally. But he claims to be utterly baffled by his wife's activities."

Sebastian brought his gaze back to the little magistrate's grim-featured face. "You believe him?"

"One can hardly call the Ambassador to the Court of St. James from the Sublime Porte a liar."

"You may not be able to," said Sebastian. "But I can."

His Excellency Antonaki Ramadani may have been devastated, but not so devastated as to forgo his usual evening ritual, which typically began with dinner at Steven's before progressing to Limmer's.

Located at the corner of Conduit and George streets just across from the Church of St. George, Limmer's was the evening resort for the sporting world. A sprawling brick edifice from the previous century, the hotel essentially served as a late-night Tattersall's. Pushing through the crowd that filled its dark, spartan public room, Sebastian found the Ambassador looking for all the world like a country squire in buckskins and high-top black leather boots, his only condescension to his presumed state of mourning being a black ribbon tied around his arm.

"Mind if I join you?" asked Sebastian, pulling out a nearby chair.

Ramadani met Sebastian's gaze, his own narrowing. Then he turned to the slim, middle-aged man beside him and said quietly, "You'll excuse us for a moment?"

Sebastian watched the former jockey walk away. "I didn't know you were a passionate follower of the turf."

"I find it amusing." The Turk settled back in his chair. "Take a glass of the hotel's famous gin punch with me, my lord? Or do you prefer port?"

"I'll have the punch, thanks," said Sebastian, watching the Ambassador signal the barmaid. "I was sorry to hear about the death of your wife."

"It is tragic, is it not? She was a very beautiful woman."

"She was indeed." Sebastian waited while the barmaid set

their punch on the table before them. "Who did she go to Queen Ann Street to meet?"

"That I do not know."

"Really?"

The Turk returned a bland stare. "Difficult to believe, I know. But nonetheless true."

Sebastian watched the Turk's face—and his hands. "I've heard the oddest rumor: that Yasmina was not your wife. That she was in fact brought here to function as a spy."

Ramadani gave him a thin, tight smile. He kept both hands wrapped around his punch, although he did not taste it. "Did you know that ambassadors posted to the Court of St. James are subjected to closer scrutiny by your government than at any other court in the world?"

"Closer even than at the Porte?"

"One might wish that we were so thorough. History tells us that Walpole spent a million pounds sterling on his secret service, and I am given to understand that such expenditures have only increased in the last seventy-five years. Our servants are bribed and hectored into becoming spies who read our private papers and report our every move. All incoming and outgoing mail is routed through the Foreign Office, where it is opened, read, copied, and then resealed before being sent on its way."

"So you're saying—what? That a nation with so little respect for the sanctity of the diplomatic corps shouldn't object when some of its guest diplomats engage in a bit of their own spying?"

"I certainly wouldn't expect such a people to stoop to murder."

Sebastian sipped his gin punch. "Are you accusing the British government of murder?"

"The government?" Ramadani pursed his lips and shook his

head. "Perhaps not. But certain members within that government? Now, that's a different matter altogether."

"Did you have anyone in particular in mind?"

The Turk gave a harsh smile. "May I suggest you address
some of these questions to your prospective father-in-law? He
is said to be omniscient, is he not? And the ruthlessness of his
methods is legendary."

"Meaning?"

"Meaning, I told you I prefer the garrote, did I not?"

"Antoine de al Rocque was garroted."

"True. But not by me," said Ramadani.

And he walked away, leaving his gin punch untasted.

Charles, Lord Jarvis, was standing at the elbow of the Prince Regent in a gaming hell off Pickering Place when Sebastian walked
up to him and said quietly, "If I might have a word with you, my
lord. Outside."

Annoyance and something else flared in the big man's eyes.
But he flattened his lips and turned to murmur his apologies to
the Prince.

"Well, what is it?" snapped Jarvis as he and Sebastian strolled
toward King Street.

"The spies in the households of the various ambassadors
posted to London," said Sebastian. "Who controls them? You?
Or the Foreign Office?"

"The Foreign Office. Why?"

"But you have access to their reports."

"Naturally."

"So you knew why the woman known as Yasmina Ramadani was sent to London as part of the Turkish Ambassador's
household."

"We had our suspicions, yes."

"Did you have her killed?"

Jarvis snorted. "I did not."

"Yet you knew she had seduced someone at the Foreign Office. Who was it?"

Jarvis's full lips curved into a smile. "Even if I knew, you don't seriously think I'd tell you, do you?"

With effort, Sebastian suppressed the urge to plant his fist in the middle of his future father-in-law's complacent face. "What about the Swede, Carl Lindquist? Did you have him killed?"

A man in a swirling evening cape walked toward them. Jarvis dropped his voice to a harsh whisper. "Don't be absurd. The Swede's death has complicated an already delicate state of affairs."

"How many people besides Ross knew of the transfer of the gold?"

Jarvis kept his voice low. "It's impossible to keep arrangements of this nature a closely held secret. By necessity it is known to individuals in the Treasury, the Cabinet . . . even some members of Parliament."

Sebastian waited until the gentleman in the evening cape had passed them, then said, "And Antoine de La Rocque? How did he figure into it?"

The King's powerful, omniscient cousin drew a gold snuff-box from one pocket and flicked open the lid. "I know nothing about de La Rocque. To my knowledge he was merely an ex-priest with a rather curious passion for collecting old books."

Sebastian smiled. "Of course."

Jarvis lifted a delicate pinch of snuff to one nostril and inhaled. "You haven't asked if I killed Alexander Ross."

Sebastian met the older man's hard gray gaze. "Would you tell me if you had?"

Jarvis closed his snuffbox with a snap. "I suppose that would depend on why I had him killed."

Lost in thought, Sebastian was walking up St. James's Street when one of Kat Boleyn's young pages found him.

Breaking the seal of her note, Sebastian read through the brief missive. Then he turned his steps toward Covent Garden.

Chapter 41

He found Kat waiting for him at the stage door.

She wore a crimson velvet cloak with the hood pulled up over her auburn-shot dark hair. He walked toward her, his footsteps echoing in the stillness, his gaze drinking in the sight of her.

She held out her hand to him. "I didn't think you were coming."

He took her hand in his, held it a moment too long, then released it. "Your page had a difficult time finding me." He searched her beautiful, beloved face. "What is it?"

"You've heard of the death of the woman known as Yasmina Ramadani?"

"Yes. Why?"

They turned to walk up the narrow lane. She said, "The friendship between France and the Sublime Porte goes back hundreds of years."

"Thanks largely to their mutual dislike of the Austro-Hungarian Empire and the grand tradition of 'my enemy's enemy is my friend.'"

"Something like that."

Sebastian glanced sideways at her. "Are you telling me that the information Yasmina collected was being shared with the French?"

"Yes."

"Via whom?"

She smiled and shook her head. "You know I can't tell you that."

He nodded. "Can you tell me who Yasmina targeted at the Foreign Office? Was it Alexander Ross? Or someone else?"

"I'm not certain, although it's possible she may have had more than one lover." Kat hesitated, choosing her words carefully. "It has occurred to you, I suppose, that it is in France's best interest to prevent an alliance between Britain and Sweden?"

"Are you saying the French acted on the information Yasmina gleaned from Ross—or someone else—and killed Lindquist in an attempt to disrupt any alliance between Britain and Sweden?"

"I'm saying it's a possibility. But do I know for certain? No."

"And Ross? Why was he killed?"

"I haven't been able to learn anything about Alexander Ross."

Sebastian blew out a long, frustrated breath. "I suppose it's possible his death isn't related to any of this at all."

"It's related," she said. "The manner of his death tells us that."

They walked along in silence for a moment, their footsteps echoing hollowly in the narrow, empty street. Then she said, "Have you considered Jarvis?"

"When one is dealing with what looks like the work of a professional assassin, the possibility of Jarvis's involvement does tend to suggest itself, yes. Although if Jarvis had Ross killed to prevent him from spilling state secrets to a Turkish spy, I don't see why he wouldn't simply admit it."

"You *asked* Jarvis if he killed Ross?"

"Yes."

She let out a peal of laughter, soft and melodic and so be-
lovedly familiar it brought an ache to his chest. "Oh, Sebastian,"
she said, "your future family gatherings ought to prove beyond
interesting, to say the least."

Then she must have read something he didn't want her to
see in his eyes, for her smile faded and she reached out to touch
her fingertips, ever so briefly, to his arm. "I know why you're
doing this, Sebastian."

He shook his head in disbelief. "How can you?"

"The British government isn't the only one who pays servants to spy on their masters. Get your bride a new abigail."

That night, Hero received an urgent note from her cousin
Sabrina.

I need to talk to you, the girl had written, her penmanship wob-
bly, agitated. *Could we meet for a walk in the park tomorrow?*

Intrigued, Hero wrote back, *Of course. I'll see you at ten.*

Then she sat for a time, her cousin's note in her hand, her
mind busy with a series of conjectures that in the end seemed to
go nowhere.

Tuesday, 28 July
The morning dawned cool and overcast, with a soft white mist
that swirled through the trees in the park.

Hero found Sabrina looking pale and heartbreakingly
lovely in a walking dress of the deepest mourning topped by a
black spencer. At first, Hero was content to simply allow the
conversation to ramble as they walked. Her abigail, Marie, followed languidly behind—thankful, Hero suspected, for the
moderating effect Sabrina's presence had on Hero's normally
brisk pace.

They spoke for a time of Alexander Ross, and Sabrina's grief, and her inability to respond with enthusiasm to Jasper Cox's plans to remove to the seaside for a few weeks.

Hero said, "I suppose you must find some comfort in your music."

Sabrina choked back a sob. "I haven't been able to play since I heard . . . since I knew . . ." Her voice trailed away.

Hero reached out to touch her cousin's shoulder in an awkward but sincere gesture of comfort. "It will come back, eventually. I know it will." Then, feeling profoundly dishonest, even contemptibly sly, she added, "You play the harp, don't you?"

Sabrina shook her head. "Pianoforte."

"Of course. How could I have forgotten?"

Hero stared off across the park, to where the waters of the Serpentine glinted in the distance. She had never actually believed sweet, dainty Sabrina capable of wrapping a harp wire around a man's neck and twisting it until his face turned purple and the veins in his eyeballs burst.

Hero wasn't so sure about Jasper.

Hero said, "Were you by chance acquainted with a French émigré named Antoine de La Rocque?"

"De La Rocque? I don't believe so. Why? Who is he?"

"He was a collector of old and rare books."

Sabrina frowned. "A rather peculiar-looking man with a long neck and a small head?"

Hero glanced at her in surprise. "Yes, that's he. So you did know him?"

"I met him once, when I was with Alexander." She sucked in a quick breath, her eyes widening with sudden comprehension. "You said he 'was' a collector of old books. Why? What has happened to him?"

"He was killed yesterday."

Sabrina shuddered and turned so alarmingly pale that for a moment Hero worried she might faint. "You mean, murdered?"

Hero eyed her warily. "Yes. I'm sorry; I didn't mean to distress you. I shouldn't have mentioned it."

Sabrina swallowed hard and shook her head. "No. You were right to tell me." She walked on in silence for a moment, her gaze on an old-fashioned closed carriage pulled by a pair of showy dapple grays that was drawing abreast of them at a sedate pace. The park was largely deserted at this hour; they could see only some children laughingly playing chase under the watchful gaze of a nursemaid, and a tall, broad-shouldered gentleman in fashionable trousers and a black coat walking briskly toward them.

"Hero," said Sabrina, as if suddenly coming to a decision, "there's something I need to tell you—"

She broke off with a frightened gasp as the tall gentleman reached out to seize her arm, spin her around, and slam her back against his chest. In his left hand he held a pistol, its muzzle pressed against Sabrina's temple.

"Do anything stupid," he said to Hero, his rough accent at decided variance with his natty clothes, "and yer cousin here gets popped. Understand?"

Hero held herself perfectly still, although she could feel her heart pounding wildly in her chest. "I understand."

"*Hero,*" wailed Sabrina, her legs buckling beneath her, her face slack with terror.

Hero's maid, Marie, had come to an abrupt halt a few feet away, her eyes wide in a sickly pale face.

"It's all right," Hero told Sabrina calmly. "They won't hurt you." She cast a quick glance at her abigail. "Marie, stay where you are."

She was aware of the showy grays coming to a stop beside them. The door of the ancient carriage flew open. Another man—his buff coat well tailored but ill fitting, his cravat clumsily tied—leapt out to seize Hero's arm in an ungentle grip. "Yer comin' wit' us," he hissed. He tried to drag her back toward the carriage, but he was a good head shorter than Hero, and slight.

"I will not," she said.

The first man pulled back the hammer of his pistol. "Do what yer told."

"Hero!" screamed Sabrina, lunging against his hold.

"I'll go with you on two conditions," said Hero.

"Oh, ye will, will ye?" jeered the buff-coated man, shoving his beard-roughened, tobacco-stained face unappetizingly close to hers. "And what are yer *conditions*, yer ladyship?"

"My cousin is allowed to leave safely."

The black-coated man with the pistol laughed. "And?"

Hero glanced down at the broken, dirt-encrusted nails digging into the fine cloth of her walking dress. "You take your filthy hand off my arm."

Chapter 42

*S*ebastian arrived in Berkeley Square to find the Jarvis household in an uproar.

"What the devil is going on?" he demanded when the harried butler finally answered his peal.

"I beg your pardon, my lord," said Grisham, his normally impassive face ashen, "but I am not at liberty to—"

"If that's Devlin," boomed Lord Jarvis's gravelly voice from the back of the house, "send him in. Now."

Sebastian followed the butler through a hall filled with milling servants, Bow Street Runners, and the steely-eyed, former-military-looking types Jarvis tended to favor for doing his dirty work. From somewhere abovestairs came the sound of hysterical weeping that inexplicably raised the hairs on the back of Sebastian's neck.

Lord Jarvis stood before the great empty hearth of his library, surrounded by a throng similar to that in the hall. "Leave us," he snapped. He waited until the others had filed from the room, then shut the door and said to Sebastian, "Hero has been taken. She was walking with her cousin in the park when they were set upon. It appears that at least two men were involved, plus a coachman."

Sebastian knew a strange numbing sensation of disbelief. As if from a great distance, he heard himself say, "Both young women were seized?"

Jarvis shook his head. "Only Hero—and her abigail. Not Miss Cox."

Sebastian took a deep breath, and when that didn't help the sudden, crushing ache in his chest, he took another. "Their object is obviously not ransom," he said, walking over to pour himself a brandy. His voice came out calm, even cold, but the hand that reached for the carafe was not quite steady.

"Obviously," snapped Jarvis. The Jarvises might be an ancient and powerful family, but most of their wealth was tied up in land. For anyone interested in extorting a fortune, Miss Cox would have been the more logical target.

Sebastian sloshed a generous measure of amber liquid into a glass. "Is it an attempt to influence you on some looming policy decision, do you think?"

"I've received no demands."

Sebastian threw him a long, cold look. "I'll take you at your word."

A flare of rage, primitive and uncharacteristically out of control, flared in the big man's eyes. "Damn you, you impudent bastard. This is my daughter we're talking about. My *daughter*."

Sebastian stared across the room at his prospective father-in-law. Once, he would have said that Charles, Lord Jarvis cared about nothing beyond his own power and the security of England and the House of Hanover. In that, Sebastian now realized, he'd been mistaken.

"I will remind you," he said quietly, "that she is also my affianced wife." *And the mother of my unborn child.*

"This is because of you." Jarvis punched the air between them with an accusatory finger. "You and this mad, quixotic quest of yours for 'justice.' You have no idea what you've mixed yourself up in this time. No idea whatsoever."

Sebastian set aside his brandy untasted. "What the devil are you saying? That Ross was involved in something *else*? Something more than the transfer of gold to the Swedish government?"

Jarvis clenched his jaw so hard, the muscles along his cheek line bulged.

Sebastian took a step toward him, then forced himself to draw up short. "*Goddamn you.* Tell me. Hero's very life may well depend upon it!"

Jarvis's nostrils flared on a deep, angry breath. "The first and fifteenth of every month, the French Minister of War provides Napoléon with what is called the Survey of the Situation of the French Army."

"Which contains what?" snapped Sebastian.

"Numerical changes in the French divisions. Billeting changes. A list of appointments to command posts. That sort of thing."

"And?"

"For some time now, a certain individual serving on the General Staff has been making copies of these briefings, which he passes to a Parisian bookseller with a stall near the Pont Neuf. From there they progress to the coast, where smugglers carry them across the channel. Until yesterday, they then passed into the hands of a defrocked émigré priest."

"Antoine de La Rocque."

"Yes."

Sebastian studied the big man's closed, angry face. "That's why de La Rocque visited Ross the Wednesday before he died? He was delivering the latest dispatch?"

"Yes."

"And then what? What typically happened to the briefings after that?"

"Generally, such documents are turned over to a dedicated section of the Foreign Office, where they are copied and studied. It's a two- or three-day process. After that, copies are distributed to the representatives of a few select allies . . . and certain friendly governments."

It was all, finally, beginning to make sense. Sebastian said, "You mean, friendly governments such as that of the Czar."

"Amongst others, yes."

"Let me guess," said Sebastian. "The Russian who typically collected the copies of the dispatches from Ross was Colonel Dimitri Chernishav."

Jarvis gave a brief, curt nod. "Their meetings excited little attention, given the long-standing friendship between them. Chernishav was scheduled to receive the dispatches Saturday night. But the transfer was never made."

"So what happened to the copies of the briefing Ross had in his possession when he died?"

"They disappeared."

Sebastian went to stare out the window overlooking the garden, one hand resting on the long library table. He was aware of a white-hot rage coursing through him, stoked by fear and guilt and a confused tumult of emotions he had no time now to analyze. "What have you discovered about the men who took her?"

"Precious little. That fool girl, Sabrina, was hysterical by the time she reached the house. A nursemaid tending some children nearby saw the entire thing but wasn't much better. All we have at the moment is a hazy description of an antiquated carriage pulled by a pair of showy dapple grays and driven by an aged, liveried coachman. That, and contradictory descriptions of two men who were not gentlemen but were dressed as if they were."

Sebastian swung to face him. "If there's anything you're not telling me—*anything!*—I swear to God, I'll—"

"Don't be a fool," snapped Jarvis. "No one is more aware than I of the gravity of the situation. I have put every available man on this, and so far they have turned up nothing. Nothing." He held Sebastian's gaze in a long, steady stare. "I can't begin to understand precisely what has developed between you and my daughter these past two months. But right now, that doesn't matter. Nothing matters except Hero. You fancy yourself adept at solving mysteries? Then solve this one. Find her.

"Before it's too late."

It didn't take Hero long to discern that the taller of the two men who'd grabbed her was the leader.

He sat beside her on the forward-facing seat, his body swaying easily with the lurching movement of the antiquated carriage, his head tipped back against the worn velvet swabs, his watchful gaze never straying far from her face. He kept his finger curled around the trigger of the pistol held resting in an easy but purposeful grip on his thigh.

He was a well-made man, handsome even, with dark curling hair and a strongly boned face. But the slant of his full lips struck her as cruel, his pale gray eyes cold and hard as he nodded toward the sobbing abigail who sat bolt upright beside his confederate on the rear-facing seat. "Make her shut up."

Hero leaned forward cautiously, one hand reaching out to touch the abigail's knee. "Marie, hush. You must hush."

The abigail stared at her with wild, unseeing eyes and wailed louder.

"That did a lot o' good," observed the buff-coated tough slouched in the corner beside the maid.

"I don't know why you brought her," said Hero.

"Don't ye?" said the dark-haired man. Sullivan, she'd heard his companion call him. "She's our insurance. Ye do what you're told, she lives, and ye live. Ye don't . . ." He shrugged. "She dies. First. Unpleasantly. It's that simple."

Fortunately, Marie was wailing so loud that the sense of most of that speech was lost on her.

Deliberately, Hero turned her head to stare out the window at the passing rows of unfamiliar shops and tradesmen's ateliers. She felt the sting of threatening tears and blinked them away angrily.

She had no idea where they were taking her, or why. She knew only that the man beside her had lied. Neither she nor Marie would be allowed to live. Otherwise, he never would have let them see his face.

Chapter 43

No one knew better than Sebastian just how ruthlessly thorough Jarvis's minions could be. But on the off chance they'd missed something, he set Tom to scouring the neighborhood of the park and asked Calhoun to make inquiries amongst some of his more unsavory contacts.

Yet barring any unexpected discoveries or a demand from the kidnappers, it seemed to Sebastian that his only hope of ever seeing Hero alive again lay in finding Alexander Ross's murderer. Quickly.

And so he went in search of the Russian, Dimitri Chernishav.

The Colonel was coming out of his lodgings in Westminster's Adington Buildings when Sebastian caught him by one arm and the back of his coat to spin him around and slam his face against a nearby brick wall.

"What the devil?" growled the Russian, heaving against Sebastian's hold. But Sebastian had the man's arm held in an iron grip and bent behind his back at a painful angle.

"Miss Jarvis," said Sebastian quietly, bringing his lips close to the other man's ear as he increased the leverage on his arm. "Where is she?"

"You are making a mistake," said Chernishav, panting.

"Diplomatically, or tactically?"

"Both. I heard Lord Jarvis's daughter has been taken. But I am not responsible. Why would I do such a thing?"

"As a distraction, perhaps?"

"From what?"

"My attempts to discover the truth about what happened a week ago last Saturday."

The Russian was silent a moment. Then he said, "I did not kill Alexander. Why would I?"

"I don't know. All I know is that your plans for that evening had nothing to do with a pint at Cribb's Parlour. You went to Ross's rooms to take delivery of Napoléon's latest war briefing."

The Russian's face twisted into a disdainful sneer. "And you are aggrieved because I failed to disclose this fact to you? I told you before, Devlin; there is much involved here of which you are ignorant."

Sebastian increased the torque on the man's arm. "So, educate me."

Chernishav gave a ragged laugh. "Break my arm if you feel you must. But it will serve no purpose. I still won't tell you anything."

"Let me help you out, shall I? The Russian Czar is pressing the British government for an active alliance that will involve a commitment of troops to help deflect Napoléon's push toward Moscow. But certain elements within the government—the Earl of Hendon amongst them—are reluctant to divert troops to Russia at a time when they may soon be needed to protect Canada. Nevertheless, despite the lack of a formal treaty of alliance, the Foreign Office has been supplying Russia with copies of the French military dispatches, which regularly make their way out of Paris via a band of smugglers in contact with a certain rare-books collector named Antoine de La Rocque."

"Ah." The Russian looked thoughtful. "That I did not know. But it does help explain why he is now dead."

"As is the Swedish trader Carl Lindquist," said Sebastian.

"I never knew Mr. Lindquist."

"Maybe not," said Sebastian. "But Alexander Ross did."

"Then perhaps, rather than assaulting diplomats in the street, you should instead consider turning your attention to someone who did have dealings with Alexander Ross, Antoine de La Rocque, and this Carl Lindquist."

"As in, someone else in the Foreign Office?"

"It seems logical, does it not?"

Sebastian shifted his hold on the Russian Colonel. "The copy of the briefing you were to receive the night of July eighteenth— what happened to it?"

"I've no idea. I'm told Sir Hyde searched Alexander's rooms the next morning, but the briefing was never found. We were given a new copy just a few days ago."

Sebastian frowned. "Ross's man, Poole, notified Sir Hyde as soon as he found Ross dead?"

"Yes. It was Sir Hyde who called Dr. Cooper."

"And subtly suggested to the good doctor that Ross may have suffered from *morbus cordis*?"

"Perhaps. I wasn't there."

Sebastian gave a grim smile. "One last question. When we met at the Queen's reception, you told me of a quarrel at Vauxhall between Ross and the Turkish Ambassador. You knew of the rumors that Madame Ramadani had seduced someone in the Foreign Office?"

"I had heard whispers, yes."

"But you didn't believe them?"

"I didn't believe it was Alexander. You didn't know him; I did. He was fiercely loyal, not only to his country but to his friends and to the woman he loved. He would never have played her false."

"So where did the rumor originate?"

"One might suspect with the man who actually did allow himself to be seduced."

Sebastian released the Russian and took a step back. "You mean, someone like Sir Hyde Foley?"

Chernishav adjusted his cravat. "I don't know for certain. But it's what I suspect, yes."

With a rising sense of urgency, Sebastian tracked Foley from Downing Street to Carlton House to Whitehall. He was just turning in through the classical screen of the Admiralty when he heard the shrill, ungenteel accents of his tiger raised above the rumble of wagons and carriages in the street.

"Gov'nor!"

Sebastian turned to see Tom darting between a ponderous coal wagon and the high-stepping pair of shiny blacks pulling a phaeton.

"Gov'nor!" The tiger skidded to a halt, breathless. "We got somethin'! The wife o' the under-keeper what lives in the lodge near the Corner recognized the carriage and dapple grays what come through the entrance to the park this mornin'. She says they belong to a livery stable on the Kentish Town Road. Seems Calhoun's ma and the livery owner is real thick, and 'e tells Calhoun the rig was let to a cove by the name o' Sullivan. Todd Sullivan."

Sebastian frowned. "Sullivan? Who the blazes is he?"

"A weery rum character, according to Calhoun. 'Angs around the Castle Tavern!"

. . .

They took her to a wretched one-room stone cottage with a tattered thatch roof somewhere to the northwest of the city.

The cottage lay at the end of a rutted, overgrown lane, its
windows broken and stuffed with rags, its yard empty and weed
choked.

The coachman—a wizened little old cockney missing one
ear—stabled the horses in a dilapidated lean-to, which told
Hero they anticipated being here for a while, at least. Then he
went to gather wood for a fire while his companions spread the
crude table with bread and cheese and salami they washed down
with ample swigs from a bottle of gin.

No one offered her either food or drink. But at least they didn't
tie her up. She was left to prowl the cottage's dark, cramped confines, conscious always of Sullivan's watchful gaze following her.
Marie collapsed in a limp heap beside the grimy hearth, her body
wracked with sobs punctuated by an occasional thin, reedy wail.

"There, there," crooned Hero, going to draw the distraught
woman awkwardly into her arms. "Don't be afraid, Marie. They're
not going to hurt us. You'll see. Everything will be all right."

She looked up to find Sullivan smiling at her through narrowed eyes. "Feel sorry for her, do ye?"

"That amuses you for some reason?" said Hero stiffly.

"Aye, it does." He took another deep swig of gin. "How ye
think we knew where ye was going to be, and when ye was going
to be there?" He nodded to the woman now sobbing quietly in
Hero's arms. "She told us. Sold ye to us, she did. For a guinea.
Just didn't know she was includin' herself in the bargain."

Marie lifted her head to display a pinched, tear-streaked
face. "I did what you asked me to do!" she wailed, her pleading
gaze fixed on their captor. "Why won't you let me go? You've
got *her*."

But Sullivan only laughed and turned away.

Hero watched him go stand in the open doorway looking out on the sunbaked yard. Then she brought her gaze back to the abigail. "Why, Marie?" she asked, her voice kept low. "Why did you do it?"

The abigail sniffed, her features hardening into what looked very much like hatred. "You think I should have been content with your cast-off gowns and a few paltry trinkets, do you? You fancy that because you pay my wages you also bought my loyalty?"

"Oddly enough, yes," said Hero, who paid her servants handsomely—for both philosophical and practical reasons.

The abigail's lip curled with scorn. "You're a fool."

"Obviously." Hero was tempted to add, *But then, under the circumstances, I would venture to suggest that the appellation applies to you, as well.* But she kept the observation to herself.

The abigail had already begun to weep again. And though Hero knew that her tears were driven as much by hatred of Hero as by fear and self-pity, Hero continued to hold the girl and do what she could to comfort her.

As the hours dragged on and the shadows in the yard lengthened, Hero found herself wondering, if Marie asked for her forgiveness, would she have the magnanimity to give it?

But the abigail never did.

They killed Marie just as dusk was beginning to send long shadows across the yard.

Nothing Hero could do would silence the woman's incessant weeping. In the end, Sullivan simply drew an ugly, curved blade from his boot and walked over to grasp Marie by the hair. Hero saw him yank the woman's head back and she looked quickly away. But she heard the maid's rasping gurgle and the soft thump of her body sinking lifeless to the flagstones.

"I take it you don't feel the need for insurance anymore?" said Hero, forcing herself to meet the tall man's gaze.

Sullivan wiped his blade on the dead maid's dress and slid the knife back into its sheath.

Chapter 44

*S*ebastian was in no mood for subtleties.

The muzzle of his pistol pressed to the temple of one of Todd Sullivan's cronies at the Castle Tavern solicited the information that Sullivan frequently made use of a ramshackle cottage on the outskirts of Barham Wood, near Elstree.

In the grip of a cold, driven purposefulness, Sebastian borrowed a bay hack from the nearby livery and entrusted Tom with a message for Bow Street.

"Why can't I come with you?" asked Tom, his head ducked, his voice strained as he tightened the saddle's cinch. "It's because o' the things I said about Miss Jarvis before, ain't it? It's because you don't trust me no more."

Painfully conscious of the daylight slipping from the sky, Sebastian paused to rest a hand on the boy's shoulder. "I trust you with my life, and you know it." He swung into the saddle. "But I could be riding into a trap. I need someone I trust to deliver this message. Now *go*," he said, and spurred the bay out the livery door.

. . .

For Hero, the darkness came all too quickly.

Only a single tallow candle set at one end of the table's rough boards lit the inside of the cottage. That, and the soft glow from the fire kindled on the hearth by the coachman.

The coachman had long since subsided into a drunken stupor in the fireplace's inglenook. But the other two men continued to drink steadily. They sprawled now beside the crude table, the remnants of their dinner—more bread and sausage—scattered across the scarred surface. They talked in desultory tones about horses and cockfights and some colleague named Jed who had recently "made a good end" on the hangman's noose. But all the while, Hero was aware of Sullivan's dark gaze following her in a way she did not like as she restlessly paced the confines of the cottage.

At one point she heard the buff-coated man lean in close to his friend to whisper, "Need to keep yer breeches' flap buttoned fer a while yet, lad. Least till we hear they won't be needin' her fer some reason." Both men laughed, and Hero felt a new rush of cold fear wash over her, followed by a hot fury that left a steady resolve in its wake.

"Hey," Sullivan called to her, raising his voice. "How about ye quit wearin' out the floor and make yerself useful by fixin' some more tea?"

Wordlessly, she prepared the cracked, brown earthenware teapot and set in on the boards between the two men. The butcher knife they'd used to slice their bread and salami still lay nearby; she'd noticed the handle of Sullivan's pistol peeking from the pocket of the coat he'd hung on a peg near the door. She was careful not to glance toward it when she went to tend the water she'd set to heat in a blackened saucepan over the fire.

She was aware of the old coachman snoring softly beside her as she waited for the water to come to a good roiling boil. Then, grasping the handle of the pot with a rag, she carried the heavy pan to the table.

"Who'd have thought," said Sullivan, smiling up at her, "that a fine lord's daughter like ye would even know how to boil water?"

"Who'd have thought?" agreed Hero, and dumped the scalding water into his lap.

She was only dimly aware of the hot water splashing up to burn her own flesh through the cloth of her walking dress. Sullivan came roaring up off his chair, both hands clasped to his wet, burning crotch, his face snarled with pain and fury. She could hear the buff-coated man stumbling to his feet behind her. But she was already spinning toward him, the saucepan still gripped in a tight hold. Throwing all her weight behind it, she slammed the hot base of the pot into the side of the second man's head with a sickening, searing *thud*. He went down.

"*Ye bloody bitch*," growled Sullivan, lunging for her. She threw the pot at him and snatched the butcher knife off the table. Clenching it in a two-handed grip, she slashed the blade like a sword across his throat.

Hot, bright red blood spurted everywhere. Streams of it. For one awful moment, she could only stand, the knife still clenched in one fist, and stare at him as his step faltered and his eyes rolled back in his head.

"Wot the 'ell?"

Looking up, she saw the coachman stumble to his feet near the hearth. Their gazes met across the room, his jaw slack with horror.

Then they both scrambled for the pistol hanging near the door.

He was closer than she, and he reached Sullivan's coat first, for she tripped over Sullivan's body on the way. But the coachman was more than half drunk and he was still trying to pull back the hammer when she buried the butcher knife in his back.

He howled and stumbled sideways, but he didn't go down. She tried to pull the knife out so that she could stab him again, only she couldn't seem to yank it free. She heard a scuffle of footsteps behind her and looked around to see the buff-coated man staggering to his feet, the side of his face burnt and blackened from where she'd hit him with the pot.

"I'm gonna make ye wish ye'd never been born," he spat, charging her.

Giving the old coachman a shove out of the way, she snatched the pistol from his loosening grip, pulled back the hammer, and fired.

Sebastian was galloping down the overgrown lane when he heard the booming report of a pistol. He checked for a moment, a sick fear seizing his gut. Yanking out his own pistol, he spurred the bay forward again.

He clattered into the yard of a tumbledown cottage softly lit by moonlight. The door stood ajar. The familiar, tall figure of a woman leaned against the outer wall of the cottage. She had her head tipped back, her eyes open wide; in one hand, she held a pistol, the barrel pressed against the blood-soaked skirts of her once elegant walking dress. "*Hero*," he said, sliding off his horse beside her. He realized he was trembling. "My God. Where are you hurt?"

"I'm not," she said, her voice unbelievably calm and steady. She nodded toward the inside of the cottage. "They're in there."

His own pistol held in a tight grip, Sebastian pushed the door open wide.

A gray-haired, liveried coachman lay facedown just to the left of the door, a butcher knife sticking out of his back. Another man, younger, wearing a buff-colored coat, was sprawled on his back halfway between the door and a crude table, a bloody hole blasted in his chest. He was alive, but barely. He breathed his last as Sebastian bent over him. A third man—taller, darker; Sullivan, Sebastian suspected—lay near the table. Someone had slashed his throat so viciously, they'd half cut off his head.

Sebastian put his gun away and walked back outside.

She was still leaning against the rough wall of the cottage. Just standing there, her chest rising and falling with her quiet but rapid breaths, her gaze on nothing in particular. At his approach, she turned her head, her eyes huge in the moonlight.

She said, "Are they dead?"

"Yes."

"Good."

He nodded toward the blood-splattered interior of the cottage. "You did that?"

She glanced down at the pistol, then up at him again. "They killed Marie."

Reaching out, he drew her into his arms.

She came stiffly, holding back. "I'm all right," she said, her voice muffled against his neck. But he could feel the faint tremors rippling through her.

He brought his hand up, hesitated, then began to stroke her hair. "I know."

"I'm all right," she said again, trying to pull away, as if ashamed of even that momentary betrayal of fear and weakness.

But he held her close, his lips pressed to her hair, his eyes squeezed shut. "Shhh," he whispered. "It's over."

Chapter 45

*S*ebastian closed the door to the old-fashioned coach and paused for a moment with one hand on the latch. The coach still stood where the kidnappers had left it, beside the lean-to of the ramshackle cottage; the body of the abigail, Marie, lay where it had been thrown by her killers, on the straw-strewn carriage floor. His fists tightening around the hack's reins, he turned to walk back to where Miss Hero Jarvis watched him from the center of the yard.

"I'm sorry," he said.

She nodded and glanced away, her lips held in a thin, tight line, her throat working as she swallowed. He had the feeling she was holding herself together with a gritty combination of pride and determination.

He said, "I can still put the horse to. You could ride on the box with me if you don't want to be inside with . . . her."

"No. Let's just . . . go."

He swung into the saddle, then slipped his foot from the stirrup and leaned down for her. She put her hand in his, and he gripped her forearm and hauled her up in a scrambling rush of ripping muslin skirts and rucked-up petticoats.

She settled easily behind him, but he was aware of her gaze drifting back to the carriage.

He said, "It's not your fault."

"No. But perhaps if I had been kinder to her . . ."

Gathering the reins, he turned the horse's head toward the lane. "I find it difficult to believe you were ever unkind to her."

"Perhaps not unkind, exactly. But if I'd been less impatient, more understanding, then perhaps she wouldn't have . . ."

He said again, "It's not your fault."

They rode through shadowy woods and empty, moon-silvered fields, the steady plodding of the horse's hooves the only sound in the stillness of the grass-scented night.

He was aware of her holding herself stiffly behind him, her hands barely touching his waist. And he found himself wishing she would simply relax and lean into him, take some measure of comfort from his warmth and his nearness. He could only guess at the horror of all that she had been through in the last twelve hours or the extent to which she was still struggling to come to terms with her own capacity for violence and the need to make that knowledge a part of her understanding of herself.

She said, "I keep thinking I should feel some measure of remorse or at least regret over the deaths of those men. But I don't. I'm glad I killed them."

"Personally, I find that perfectly understandable. I see no reason for you to feel remorse. But then, my own propensity for violence is considered by some to be excessive."

She surprised him with a soft, ragged chuckle. "And you are a man. Our society expects women to be gentle and forgiving. Not ruthless and . . . lethal."

"Gentleness and forgiveness have their place. This was not one of them."

Her hands shifted subtly at his sides. She said, "I'd like to think I killed them because of what they did to Marie. But that's not true. I killed them because they made me afraid. I don't think I've ever been that afraid."

Her admission both touched him and surprised him. He said, "I was afraid too."

There was an awkward pause. Then she said stiffly, "Under the circumstances, I will understand if you wish to withdraw your offer of marriage."

It took him a moment to grasp what "circumstances" she was referring to. "That's very kind of you," he said, keeping his voice light with effort. "But I have no intention of allowing you to cry off at this late date."

"I am not attempting to cry off," she said with some heat. "But you must realize that what happened today will inevitably become known."

"Your kidnapping is known already."

"So."

"So?"

"You know what people are like—what is no doubt being whispered at this very moment in nearly every drawing room and club in London. People will say you married soiled goods. And in time there will be sly suggestions that this child is not yours."

He drew up and swung to face her. "Do you seriously believe I would refuse to marry you because of today?"

"People will say—"

"Not if they value their lives."

"What are you suggesting? That you challenge half of London to a duel?"

"Somehow I doubt it will come to that." He moved the bay forward again.

She said, "I would like to make it quite clear that those men did not . . . I mean, that nothing of that nature occurred . . ."

"Miss Jarvis, believe me when I say that even if it had—"

"*It did not!*"

"Even if it had, it would in no way influence my determination to make you my wife."

Silence fell between them again. This time, he was the one to break it. "Did you hear nothing that might indicate who hired those men?"

"No."

"Your father sees the dark hand of Napoléon's agents."

"*Napoléon?*"

"It does make sense."

"The idea being that some French agent is the killer, and if you were busy looking for me then you wouldn't have time to pursue him?" She paused as if considering this. "It's possible, I suppose, if the intent were to buy time for the murderer to flee the country. Otherwise, what would be the point? De La Rocque and Ross are already dead."

Once again, he drew up to look at her over his shoulder. "You knew de La Rocque was passing the French War Ministry's briefings to Alexander Ross?"

"I did."

"And you didn't tell me—why, precisely?"

"I am not in the habit of betraying confidences."

He made a noncommittal sound and urged the horse forward again.

She said, "I hardly see how you can complain, since it's exactly the same reason you refused to tell me how you knew Ross died from a stiletto thrust to the back of his neck." When he remained silent, she added, "I've figured it out, you know."

"You have?"

"Mmm. It wasn't difficult, given the condition of the body when it was exhumed."

"You heard about that?"

"All of London has heard about it." The church spire of the village of Elstree appeared above the treetops before them. She said, "You also didn't tell me about Ezekiel Kincaid."

"I didn't?"

"You didn't."

"That, I can assure you, was mere oversight."

"So tell me."

"Very well."

She listened to him in silence, then said, "Even if the French did kill Ross and de La Rocque—and Lindquist—I see no reason for them to kill either Kincaid or Yasmina Ramadani."

"Not unless we're missing something," he agreed. The horse shied at a pig scuttling across the road before them, and he steadied it with a murmured word. "I'm beginning to think that while the most recent murders are in some way related to Ross's death, they may actually have been committed by a different person."

"What are you suggesting? That we're dealing with *four* different killers?"

"Not four, no. But there could be two."

The cottages of the village were closing in around them. She said, "One, the mystery man with the stiletto who killed Ross and Kincaid for some reason we don't yet know—"

"Something *we* don't know? Or something *I* don't know?"

"And someone else," she continued, ignoring the jibe, "who coincidentally killed de La Rocque, Lindquist, and Yasmina? I thought you didn't believe in coincidences."

"Not coincidentally." He turned into the yard of a rambling, half-timbered inn at the top of the village's high street. "Tangentially."

She stared up at the inn's surrounding galleries. "Why are we stopping here?"

"To inform the local magistrate that he has several bodies out at Barham Wood to deal with." He reined in beside the worn old mounting block in the corner of the yard. "And because Miss Hero Jarvis cannot ride into London on the back of a mud-splattered, hired hack."

She slid off the bay's back onto the high, flat stone. "I suppose we should also send word to Bow Street."

"I already did."

She looked up from straightening her skirts. "You did? When?"

"When I discovered where you were being held. I thought I might need help." He met her frank gray eyes and found himself smiling. "I didn't expect you to rescue yourself."

"Feeling better?"

Hero smiled at her father. "Yes, thank you."

She sat curled up beside a roaring fire in the library; Jarvis occupied the chair opposite, his gaze on her face. Around them, the house was quiet, the servants long since retired to bed. Since her return from Elstree, she had bathed and eaten a hearty meal, and spent considerable time consoling her hysterical, prostrate mother. Now she was quietly sipping a cup of tea liberally laced with brandy.

Devlin had insisted on remaining in Elstree to deal with the authorities, while sending her back to London in a hired coach. She'd argued, of course, but in the end she'd allowed herself to be persuaded. She was bone weary and emotionally drained, and beyond caring that he knew it.

"What can you tell me about whoever was behind this day's work?" Jarvis asked now.

"Very little, I'm afraid. You may find something by investigating the contacts of that man, Sullivan. But I'll be surprised." She had no doubt he would be both thorough and ruthless in his determination to find the man or men responsible for kidnapping his daughter. But she also suspected that whoever they were dealing with had foreseen that—and made his moves accordingly.

Jarvis nodded. "It might have helped if you could have left one of them alive."

She gave a soft chuckle. "So you could have interrogated him? Yes, I should have thought of that. Shockingly careless of me, wasn't it?"

She won from him a wry answering smile. He said, "I am proud of you, you know. There aren't many women who'd have the courage and fortitude to do what you did."

"I think you might be surprised."

He grunted and shifted in his chair to draw his snuffbox from his pocket. Flipping it open, he held a pinch to one nostril and sniffed. Then he sat thoughtfully for a time, one finger tapping the figured gold lid. He said, "I'll never forgive him for this."

"Devlin, you mean? He did find me."

Jarvis's jaw tightened. Watching him, it occurred to Hero for the first time that it rankled with her father, that despite all his spies and informants, Devlin had succeeded where he had failed.

"You wouldn't have needed finding if his damnable habit of involving himself in murder investigations hadn't caused you to be kidnapped." He shot her a piercing look from beneath lowered brows. "You're still determined to see this wedding go forward?"

"I am."

He started to say something, then glanced away. And she

suddenly thought, *Good heavens, he knows about the child.* Then she decided she must simply be overwrought and tired, for how could he?

Her father said, "He is my enemy. Yet you would make yourself his wife?"

"I suspect you are more his enemy than he is yours. He does not hesitate to stand against you when he believes you are in the wrong. But I do not believe he would go out of his way to cause you harm."

He brought his gaze back to her face. "And you? Would you stand beside him? Against me?"

"I will stand for what I believe to be right, as I have always done. But I am your daughter, and ever will be."

He pushed to his feet. "If anything should ever happen to you because of him, I'll kill him." He tucked his snuffbox back into his pocket. "Good night, my dear."

She sat for a time after he had gone, her tea grown cold in her cup, the fire burnt low on the hearth. She'd told her father the truth when she said she didn't believe Devlin would ever work against him without provocation. But she had no doubt that the day would come when the two men stood once more against each other. And what would she do then, as Jarvis's daughter and Devlin's wife?

She pondered the question long after she had retired for the night. But in the end she came no closer to a conclusion.

Later that night, Sebastian sat in one of the worn old chairs beside Gibson's hearth. He had his head tipped back against the cracked leather upholstery and a brandy in one hand.

It was not his first brandy.

Gibson said, "Is she going to be all right, do you think?"

"Miss Jarvis? Aside from a measure of guilt over the death of her abigail, I think so, yes. She's a remarkable woman." *And very much her father's daughter*, he thought, although he didn't say it.

Gibson frowned. "Guilt? Whatever for? The abigail betrayed her."

"I doubt the abigail knew what those men intended."

"Probably not." Gibson took a long drink. "I still can't believe Miss Jarvis killed all three of them. My God."

"I offered to take responsibility for the deaths myself, to spare her the unpleasantness and notoriety that will inevitably result. But she would have none of it."

"I'd like to have seen Lovejoy's face."

Sebastian gave a soft laugh. "I think she frightens him."

"You're the only man I know whom she doesn't frighten."

Sebastian saw no reason to shatter his friend's illusions.

Gibson said, "There'll be an inquest, I suppose."

"Yes. But it will be largely perfunctory."

They drank in companionable silence for a while, each lost in his own thoughts. Then Sebastian sat forward, his elbows on his knees. "You've seen the bodies, Gibson; do you think it's possible we're dealing with two killers? One who murdered Kincaid and Ross, and someone working for the French who killed Lindquist, de La Rocque, and Yasmina?"

"It's possible, yes. But"—Gibson took a deep swallow of his brandy, his lips pursed as he considered this—"why would the French kill Yasmina?"

"Perhaps she became restive and threatened to betray what she was doing."

"That seems unlikely."

"The only alternative I can come up with is that we're talking about *three* killers . . ." Sebastian scrubbed his hands over his face and slumped back. "Oh, bloody hell."

Gibson stood up, staggering slightly as his weight came down on his peg leg. "Maybe some more brandy will help."

Wednesday, 29 July

The pounding went on and on, loud and insistent.

It took Sebastian some moments to realize that the pounding in his head was not, in truth, in his head, but the result of a fist beating a lively tattoo against a distant door.

He opened one eye. His gaze traveled from the row of grotesque specimens lining Gibson's mantel to Gibson's gently snoring face. The golden light of late morning streamed in through the room's narrow window. At some time during the night he had decided there was no point in making his way back to Brook Street. But he couldn't fathom why he hadn't at least made it from the damned chair to the sofa.

The pounding continued. Where the bloody hell was Mrs. Federico?

He pushed up from the chair, wincing as he straightened his cramped, stiff limbs. Rubbing the back of his neck, he wove his way down the narrow hall to yank open the door. "What do you w—"

He broke off.

Miss Hero Jarvis stood on the doorstep.

Chapter 46

*H*is betrothed was, as always, exquisitely turned out in a walking dress of teal silk with medieval sleeves slashed with strips of yellow. She wore pale yellow kid half boots that laced up the back and coordinated nicely with her yellow kid gloves and a teal silk reticule embroidered with tiny primroses. To top it off, she wore a hat trimmed with three peacock feathers. There was nothing in either her appearance or her manner to suggest that she was suffering any ill effects from either yesterday's kidnapping or its bloody ending. The Jarvis town carriage with its two footmen waited nearby; a very young, very frightened-looking housemaid hovered at her elbow.

"Ah, there you are, my lord," Miss Jarvis said, brushing past him into the hall. "When I couldn't find you at Brook Street, I spoke to Sir Henry. He suggested you might be here."

"Miss Jarvis—"

She went to stand in the doorway to the parlor. Gibson was now snoring gustily. She turned to face Sebastian, her eyes narrowing as she surveyed him critically. "I take it you haven't heard the news."

He scrubbed one hand down over his face, painfully conscious of the rasp of his day's growth of beard. "Good God. Not another murder?"

"What? Oh, no. Nothing like that. My father has been closeted with the Prince and his ministers at Carlton House since dawn. A ship docked this morning from Canada with news that the United States have attacked us. According to the captain, the Americans declared war six weeks ago, on June eighteenth."

He stared at her, his sleep-fuddled brain slowly beginning to move.

She said, "You do see the implications, do you not? According to what I have been able to discover, the *Baltimore Mary* sailed from America on June fifth."

"But that would have been before war was declared. And it's no use saying they could have heard rumors of war before they sailed, because the rumors have been flying for months now."

"Yes. But I've also discovered that the *Baltimore Mary* didn't sail directly to London. It stopped in Bermuda. Now, think about this: Say I'm the captain of an American ship—let's call it the mystery ship, shall we?—with a cargo bound for Bermuda. Just as I am ready to set sail, word reaches me that Congress has declared war on Britain. I know that if I land in Bermuda after news of the war has reached there, the British colonial officials will confiscate my ship. But I also know that my government is in no hurry to send notice of their war declaration to the British, because Washington is planning an attack on Canada and they want to take the forces there by surprise. So I decide to set sail immediately, hoping to make landfall in Bermuda, unload my cargo, and be gone again before word of the war reaches there."

"Risky," said Sebastian. "But tempting. Yes, I can see that. So you're suggesting—what? That this mystery ship landed at Bermuda and found the *Baltimore Mary* still there?"

She nodded. "And if so, wouldn't I—in my role as this unknown American sea captain—warn my fellow compatriots of the outbreak of war?"

He realized suddenly that he was still in his shirtsleeves and scrambled quickly into his coat. Gibson stirred, murmured something, then fell back to sleep.

Sebastian hunted around for his cravat. "It would certainly explain why the *Baltimore Mary*'s captain was in such an unnatural rush to unload his cargo and why he sailed again without reloading or even refitting. He wanted to get away before word of the declaration of war reached London."

She nodded. "What I don't understand is why knowledge of the declaration of war didn't leak out. All it would take is one drunken sailor."

"The ships' officers wouldn't have told their crews—not if they could help it. They had too much riding on maintaining the secret." He went into the kitchen, poured himself an ale, and downed half of it in one long pull. "That's the link. The link between Kincaid and Ross. As Cox's agent, Ezekiel Kincaid would immediately have hurried off to the West End to warn his employer of the declaration of war."

"Which he did."

Sebastian stared out over Gibson's unkempt garden with its secret, unmarked graves. "Which, thanks to the landlady of the Bow and Ox, we know he did."

Miss Jarvis said, "So what happened after that? Obviously—somehow—Ross heard about the declaration of war. But then what?"

"I'm not entirely certain. But we now know that Jasper Cox had a damned good reason to kill both men: to keep them quiet."

Chapter 47

"Jasper Cox is my cousin," she reminded Sebastian as they drove through the crowded streets of the City in her carriage.

"All the more reason for you not to be present when I confront him with this."

She raised one eyebrow in an expression that was unfortunately reminiscent of her father. "I'm sorry, but I don't see that."

He chose his words carefully. "There are times when men are simply more comfortable talking to men. Reprehensible, I know, but nevertheless true."

He watched her nostrils flare on a quickly indrawn breath, saw her eyes narrow. But however much she might rail against the realities of their society, she was no fool and she knew he was right.

"Very well," she said as the carriage drew up before his Brook Street house and the footman pulled open the near door. "But you will tell me what you discover."

It was not a request. Torn between exasperation and amusement, Sebastian paused with one hand on the doorframe to look back at the woman who, in less than twenty-four hours, would become his wife. "I will tell you what I discover," he promised. "After all, it's the least I can do." He hesitated a moment, then added, "And thank you."

Some forty-five minutes later, freshly arrayed in the buckskin breeches and dark blue coat that served a gentleman of the ton as morning wear, Sebastian knocked at the shiny black door of the Coxes' impressive house on Bedford Square.

The door was opened by a stout, disdainful-looking butler, who listened to Sebastian with a bored air before intoning dismally, "I am sorry, my lord, but Mr. Cox is not at home this morning."

"No?" said Sebastian, pushing past him. "You don't mind if I have a look myself, just to be certain?"

"But . . . My lord!" protested the butler, staggering at the effrontery. "What are you *doing?*"

Striding down the hall, Sebastian threw open the door to the library. Finding it empty, he turned to mount the stairs two at a time to the first floor.

"My lord!" wailed the butler, panting noisily as he labored in Sebastian's wake. "Please! I do most humbly beseech you! *Come back.*"

"Where the devil is he?" Sebastian demanded, throwing open first one door, then the next. "The morning room? His dressing room? You may as well tell me, because I—"

"May I help you?" said a pleasantly modulated female voice behind him.

Sebastian turned.

It was the young woman from the silhouette. Small and dainty, with a winsome face framed by short dark curls, she wore a well-cut but painfully plain black mourning gown caught up high under her breasts by a simple black satin ribbon.

"Miss Cox?" he said.

She was pale but surprisingly self-possessed. "Yes. You're Lord Devlin, aren't you? You're looking for my brother?"

"I am."

"I keep telling his lordship that Mr. Cox is not at home, but he won't listen to me," said the butler, wheezing as he reached the top step.

"Thank you, Heath," she said to the butler. "That will be all." She led the way into a drawing room, where an older woman in a mob cap—whom Miss Cox introduced as her former governess—sat working on a chair cover in a seat overlooking the rear garden. The woman looked up, squinted at Sebastian, then went back to her needlework.

"My brother left yesterday for Southampton," said Miss Cox. "Is there something I can help you with?"

Sebastian cast a questioning look at the governess.

"Mrs. Forester becomes quite oblivious when she's involved in her needlework," said Sabrina. "You may speak freely."

Sebastian took up a position before the empty hearth. "A week ago last Saturday, a man came to see your brother—an American named Ezekiel Kincaid. Blond hair. Prominent teeth."

If Sabrina Cox had been pale before, she was now ashen. "Kincaid?" she said vaguely, sinking into a nearby chair. "No, I don't recall anyone by that name visiting us. Perhaps—"

"I beg your pardon, Miss Cox, but you are a terrible liar."

"I think you should leave now," she said abruptly, thrusting to her feet again.

Sebastian stayed where he was. "Did you know Kincaid is dead?"

"*Dead?*"

"Murdered. The same night as Alexander Ross. And in exactly the same way."

She sank back to the edge of her chair, her hands gripped together in her lap. "No," she said in a small voice. "I did not know."

"Ross was here that day, wasn't he?" said Sebastian. "He came to see you, but somehow he overheard Kincaid telling your brother that the United States had declared war on Britain."

She shook her head back and forth, her lips pressed tightly together, her face crumpled with distress.

Sebastian said simply, "He was here."

She bowed her head, her voice a torn agony. "I didn't know anything about it at the time. Alexander and I were here, in the drawing room. But he went downstairs for a moment to ask Jasper some question—I don't recall what about now. It wasn't important. He was gone only a moment, but when he came back, he behaved strangely. It was obvious he was distressed, but he wouldn't say what about. He left almost immediately afterward. It wasn't until later, when Jasper told me about Kincaid's visit, that I realized Alexander must have overheard them speaking." She swallowed, hard. "Jasper was . . . Jasper was in the midst of some delicate business transactions that would have been adversely affected had news of the declaration of war become common knowledge before he could make certain . . . adjustments. It was dreadfully important that the information be kept quiet. Not for long, you understand, just a day or two."

Sebastian glanced up at the life-sized portrait of Jasper Cox that hung over the mantelpiece. He had no doubt that an investigation of Mr. Cox's activities over the past twelve days would reveal an interesting flurry of buying and selling.

He said, "So you went to him that evening, didn't you? You put on your plainest cloak and a heavy veil, and you took a hackney to Ross's lodgings in St. James's Street to beg him to keep what he'd heard quiet. Only, he refused."

She nodded, her chest rising and falling with her rapid breathing. "He was horrified that I would even ask him—that I would think him capable of doing something so dishonorable, so . . . dishonest. I tried to make him understand how vitally important it was—how much was at stake. It would only have been for a few days! But he was appalled at the suggestion that he even consider putting personal financial interests ahead of his duty to his country."

"So your brother had him killed," said Sebastian. "Had them both killed."

Her eyes went wide with horror. "No!"

She must have read the disbelief in his face, because she rose from her chair to stand facing him. "No, you're wrong. Jasper would never do anything like that."

"Even with tens of thousands of pounds at stake?"

"No! You don't know him. He's ruthless in business, yes, but he's not . . . evil. Besides, he . . . he couldn't have done it. He was at a dinner given by the Lord Mayor that night!"

"I'm not suggesting he did it personally," Sebastian said quietly.

"You think he hired someone?" It was obvious this possibility had never occurred to her. She was silent a moment, then shook her head. "No. I still don't believe it. You say the American, Kincaid, was killed that same night, in the same way. Well, don't you see? Jasper had no reason to kill Kincaid. Ezekiel Kincaid had as much interest in keeping the information quiet as Jasper—if not more."

Sebastian said, "The only link between Alexander Ross and Ezekiel Kincaid is this house and the sensitive information both men possessed. The only one who knew they had that information was your brother. And you."

"But other people did know! By the time I talked to him, Alexander had already told several people."

"Who?"

She took a quick turn around the room, one hand brushing the curls off her forehead in a distracted gesture. "Sir Hyde Foley, for one. When Alexander left here that evening, he went straight to Sir Hyde's house."

"You seriously expect me to believe that the Undersecretary knew the Americans had declared war on us and kept it quiet for nearly two weeks?"

She turned to face him, her fists clenched to her sides. "I don't understand it myself. But it's true."

Sebastian studied her pale, strained face. "You said Ross told several people. Who else?"

"Some Americans he knew. A man and his daughter—I don't recall their names. The man's son is a seaman who has been impressed by the British Navy, and Alexander had volunteered to see what he could do to help get the son released."

"You mean, the Batemans? Why would Ross tell them?"

"Yes, that was their name: Bateman. Alexander said he wanted to warn Mr. Bateman to keep quiet about his son's nationality, since once it became known that Britain and the United States were at war, any seaman identified as an American would probably be thrown in the brig. He thought Bateman would have a better chance of surviving the war as a British seaman than as a prisoner on some fever-infested hulk on the Thames."

Sebastian could understand why the Batemans would decide to keep their knowledge of the outbreak of the war to themselves. But he wondered why they had in the end ignored Ross's recommendation and asked Sebastian for help in petitioning the Admiralty. Then he realized that as the weeks passed, father and daughter had no doubt come to the conclusion that Alexander Ross's warning of war had been nothing more than a false rumor.

By now, of course, they would know the truth—that war between the two countries had indeed broken out, and that their attempts to save their loved one from the clutches of the British Navy had perhaps succeeded only in putting his life at even greater risk. Sebastian intended to hold firm to his promise to do what he could for the man—although under the circumstances, he wondered exactly how much he could do to help.

Sebastian glanced again at the governess, Mrs. Forester, her head still bent over her embroidery as if she were indeed oblivious to the conversation in the room. He said, "Who else did Ross tell? Besides Foley and the Americans?"

"I don't know of anyone else. But don't you see? Word of the declaration of war never did become known. Which means that both Foley and the Batemans kept the news quiet for some reason." She was shivering now, trembling with the need to persuade him—and herself—of her brother's innocence.

But in truth, Sebastian was far from convinced of Jasper Cox's guilt. Because while Jasper Cox might have had a powerful motive for silencing Alexander Ross and Ezekiel Kincaid, the fact remained that the wealthy, ruthless merchant had no conceivable reason to kill Carl Lindquist, Antoine de La Rocque, or Yasmina Ramadani. In fact, as far as Sebastian knew, Cox was completely unaware of the existence of any of the other three.

Sir Hyde Foley, on the other hand, was now clearly linked to all five victims.

Chapter 48

"So I was right," said Miss Jarvis from where she sat on the high seat of Sebastian's curricle. "Both Kincaid and Alexander Ross did know of the American declaration of war."

"You were right." Sebastian leaned against the iron fence of Berkeley Square, his arms crossed at his chest. "They did indeed."

They were outside Gunter's Tea Shop, which was the only establishment for refreshment where an unmarried young lady could be seen in the company of a gentleman who was not a relative without fear of provoking a scandal. The lady stayed in the carriage, while the gentleman lounged in the street beside her. Sebastian had noticed that however scornful Miss Jarvis might be of society's strictures, she was still careful not to fall afoul of them.

"And now you think the killer is Sir Hyde, don't you?" she said, watching their waiter dart across the street toward the curricle. She didn't sound as if she agreed.

"It makes sense, doesn't it?" Sebastian waited while the tea shop's boy handed a cup of chocolate ice up to Miss Jarvis.

"News of the American declaration of war has effectively ended all talk of committing British troops to support the Russians. That's a powerful defeat for people like Foley who've been pushing for an active alliance." He hesitated, then added, "People like Foley and your father."

"My father did not kill Alexander Ross and Ezekiel Kincaid."

"Probably not," Sebastian agreed.

She let out a soft *hmph*. "I find it difficult to believe that even Foley would delay the dispatch of reinforcements to Canada for weeks longer than necessary, simply to buy extra time to convince the doubters in the government to back an active alliance with the Czar."

"Yet he has, hasn't he? Kept quiet about it, I mean."

Miss Jarvis thrust her spoon into the ice. "Ross could have told Sabrina a lie to make her give up and stop pressing him. Perhaps he intended to tell Foley but hadn't yet done so."

"I suppose that's possible," Sebastian conceded.

"And while I can imagine Foley might well kill Yasmina if he discovered she were a spy, why on earth would he kill de La Rocque? The book collector was a vitally important link in the transfer of the French dispatches from Paris to the Foreign Office."

Sebastian stared out over the gently rustling tops of the maples in the square. "I think de La Rocque told Ross about Foley's indiscretions with Yasmina."

"I thought de La Rocque suggested to you that Ross was the one ensnared by Yasmina?"

"He did. But bear with me here. We know that de La Rocque met with Ross on Wednesday, to deliver the latest dispatches. I think that's when he told Ross about Foley and Yasmina. Ross wouldn't simply have taken the accusation at face value, but he certainly would have investigated the possibility that de La Rocque was onto something. I suspect that by the time Ross encountered Ramadani at Vauxhall Gardens that night, he either knew it was true or had strong suspicions."

Hero swallowed another spoonful of her ice. "Which actually gives Ramadani a motive for the murders of Ross, Jasmina, and de La Rocque, although not Lindquist and Kincaid."

"Can we just focus on Sir Hyde and de La Rocque for a moment?" said Sebastian, pushing away from the fence. "The way I see it, de La Rocque knew Sir Hyde's sexual indiscretions were putting his own activities at risk. That's why, when he delivered the dispatches to Ross on Wednesday, de La Rocque demanded more compensation. It's also why he went to see Ross again on Friday—because he was expecting more money. But for some reason, Ross refused."

Hero said, "The only way Ross could have increased de La Rocque's remuneration would have been to go to Foley himself—which he obviously couldn't do in this situation—or to go over Foley's head, to Castlereagh. So why didn't he do that?"

"Because Foley killed him before he had gathered enough evidence. Ross wouldn't have made that kind of accusation lightly."

She pressed a thumb and forefinger against the high arch of her nose and looked pained.

Sebastian smiled. "That's what happens when you eat ices too fast."

"It's melting in this heat." She kept her fingers pinched on her nose. "So why did de La Rocque lie to you?"

"Because by that point he'd come up with what he thought was a clever scheme: He was going to blackmail Foley. And *that's* why Foley killed him."

She resumed eating her chocolate ice and considered this in silence. "I'll admit it makes sense, except for Carl Lindquist. Why would Foley kill him? The payments to Sweden were an important part of Sir Hyde's push for an alliance between Britain and Russia."

Sebastian blew out a long breath. "That's the one part that's difficult to fit."

Miss Jarvis scraped the bottom of her cup. "The way I see it, the only ones with any motive to kill Lindquist are the French. His death obviously won't stop the transfer of gold to Sweden, but it will delay things—and make future clandestine arrangements between our two nations more difficult."

Sebastian handed the empty cup to the passing waiter, then leapt up onto the seat beside her to take the reins. "Ah, yes; the nameless, faceless French agents," he said as Tom stepped away from the horses' heads and scrambled back to his perch.

She gave Sebastian a long, steady look. "Some of them have names. And faces."

He stared back at her, wondering if she meant who he thought she meant. Then he reminded himself that she was Jarvis's daughter, and he realized that she probably did.

But she simply opened her parasol and tilted it toward the sun as they moved out from beneath the dappled shade cast by the leafy maples in the square.

Sebastian was concerned that Miss Jarvis might insist on accompanying him to Downing Street. Instead, she seemed almost anxious to bid him adieu.

Arriving in Westminster, he found the entire stretch of Whitehall from Charing Cross to the Houses of Parliament in an uproar, with a stream of panting runners carrying messages back and forth between the Foreign Office, the Horse Guards, the Admiralty, Parliament, and Carlton House. Sebastian pushed his way through the crowded labyrinth of corridors to the chambers of the Undersecretary.

"Sir!" yelped a tall, emaciated clerk as Sebastian strode through the antechamber toward Sir Hyde's office. Sebastian kept going.

Trembling, the man thrust up from his seat and scrambled out from behind his desk. "You can't go in there! Sir Hyde is composing an important briefing and he's been most insistent that he not be disturbed. *Most* insistent."

"I'll tell him I held a gun to your head," said Sebastian, and threw open the door.

Sir Hyde paused in the act of reaching his pen toward the nearby inkwell and looked up. "What the devil?"

Sebastian closed the door in the face of the still-pleading clerk. "We need to talk. Now."

Sir Hyde slammed down his quill. "Are you mad? I've no time for this! Have you not heard what has happened?"

"I have," said Sebastian, tossing hat, gloves, and walking stick onto the littered surface of the desk. "I've also just learned that Alexander Ross discovered nearly two weeks ago that the Americans had declared war. But then, you knew that, didn't you?"

"Ross *what?* But . . . how is that possible?"

For a moment, the look of utter astonishment and incredulity on the Undersecretary's face gave Sebastian pause. "He had it from an American ship called the *Baltimore Mary* that docked in Rotherhithe the day he died. As soon as he heard, he went straight to your house, to tell you. And that's why you killed him—him and the American who brought the news."

"But . . . that's absurd! What possible reason could I have to do such a thing?"

"Because war with America means the end of any chance of sending British troops to Russia—something you have been working very hard to achieve. In fact, you've virtually staked your career on it." Sebastian watched the Undersecretary's jaw tighten, and knew he'd touched a raw nerve. "What exactly did you think? That you were close enough to achieving your aim that you could force through a commitment before official news of the American war declaration reached London?"

"We were close. So bloody close. If it hadn't been for Hendon, the alliance would have been signed weeks ago." Foley pushed up from his desk and went to stand at the window overlooking the courtyard below. He was silent for a moment, his lips pursed as if in thought. Then he said, "Ross did come to my house that Saturday evening—I'll not deny it. But I wasn't home. He left a note claiming he had something urgent to tell me. Only, when I went round to his lodgings some hours later, he wasn't there—or at least, he didn't answer the door. If he had early warning of the declaration of war, this is the first I've heard of it."

Sebastian frowned. "What time was this?"

"That I went round to his rooms? I don't know. Midnight, perhaps?"

Sebastian drew in a deep breath as a new possibility occurred to him.

Foley said, "You do realize how preposterous your suggestion is, don't you? You obviously forget that Ross worked under me. Had I wished him to keep his knowledge of the war silent for a time, all I'd have needed to do would be to give him an order. No need for murder."

"According to everything I've learned, Alexander Ross was a passionately honorable man. I'm not convinced you could have prevailed upon him to keep quiet."

"It's all in the way you phrase things. Good of the realm and all that rot." Foley smiled. "It's the earnest, honorable ones who are the easiest to manipulate."

Sebastian was aware of his hands curling into fists at his sides; he forced them to relax. "I'm curious about one thing: If you didn't kill Ross, why not tell me about the message he'd left at your house that night? Or your visit to his rooms at—what time did you say? Eight?"

"Midnight." Again, that tight little smile. "Do you take me for a fool? I'm perfectly aware of how it would have looked."

Sebastian studied the other man's thin, sharp-featured face. "Are you saying that when Ross's valet called you to his master's bedside that next morning, you knew he'd been murdered?"

"I didn't *know* it, no. But I had my suspicions, yes."

"When you searched his rooms, did you find the copy of the French briefing that Ross was to deliver to Chernishav the previous night?"

"Unfortunately, no."

"You don't find that curious?"

"Of course I find it curious. Obviously, whoever murdered Ross took the briefing too."

"Perhaps," said Sebastian. "What about the intruder who died breaking into Ross's rooms the night of Sir Gareth Ross's return to Oxfordshire? Was he one of your men?"

"I don't know what you're talking about." Foley cast a quick glance at the elaborately carved wooden clock hanging on the far wall and turned to gather his papers. "Now, my lord, you'll have to excuse me. Castlereagh has been closeted with Liverpool in his offices since news of this latest crisis arrived, and I'm scheduled to meet with them again at three."

According to Miss Jarvis, Castlereagh and Liverpool had been in seclusion with the Prince at Carlton House since early morning. But all Sebastian said was, "You actually had two reasons to kill Ross."

Foley laughed. "Another reason? You can't be serious."

"Mmm. Something that had nothing to do with those pesky upstart former colonials. Ross knew about your indiscretions with Yasmina Ramadani."

Foley paused in the act of shoving his papers into a case. Then he very deliberately fastened the buckles and lifted the case off his desk. "Again, I don't know what you're talking about." He turned toward the door. "Perhaps we could continue this conversation at another time?"

.   .   .

Sebastian stood in the shadowy doorway of the Cat and Bagpipe, his gaze on the bustling, crowded flagway across the street. Tom held the chestnuts nearby.

They had not long to wait. A moment later, Sir Hyde Foley exited the Foreign Office and turned toward Whitehall. At the top of the street he paused for a moment to take a nervous look around. Then he turned right, walking quickly toward the hackney stand on Parliament Street.

Chapter 49

*D*riving his curricle, Sebastian trailed the Undersecretary's hackney through a snarled throng of wagons, carriages, and carts. Drivers shouted; horses snorted and sidled restlessly; dogs barked. He was careful to keep well back from his quarry, lest Foley chance to glance around and see him. As a result, he nearly lost him first on the Haymarket, then again on Piccadilly.

"Where is he going?" muttered Tom from his perch at the rear of the curricle as they followed Foley onto Park Lane.

"Wherever it is," said Sebastian, "I doubt we're going to find either Castlereagh or Liverpool awaiting him."

They were just swinging onto Oxford Street, headed toward the Tyburn Turnpike, when Sebastian reined in hard. A milling herd of sheep filled the rutted roadway, the angry voices of their drover and the gatekeeper drifting over the plaintive chorus of *baa*s and bleats.

"Four pence? Four pence, you say? Can't you count? There's thirty sheep 'ere, not forty!"

"You're the one who can't count! It's four pence, I say."

"Bloody hell," swore Sebastian as he watched Foley's hackney bowl away up Uxbridge Road. He handed the reins to Tom, along with ten pence for the toll. "Here. Follow as soon as you can."

"Aye, gov'nor!"

Slipping past the toll gate on foot, Sebastian pushed his way through the last of the bleating, crowding sheep. Then he began to run, his Hessians kicking up little eddies of dust in the unpaved road.

From here, the vast acres of Hyde Park and Kensington stretched away to the south; to the north, facing the parklands across Uxbridge Road, rose the new blocks of St. George's Row. But beyond that lay only the burial grounds, a few more scattered houses, and then the open fields of Paddington.

Where in the bloody hell was Foley going?

Then he realized the hackney was pulling up before the cemetery's plain, small chapel. Sebastian slowed to a walk. As he watched, Foley paid off the jarvey, pulled his hat low, and strode quickly through the gates to the burial ground.

Sebastian followed him.

He was aware of an aged landau with two footmen parked farther up the leafy lane that ran along the far side of the burial ground. There was something vaguely familiar about the liveried coachman on the box, but Sebastian couldn't place him.

Pausing in the shadows cast by the chapel's high walls, Sebastian watched Foley slip from one monument to the next, being careful to keep to the long, rank grass rather than the graveled path.

What the hell was he doing?

Then Sebastian realized there was someone else in the cemetery, near a massive weeping willow that shaded what looked like the oldest section of graves. A small, slim woman in a gray walking dress trimmed at the neck with a narrow band of simple lace, she clutched a bulky gray reticule in one hand; a black silk patch covered her right eye.

Angelina Champagne.

Pressing himself flat against the chapel wall, Sebastian watched Sir Hyde Foley crouch behind a massive classically columned monument.

The Frenchwoman had paused beside one of the low, lichen-covered vaults. Much of the tomb's weathered concrete surface had crumbled and fallen away, exposing the brick structure beneath. She cast a quick glance around. But the burial ground was quiet, the only sounds the breeze rustling the leaves of the willow and the cheerful chirping of an unseen sparrow high above them.

Stooping low, she stripped off her fine kid gloves, then eased one of the bricks from the old tomb's lower course. It was obviously loose, for it came out easily. Setting it aside, she reached her hand into the small dark opening now revealed. From where he stood, Sebastian could see her stiffen.

She withdrew her empty hand and cast another darting look around.

"It's nice to know that Yasmina told me the truth," said Sir Hyde Foley, stepping out from behind the monument to stroll toward her. "In the end."

Angelina Champagne held herself very still. "You killed her."

"I did, yes. But before she died, she provided me with some very useful information." He nodded to the tomb beside them. "The location of your drop point, for instance. The clever signal she used to let you know she'd left information there." He paused. "And of course your identity as an agent of Napoléon. I suspect she hoped if she told me what I wanted to know, I might allow her to live. "

Angelina Champagne let her head fall back, her remaining eye narrowing as she watched Foley walk up to her. "How did

you discover that Yasmina's motives for seducing you had nothing to do with your *beaux yeux* and everything to do with your
propensity for bragging about your knowledge of state secrets?"

A quiver of fury, quickly contained, flickered across the Undersecretary's sharp-featured face. "As it happens, Ross told me.
He confronted me with his suspicions the day before he died. I
denied everything, of course. I'm not certain he believed me, but
it gave him pause."

"Alexander knew?" She frowned. "How could he have known?"

"De La Rocque."

"Ah." She pushed carefully to her feet, her reticule and gloves
clutched in her hands. "He was cleverer than I thought."

"Not so clever in the end. The fool attempted to blackmail
me. I had every intention of quietly silencing him myself, only
someone else—you, perhaps?—was kind enough to take care of
it for me."

A faint whisper of a sound—like cloth shifting against cloth,
or perhaps a soft kid shoe brushing against stone—drew Sebastian's attention to one of the newer tombs that lay in the dappled
shade of the willow. It was obvious that neither Angelina Champagne nor Sir Hyde Foley had heard anything. But then, Sebastian's senses were unusually acute.

Squinting against the glare of the sun, he studied the tall young
woman who stood motionless in the shade of the giant old willow.
The glorious teal and yellow walking dress he'd admired earlier
had been replaced by a more subdued muslin gown worn with a
lightweight, moss green spencer and a small chip hat devoid of
feathers. But it was undoubtedly his betrothed. He remembered
the landau with the familiar coachman he'd noticed waiting in the
lane and wondered what she had done with her maid.

He also wondered what the bloody hell she was doing here.

He heard Angelina Champagne say, "So it was you who
killed Ross."

Foley drew up beside her. "No. I assumed it was you."

"I liked Alexander. And I had no reason to kill him."

"But you would have killed him, had it become necessary. After all, you killed Lindquist."

"We did." She gave a wry smile. "Although in a sense, one could say that you did. If you hadn't bragged about the gold transfers to Yasmina, we never would have known where to look for him."

Sebastian saw Foley's shoulders bunch, saw the flash of the knife blade in the man's hand. *"Look out!"* he shouted and came from behind the chapel at a run.

He was too late.

Reaching out, Foley grabbed the Frenchwoman by her upper arm and plunged the knife into her breast.

"Bloody hell," swore Sebastian. Then he swore again, throwing himself flat as the booming explosion of a pistol echoed around the burial ground.

Foley turned a strange, slow pirouette, his body tense, a look of shock and surprise on his face, the front of his white silk waistcoat a sheet of dark shiny wetness. He took one step. Then his eyes rolled back in his head and he fell in a limp sprawl against the side of the tomb.

Sebastian's gaze jerked back to the Frenchwoman. She still had one hand in her reticule. He could see the charred hole in the side of the cloth and realized she must have hidden a small pistol there. For a moment, her startled gaze met his.

She crumbled slowly.

He pushed up, aware of the patter of running feet as Miss Jarvis rushed forward. Sebastian reached the fallen woman first.

He gathered her gently into his arms. She was still conscious, her eye filming with tears, one hand coming up to grip his forearm.

"How did you come to be here?" she asked.

"I followed Foley."

"Ah." There was a pause. "You heard?"

"Yes."

"It's true, what he said. We killed de La Rocque and Lindquist, too—both were agents of the enemies of France. But I swear to you, I had nothing to do with the death of Alexander Ross." She coughed, and a trickle of blood spilled down her chin. "*Je ne regret rien,*" she said softly. "We are at war."

He was aware of Miss Jarvis drawing up at the edge of the tomb. She made no move to come any closer.

Angelina's grip on his arm tightened. She said, "I never did tell you about your mother."

Sebastian felt his breath catch in his throat. "Tell me what?"

She shook her head. "You look so like her. Except for the eyes. She told me you had his eyes."

"What? Whose eyes?" But he realized she had slipped beyond hearing him.

He held her as she breathed her last, as her heart slowed and stopped and the life eased from her body. Then he laid her gently into the long grass and turned his head to fix his betrothed with a hard stare.

"Why are you here?" he demanded.

She returned his gaze steadily. "I followed her."

"You *what?* Why?"

"I thought you were wrong about Foley—"

"I was. Partially."

"And it occurred to me that Madame Champagne may have heard far more of Ross's argument with de La Rocque than she led you to believe. I thought I might try speaking to her myself, only she was just leaving as I drove up. I thought she looked . . . strangely furtive. So I followed her."

Sebastian stared down at the Frenchwoman's limply curled hands. The calluses on the fingertips were plainly visible.

Miss Jarvis followed his gaze.

He said, "She told me once that she loved music, but . . . surely she's too small to have strangled anyone."

"She did say, 'we,' did she not? Somewhere, she must have a confederate. The gray-bearded man who worked for her at the coffee shop, perhaps?"

"Perhaps." That would be for the authorities to deal with. Sebastian pushed to his feet. "What have you done with your maid?"

"She's in my grandmother's landau. I thought it would be less conspicuous than the barouche."

"Is that why you changed your dress? So you'd be less 'conspicuous'?"

"Under the circumstances, peacock feathers seemed somewhat inappropriate."

He found himself smiling. Then his gaze fell to the dead woman beside them, and his smile faded.

"Her death saddens you," said Miss Jarvis in a tone that told him she was both confused and disapproving.

"I liked her."

"She was a traitor—"

"Not to France."

"And a killer."

"That's what people do in war. We kill."

"This was different."

Sebastian shook his head. "No. Only less indiscriminate."

She nodded to the sprawled, bloody body of the Undersecretary. "One could say the same of Foley. He killed the agents of his country's enemy."

"Foley didn't kill for Britain's sake. He murdered to protect himself—to cover up his betrayal of his own country. Madame Champagne was right: In a sense, he killed de La Rocque and Lindquist, even though he didn't actually tighten the garrote or wield the cudgel. It was his vain, self-indulgent indiscretion that led to their deaths."

Her gaze drifted back to the Frenchwoman's now serene features. Sebastian saw two frown lines form between Hero's eyes. She said, "I don't understand how she could have been working for France. After what the Revolution did to her. To her son. Her husband . . ."

"That was the France of 1792, of Robespierre and the Jacobins and the Terror. Not the France of Napoléon and the Grand Empire. It's not unusual for those who love France to see the Emperor as a savior rather than—"

"A monster?"

"Well, yes." Sebastian found himself wondering for how long Angelina had been an agent of the French. Since the days of the Directoire, perhaps? When she'd been in Venice and Spain?

When she'd known his mother?

"It still doesn't make sense," said Miss Jarvis. "If Angelina Champagne killed Lindquist and de La Rocque, and Sir Hyde killed Yasmina, then who killed Alexander Ross and Ezekiel Kincaid?"

"Ross's Russian friend, Colonel Dimitri Chernishav. The problem is, I can't prove it. And even if I could, the bastard has diplomatic immunity."

Chapter 50

$\mathcal{B}$y the time Sebastian had finished with all the inevitable unpleasantness attending the violent deaths of an Undersecretary of State for Foreign Affairs and a French spy, a stormy, windblown darkness was falling over the city.

Arriving at Colonel Dimitri Ivanovich Chernishav's lodgings in Westminster, he found a two-wheeled covered cart drawn up in the pool of fitful light cast by the oil lamps mounted high on the walls of the Adingdon Buildings. Dressed in a long, flowing cape and with a silver-headed walking stick tucked up under one arm, the Russian was supervising the loading of a small ship's desk onto the back of the mule-drawn cart.

"Going someplace?" asked Sebastian, eyeing the pile of portmanteaux, bandboxes, and trunks that still littered the flagway.

Chernishav looked around. "I've been recalled to Russia."

"Oh? Problems?"

"My father. I fear he is gravely ill."

"I'm sorry to hear that."

Chernishav acknowledged his condolences with a small

bow. "There is a ship leaving for St. Petersburg with the morning tide. The *Staryy Dub*."

"How fortuitous." Sebastian studied the Russian's florid, pleasant face. "You've heard about the deaths of Sir Hyde Foley and Angelina Champagne, I presume?"

"I have heard the dozen or so different versions of the tale making the rounds of the clubs, yes. None of them entirely accurate, I've no doubt, although one can of course guess at the truth. Poor Alexander. Who'd have thought he'd fall victim to the French here, in London, of all places?" Chernishav shook his head, his lips pressed into a sad smile. "At least you have brought him a measure of justice."

"Not quite. You see, neither Foley nor Angelina Champagne killed Alexander Ross." Sebastian paused. "You did."

The Russian gave an incredulous laugh and turned to hand a bandbox up to the waiting man in the cart. "What possible reason could I have to kill Alexander?"

"You were never supposed to meet him at Cribb's Parlour that night. Instead, he was waiting for you at his lodgings—at around eight, not midnight—and you found him very much at home and alive. He invited you in, perhaps even offered his old friend a glass of wine. After all, he'd just learned from Ezekiel Kincaid that the United States had declared war on Britain and he was doubtless concerned about what effect this new development would have on Russia's chances of cementing an active alliance with Britain. Ross liked Russia; he had good memories of his time there and he wanted to see British troops deployed to help stop Napoléon from reaching Moscow. He had tried but failed to get in contact with Foley, so it makes sense he'd be anxious to discuss this latest development with his old friend." Sebastian paused. "He didn't expect his old friend to thrust a stiletto blade into the base of his skull."

"This is ridiculous," said Chernishav, turning to toss a portmanteau into the back of the cart.

Sebastian said, "I suppose it was an act of desperation, a spur-of-the-moment decision to kill Ross before he had a chance to pass his information on to his superiors at the Foreign Office. The ironic thing is, I'm not convinced Sir Hyde Foley wouldn't have ordered Ross to keep the information to himself, even if Ross had lived long enough to report to him. But you had no way of knowing that, and I suppose it was a risk you felt you couldn't afford to take. So when your good friend turned his back on you—perhaps to pour you another drink?—you quietly slipped your stiletto from your walking stick and drove it into the base of his skull. Then you stripped the bloody clothes from your good friend's body, placed him in bed to make it look as if he had died naturally, and carried the bloodstained clothing away with you. You figured you could trust Jasper Cox to guard the secret for his own reasons, but you weren't so sure about Ezekiel Kincaid. So you tracked him to the Bow and Ox in Rotherhithe and sent him a note purportedly from Jasper Cox, asking that he come to the St. Helena tea gardens—"

"This is preposterous!"

"Where you waylaid him and killed him, too. Probably also unnecessary, under the circumstances, but you're nothing if not thorough. You drove his body to Bethnal Green wrapped in a tarp on the floor of your curricle and dumped him in a ditch. Then you had Ross's bloodstained clothing cleaned and, after Sir Gareth Ross had returned to his home in Oxfordshire, you slipped the items back into his cupboards. Nice attention to detail, by the way. The only thing that confused me for a while was the intruder I encountered in Ross's room. Then I realized he was probably sent to make certain Ross hadn't left any written record of what he'd learned from Kincaid."

Chernishav had given up all pretense of loading the cart. "An interesting theory," he said. "Except of course it is only that—a theory, with no proof. You're grasping, Devlin. And why? Madame Champagne is dead. Let it all end with her."

Sebastian shook his head. "Taking the copy of the French War Minister's dispatches from Ross's rooms was a mistake. So was dumping Kincaid's body in Bethnal Green. It was dark that night, but not that dark. You were seen."

The Russian's nostrils flared on a quickly indrawn breath. "This is nothing more than a pitiful attempt to disrupt relations between our two countries by unjustly accusing me of this barbarous crime. Yet even if it were true—which it is not—you forget that I am a member of my country's diplomatic posting. According the Diplomatic Privileges Act of 1708, your law can't touch me. I have diplomatic immunity." He reached for a bulky portmanteau, his fist tightening around the handles as he straightened. "When the *Staryy Dub* sails in the morning, I will be on it. "

His gaze on the silver-headed walking stick tucked under the Russian's arm, Sebastian showed his teeth in a smile. "Your third mistake was in trying to distract me by kidnapping Miss Hero Jarvis. No one has immunity from Jarvis . . . or me."

Chernishav swung the leather portmanteau at Sebastian's head.

Sebastian threw up his arms and caught the heavy blow with a block, staggering as the impact reverberated through his body. He saw the flash of the Russian's boot heel aimed at his groin and leapt backward, crashing into the pile of bandboxes and trunks. He stumbled and went down.

The Russian tossed the portmanteau at him and turned and fled into the gathering gloom.

"Hell and the devil confound it," swore Sebastian, bandboxes tumbling around him as he struggled to his feet.

He could hear the clatter of boot heels on cobbles as the

Russian darted up the passage that ran along the side of the Adington Buildings. Sebastian pelted after him into a damp, narrow alley that erupted onto a deserted wharf littered with coiled hemp and piles of crates and a cluster of white gulls that rose up, screeching, as Chernishav raced across the weathered planks.

This was a part of Westminster where the stately streets surrounding the Houses of Parliament and the abbey degenerated rapidly into a warren of age-blackened houses. Distilleries and blacksmiths' forges and scrap ironmongers' shops opened onto coal yards and a long string of wharfs where barges from the counties upriver unloaded everything from hay to stone and timber. Now, in the rapidly descending darkness, the waterfront stood empty, the barges riding at low tide and battened down against a storm that sent streaks of lightning flickering over the roiling horizon.

With Sebastian some thirty feet behind him, Chernishav sprinted across an open stretch of planking to where the looming high walls of a riverside brewery rose, dark, soot-streaked brick against a rapidly darkening sky. The heavy, pungent smell of fermentation and hops mingled with the scent of tar and the smells coming off the water. Rows of casks turned on their sides and stored in towering stacks three and four high threw dark shadows across the yard. Chernishav ducked between the rows of casks, and a sudden stillness settled over the deserted waterfront.

The Russian had stopped.

Sebastian drew up sharply as thunder pealed slowly across the water. Then his preternatural hearing caught the quiet hiss of a well-oiled blade being pulled from its sheath.

He crept forward, his senses alert to the least flicker of movement, the betraying whisper of an indrawn breath. He had just reached the end of the first row of barrels when he heard the faint scrape of wood against wood. He leapt back and felt a gust of wind as the wall of casks beside him began to move.

They crashed down around him in a rolling, clattering, bouncing cascade of shattering staves and ringing iron. A dog began to bark hysterically, its chain rattling; a watchman shouted in the distance.

Sebastian caught the patter of footsteps running away fast. He clambered over the piles of shifting, broken barrels in time to see the Colonel disappear around the edge of the brewery.

Bloody hell.

He chased the Russian through a stone wharf, with its towering walls of roughly quarried granite and sandstone, and into the yard of a pottery factory. A flash of lightning lit up the waterfront, limning a long rambling building of rough brick with a low-slung tile roof and towering twin chimneys. Sebastian drew up abruptly at the base of a high, platformlike shelf that stretched along the end of the building and was stacked with massive earthenware pots.

The Colonel had stopped running again.

Sebastian heard a soft thump followed by a faint *clink*, as of unglazed, fired clay tapping against its neighbor. Looking up, he grasped the edge of the wide shelf above his head and carefully levered his weight onto the high platform. The rain was falling harder now, pocking the heaving dark surface of the river and pinging noisily against the stacks of pots and urns, pipes and culverts. Moving quietly, he swung up onto the overhanging roof, then rose to a crouch.

Beneath the smooth leather soles of his boots, the old tiles were wet and slippery with moss. He moved cautiously up over the ridge of the roof. He could feel the residual heat from the kilns' soaring chimneys warm on his back as he hunkered low at the far edge of the slope.

From here he looked down on the wide raised platform that ran along the back of the workshop. At the far edge of the platform, Chernishav waited, motionless, his form all but lost in the shadows cast by the hundreds and hundreds of four-foot lengths of fat drainpipe stored on end beside him. A jagged arc of lightning flashed across the sky, and Sebastian saw the gleam of the stiletto in the Russian's hand. Around them, the rain poured, filling the air with the scent of wet clay.

Loosening his own dagger in its sheath in his boot, Sebastian dropped to the near edge of the shelf below. The impact shook the nearest row of drainpipes. Sebastian gave them a helpful shove.

They toppled slowly, the first row falling against the next, which in turn collapsed onto the next row until the entire mass of drainpipes tumbled over like dominoes in a rolling crescendo of clattering, shattering earthenware. Chernishav swung around, saw the wall of pipe crashing toward him, and leapt off the platform into the yard below.

Sebastian landed in a crouch a few feet from him, his dagger in his hand. The Russian pirouetted gracefully, his stiletto extended like a foil, his left arm curled in the classic fencing pose.

"So," said Chernishav, his teeth bared in a smile. "Here we are."

"You fence, I take it?" said Sebastian.

"Since childhood," said Chernishav, flexing his wrist. "I hear you were a cavalry officer. Unfortunately, your saber is a little short."

"So's your foil," said Sebastian.

"True."

The two men circled each other warily. They were equally matched, of much the same height and build, both well trained in the arts of war. But each held a very different type of blade. The Russian's stiletto was a thrusting weapon with no edge, while Sebastian's dagger had carefully honed edges but was considerably shorter.

Chernishav struck first, lunging forward like a fencer thrusting with a foil, his stiletto aimed for Sebastian's heart.

Sebastian sidestepped the thrust, dancing away easily to the right, his boots sliding over the muddy wet cobbles of the pottery yard. Lightning played across the heavy clouds pressing down on the waterfront; the rain pounded.

"The advantage is mine, I think," said Chernishav. "You don't have to do this, you know. Why make Miss Jarvis a widow before you have the opportunity to make her your wife?"

"You'd have me simply walk away?"

"Why not?"

Thunder rumbled in the distance. Sebastian said, "I told you why not."

With a grimace, Chernishav struck again. Again, Sebastian skittered to the right. The repetition was deliberate; he was setting up the expectation of the pattern in the Russian's mind.

The Colonel lunged a third time, expecting Sebastian to once more fall away to the right. Only this time, instead of dancing away, Sebastian stepped into the Russian's lunge. It was a street fighter's trick: Clamping his left fist around the man's right wrist, Sebastian yanked the Colonel forward and stepped in to plunge his dagger up under the man's sternum. Driving straight toward the heart.

He saw the Colonel's eyes widen in surprise. Sebastian stepped back. Chernishav dropped to his knees, his hands coming up to clutch his chest as he toppled forward.

"So much for your bloody immunity," said Sebastian, and swiped the dripping rain from his face.

Chapter 51

*T*he chapel of the Archbishop's palace at Lambeth was small but graceful, with soaring lancet windows, a black-and-white-tiled marble floor, and delicate stone tracery that seemed to have captured and held the scent of some five centuries' worth of burning incense.

Charles, Lord Jarvis, stood just inside the chapel door, his snuffbox clasped in one hand, a frown lowering his brows. Slowly and deliberately, he nodded to the man known to the world as the groom's father. Hendon responded with the smallest of bows. Neither man smiled.

Owing to the hasty nature of the ceremony, the guest list was necessarily small. Devlin's only surviving sibling, Lady Wilcox, had evidently chosen not to attend—if indeed she had been invited. But the redoubtable Dowager Duchess of Claiborne was there, looking fierce in puce satin and a towering feathered turban. Also in attendance were a peg-legged Irish surgeon of doubtful antecedents and a Bow Street magistrate, of all things.

The bride's only living grandmother, the cantankerous old Dowager Lady Jarvis, had condescended to put in an appearance, as had Jarvis's two bird-witted sisters. The three women huddled together to one side, their eyes wide with vulgar curiosity as they whispered speculatively behind their fans. It occurred to Jarvis that the only member of the assembled company who actually looked happy about the coming nuptials was his own half-mad wife, the bride's mother, who stood with her face suffused with an idiotic kind of joy. And he found himself wondering how many of those in attendance—if any—knew the real reason for the quickly arranged wedding.

The truth would be obvious soon enough.

He transferred his gaze to his daughter. She was looking exceptionally lovely in an exquisite gown of white silk with a high-waisted bodice and small puffed sleeves embroidered with tiny blue rose sprays. Hero had always possessed unerring taste. A scoop neck edged in lace flowed into a V-shaped, charmingly gathered back, while a row of slightly larger rose sprays trimmed the hem above a long flounce of delicate lace. She had crimped her fine brown hair into soft curls that framed her face charmingly. Around her neck she wore a single strand of pearls with a sapphire pendant, a wedding gift from her husband. Devlin had clasped the necklace around her throat just moments ago. Jarvis had watched his daughter color faintly at her future husband's touch.

It was a reaction Jarvis would not have expected.

Jarvis transferred his gaze to the groom, who stood now near the altar, his head tipped to one side as he conversed in low tones with the Archbishop. Devlin looked relaxed and remarkably untroubled, although Jarvis noticed he had done little more than nod to Hendon.

Devlin and Jarvis himself had exchanged only the coldest of unsmiling bows.

Flicking open his snuffbox, Jarvis raised a pinch to one nostril and inhaled sharply. Then he closed the box with a snap and tucked it away. Walking up to his daughter, he held out his arm. "Ready?" he asked.

She put her gloved hand on his crooked elbow. For a moment, her gaze strayed to the tall young Viscount near the altar. Then she brought her gaze back to her father's face and surprised him by giving *him* a reassuring smile.

"Ready."

That night, long after the wedding breakfast with its awkward strained silences and thinly veiled hostilities, and long after Sebastian had brought his new bride home and shown her to her rooms, he stood at the open window of his bedchamber, his gaze on the darkened rooftops and church spires of the city, the air cold against his naked flesh.

Swept clean by a brisk wind off the North Sea, the sky was unusually clear and full of stars, the streets below now quiet and empty. He could smell the hot oil from the lamps left burning at the top of his front steps, hear the distant cry of the watchman. "One o'clock on a fair night, and all is well."

He held a glass of burgundy in his hand, but he had not tasted it, for he knew with quiet resignation that this was but the first of an endless string of lonely nights that stretched before him. He was a young man with all of a healthy young man's appetites and a wife who was a wife in name only. A different kind of man might take that as a license to dishonor his marriage vows, but not Sebastian.

Yet, somehow, he had not expected the thoughts and images that now tormented him. The remembered warmth of her body beneath his on a stolen afternoon. The faint, evocative scent of starch mingled with honeysuckle. The way the morning light had quivered on the tops of her breasts when her gaze met his across the length of the chapel and she drew in an unexpectedly quick, nervous breath.

He raised the glass to his lips and then paused, his head turning as he caught the opening of a distant door, the sound of soft footsteps in the hall. His door swung slowly inward and Miss Jarvis—*no*, he reminded himself; *his wife, the new Viscountess Devlin*—stood on the threshold.

She wore only a thin chemise, her bare toes curling away from the cool floor, her eyes wide and dark in the night. "If you don't want me here," she said, "just say so."

The wind billowed the curtains at the window and fluttered the loose hair about her face. He set aside his wine and went to her. If his nakedness caused her either embarrassment or alarm, she did not show it. He breathed in the familiar scent of her, and she lifted her face to him.

He covered her mouth with his and felt her hands slide up his bare back, pulling him close. He tangled his fingers in her hair, his thumbs brushing the soft flesh beneath her chin as he deepened the kiss. She pressed against him, and he felt the warm, remembered firmness of her body. Her breasts were small and high, her stomach gently rounded, her hair fragrant with the scent of flowers when he buried his face in her neck.

She threaded her hand with his and walked with him to his bed. He gazed into her eyes, saw her lips part. Reaching out, surprised to find himself trembling, he slipped the straps of her chemise from her shoulders.

"'When her loose gown from her shoulders did fall,'" he quoted softly with a smile, "'and she me caught in her arms long and small . . .'"

She stopped his words with her kiss, and he bore her down beneath him onto the tangled sheets of his bed. The wind filled the room with the scent of the distant sea and in concert with the moon set strange shadows to dancing around them. He was only dimly aware of the clatter of horses' hooves and the rattle of carriage wheels passing in the street below. For his world had narrowed down to the silken hair that slid across his belly and the heated invitation of her legs wrapping around his hips and the gentle wonder with which his wife whispered, *"Sebastian . . ."*

Author's Note

$\mathcal{A}$s difficult as it is to believe in this age of instant communication, word of the United States' declaration of war on Great Britain, which occurred on 18 June 1812, did not reach London until 29 July—and even that was unofficial. The *Baltimore Mary*, which in *Where Shadows Dance* brings word of the war nearly two weeks earlier, is my own invention.

The United States was still treated as a plural noun in 1812; thus, Englishmen at the time said, "The United States *have* declared war on us."

The diplomatic maneuverings of the summer of 1812 that form the background of this story were real, although far more complicated than portrayed here since they also involved Austria and Prussia. England did indeed bribe the Swedes with gold and promises of Norway—which at the time was part of Denmark—in exchange for Finland, which Sweden had recently lost to Russia. The Czar was indeed pushing—unsuccessfully—for a strong, active alliance with the British.

Richard Trevithick ran a London Steam Carriage from Holborn to Paddington in 1803; in 1808 he constructed his Steam Circus in Bloomsbury. The New Steam Circus described here in 1812 is my own invention.

Antonaki Ramadani was a real man, although he was actually the Chargé d'Affaires from the Sublime Porte, not the Ambassador. Yasmina Ramadani is my own invention. The extensive spying activities directed toward ambassadors to the Court of St. James that Ramadani describes were quite real.

The Surrey Docks in Rotherhithe were the center of the Arctic whaling expeditions that set sail from London. Rather than being boiled aboard ship as became the practice in later years, the blubber was cut into blanket pieces and brought back to London to be melted down. But by the early nineteenth century, the whales that had once filled the seas near England were nearly extinct and the industry came to be dominated by the American whaling fleets.

The intrigue surrounding the Survey of the Situation, provided to Napoléon on the first and fifteenth of each month by the French Minister of War, was inspired by a real event. From 1811 to 1812, a traitor in the General Staff of the French Army was slipping copies of these reports to an officer attached to the Russian Embassy in Paris named Alexander Ivanovich Chernishav. The smuggling of these reports to London is my own invention, although I have referenced the real event by using Chernishav's name for my Russian colonel.

The story of Nathan Bateman is based on the autobiographical account left to us by Joseph Bates, an American sailor impressed into the British Navy during the Napoleonic Wars. Thousands of American sailors suffered his fate. And yes, Bates was sent to London as a prisoner and thrown into a hulk on the Thames after the United States declared war on Britain. He survived to become a ship's captain, a revivalist minister, and a strong champion of abolition and the separation of church and state, before dying an old man in 1872.